Other Girls

a love story about second chances

Avery Brooks

Ann Arbor
2019

Bywater Books

Copyright © 2019 Avery Brooks

ISBN: 978-1-61294-167-7

Bywater Books First Edition: December 2019

Printed in the United States of America
on acid-free paper.

Cover Design by Ann McMan, TreeHouse Studio

Bywater Books
PO Box 3671
Ann Arbor MI 48106-3671

www.bywaterbooks.com

This novel is a work of fiction.

This book is dedicated to everyone who has ever felt not good enough, and yet found the strength to own their truth and face another day anyway.

"The wound is the place where the Light enters you."

—Rumi

Chapter 1

As they left Pizza Luna and turned down Magazine Street, Sam took Jake's hand in hers and smiled down at him. "So, what next, honey?"

Jake smiled his toothy grin, and began swinging their arms back and forth as they walked. He looked toward the sky with a thoughtful expression and bit his bottom lip—his thinking face.

They walked along the sidewalk, dodging people out enjoying their weekend despite the brisk weather. Magazine Street was one of the main arteries of New Orleans—packed with rows of boutiques, galleries, and restaurants. The wall of storefronts on each side of the road displayed classic New Orleans style—an amalgamation of different centuries-old architecture with archways and adornments that gave an air of sophistication and heritage, bold paint colors that exhibited the city's zest for life, and second stories demarcated by intricately decorated, black wrought-iron balconies.

Sundays were their days to explore, relax, and goof around. It was the one day Sam got to just enjoy being with her son and not worry about balancing work and motherhood or things she might be missing out on while she was working. She hoped these days lessened any void Jake might still feel from having only one parent.

They went to museums, the zoo or played miniature golf, during which Same often had to remind herself: *don't be so competitive.* Today began with the zoo, then an early dinner at their favorite pizza place. It was still fairly early so they had time to fit something else in before heading home.

"Ice cream!" Jake squealed.

For late February, it was still a bit cold for ice cream. Sam looked at her son, engulfed by his bulky green winter jacket, and decided not to be a killjoy. She smiled down at Jake. "You got it, mister."

They had just walked a few blocks along the uneven and often missing pavement of New Orleans, dodging the occasional tree root mixed in to trip up less wary pedestrians, when Jake shouted, "Tony! I forgot Tony!" The three-inch tall, blue and gray Transformer was Jake's favorite toy. He took it wherever he went—often leaving it behind, as well. He halted, stopped swinging his arm, and stared up at Sam with large, sad brown eyes. "Mom, we have to go get him. What if someone takes him?"

"Don't worry, honey, we'll go get him," Sam reassured him. They turned around and headed back to the restaurant to save their abandoned comrade.

Inside the restaurant, Sam looked across the crowded room, packed with families sitting at tables draped in red-and-white checkered vinyl. She saw two women sitting at their former table near the far wall.

Great, I'll have to interrupt some strangers' meal and search the table and floor for Jake's plastic hero. She couldn't leave Tony behind.

They approached the table, occupied by two blonde women who were dressed a step above most of the other patrons in the family restaurant. They were leaning toward each other as they talked, probably trying to hear each other over the loud hum of conversations and the occasional screaming child.

Sam groaned, figuring the last thing the women would want was some lady and her kid sabotaging whatever intimate moment they were sharing. Jake ran ahead and stopped abruptly beside the table, causing the two women to jerk away from each other in surprise. The blonde with the longer, shoulder-length hair gazed up at Sam with a confused expression.

Sam was only a few feet behind Jake, but when she met the woman's gaze, she stopped dead in her tracks. The air escaped her lungs. *Ashley.* Sam hadn't seen her in years, but there was no mistaking those green eyes. They had been so cold—icy—back in high school. But there was something different about those eyes now. They seemed warmer as they held her startled gaze. And was that a slight smile on Ashley's lips? *Does she even remember who I am?*

"Hey, there's Tony!" Jake said loudly to no one in particular as he pointed at the table. Sam's attention snapped away from those eyes and glancing at the table she realized Ashley was holding the toy, bending his legs back and forth.

"Oh, is this yours?" Ashley asked Jake, holding up the toy in her hand.

"Yeah! His name is Tony. Do you want to see what he can do?" Jake asked excitedly.

"Sure!" Ashley responded with a grin, handing Tony back to his rightful owner.

Sam stood there, rooted to the spot, staring at the exchange. Alarm bells sounded in her head—the same kind you hear when your child is in immediate danger. Her body buzzed with adrenaline and yet she couldn't move. She swallowed hard, forcing herself to notice the families around them, reminding herself where they were and that nothing bad was going to happen. *Right?*

Jake was engrossed with Tony, contorting the tiny man into a small jet, then making engine noises as he pretended to fly it through the air. He had no idea his mom was having an emotional breakdown only a few feet away.

"That's pretty impressive," Ashley said. She looked back up at Sam and smiled. "Hello, Samantha. It's been a long time."

Bile worked its way up into Sam's throat as the alarm bells rose to nuclear strength.

Fuck. She does remember me.

"Come here, Jake!" Sam nearly shrieked, in an octave usually reserved for times she found herself alone in the shower with a spider.

Jake's body instantly stilled at the sound of Sam's voice and he scurried the few feet back to her side. Sam wrapped her arm across his chest, holding him close.

The sirens in Sam's head quieted as Ashley held her gaze. Ashley glanced at the other blonde woman at the table, who was watching Sam with a look of concern on her face.

"Samantha?" Ashley asked with hesitation, the smile fading from her face.

3

Sam swallowed again. "Hi . . . Ashley. It has been a long time," she managed to stammer.

Ashley's smile returned, which was . . . confusing . . .

"Anyway . . . sorry to interrupt. Have a good dinner," Sam blurted out before turning and charging toward the exit, holding Jake's hand a bit too tightly. When they reached the door, she risked a glance back. Ashley was watching her, but the smile had faded. Sam couldn't identify the expression.

Outside, Jake peered up at Sam. "Mom, who was that?" he asked with concern.

"Just someone I used to know, honey." Sam squeezed his hand reassuringly and forced a smile. "Let's go get that ice cream."

When Ash turned back to face her dinner companion, the look on Ali's face caught her attention.

"What?" Ash asked sheepishly.

Ali arched an eyebrow, intensifying her already suspicious gaze. "You want to tell me what that was all about?"

Ash's face fell. "What do you mean?"

Her attempt to feign innocence must've been believable because Ali backed down. A little. Ali's face softened. "You look like you've seen a ghost."

Could this day get any worse? Not only had she been nervous all day about going on this date with Ali—it had been almost two years since she had dated anyone—but her worst nightmare was coming true: running into Samantha. *Man, karma is a twisted bitch.*

Ali cleared her throat and arched her eyebrow again, something Ash was quickly growing weary of. Clearly she was expecting some sort of explanation.

"It's complicated." Ash sincerely hoped Ali would prove herself to be an understanding person. It was their first date, after all. How many expectations could one person have on a first date?

Ali sat back in her chair. She managed to retain her rigid posture and nodded at Ash. "Try me."

Ash blew out a breath. *Apparently, a lot of expectations.* She watched a family enjoying their pizza at another table, wishing she could escape her present situation. After a moment, she mustered the courage to meet Ali's hard stare.

"She's just someone I used to know."

Ali's eyes flashed bright. "Like an ex?"

"What? No! God, no." Ash shook her head.

Ali's eyes narrowed. "I feel like there's something you're not telling me."

Ash sighed. "It's really nothing. I'm still getting used to running into people from so long ago." As Ali opened her mouth to speak, Ash interjected. "Can you finish telling me the rest of that story?"

The frown plastered on Ali's face slowly gave way to a small smile before she launched into a highly detailed retelling of one particular court case. Ash tried hard to be present—to nod, smile, and even shake her head at appropriate moments. But there was only one image her mind was truly focused on—Samantha staring at her, clutching someone Ash assumed to be her son, and the look of sheer terror in her eyes. Every detail was new, except that look. She had seen that look many times before. But now, it only made her want to throw up.

Ali stopped talking suddenly and placed her hand on Ash's arm. "Are you okay? You turned really pale all of a sudden."

Ash swallowed the lump in her throat and tried to force a small smile. "Yeah, I'm not feeling too great. Do you mind if we continue this another night?"

Sam watched Jake as they sat at their small kitchen table. He took a scoop of mac and cheese from his plate and eyed the burnt pieces.

"It's not my best work. Sorry." Sam frowned.

Jake gave her an encouraging smile. "It's okay, Mom." He picked the black bits off his spoon and ate the rest.

Sam smiled and shook her head, wondering for the billionth time how she had lucked out with such a good kid. She knew lots of kids were picky eaters, but not Jake. Even though her lackluster cooking skills gave him good reason to be. "Did you and Lauren do anything fun after school?" Sam reached over and brushed the shaggy brown hair out of his eyes.

Jake nodded enthusiastically. "We played hide and seek."

"Oh yeah? Did you find a new hiding place?"

He nodded.

"Cool, where is it?"

Jake pretended to think. "Not telling. It's a secret. If I tell you, it won't be a secret anymore."

Sam smiled at him. "Okay, you're right. I'll just have to figure it out on my own."

"Good luck," Jake said confidently, grinning at her.

Sam's jaw dropped. "Excuse me, mister." She proceeded to tickle him until he screamed for mercy through his giggles. Sam laughed. "That's what I thought."

Jake ate the last slice of his apple and took a final gulp of milk, leaving a mustache on his upper lip.

Sam couldn't help but grin at him. "You done?"

He nodded.

"You got a little somethin'…" She indicated his lip. "Want me to get it?" Before he could answer, she was up and wiping his face and then wrapping him in a big hug.

"Mo-om," Jake whined as she let him go.

"You can play with your LEGOs while I clean up, then it's bath time."

Jake was out of his chair and almost to the living room before Sam spoke.

"Make sure you clean them all up when you're done," Sam called after him as she picked up the lime-green plastic plate of burnt mac and cheese bits and sighed.

After she had cleaned the dishes, she texted Drea to let herself in, and went to get Jake for his bath. She hadn't had time yet to fill her best friend in on the Ashley run-in yesterday and it was eating her up inside.

"Hello?" Sam heard Drea call from the entryway a short time later.

"We're in the bath," she called back.

A moment later, Drea burst through the open doorway—one hand covering her eyes and the other feeling out in front of her. "Is he decent?"

Sam had to stifle a laugh when she saw Drea's hair. Her dark curls were splayed out several inches from her head. "There are bubbles."

Drea peeked through her fingers at Jake. "Nope, need more bubbles. I have a reputation to uphold, ya know."

Sam arched an eyebrow and handed over the bottle of bubbles. "Oh, everyone is aware of your reputation, Drea." She turned the faucet back on.

Drea kept her eyes to the ceiling as she squirted the bubble liquid generously all along the tub. Jake giggled as she got his head.

She bent down, worked up the bubbles, and then corralled them into one huge heap as high as Jake's chin. When she was finished, she and Jake high-fived.

"That was all a ploy for more bubbles?" Sam asked in disbelief.

"Of *course*." Drea dragged out the words to emphasize the 'duh' she didn't say, and rolled her eyes at Jake. She made an elaborate bow and hand gesture toward him. "Good evening, my lord."

Jake did his best to mirror her actions. "Good day, my lady."

Sam narrowed her eyes at Drea. "This better not mean you're watching *Game of Thrones* with my five-year-old son again."

Drea scoffed once. It was almost believable until she scoffed again and pointed to her chest. "Me?"

Sam shook her head as Drea winked at Jake.

Drea lowered the toilet lid and sat down. "Lord Pickles sends his regards." Drea's rust-colored tabby cat, who Jake had named—unfitting as it was—was pretty much Jake's favorite being on the planet.

Jake's face lit up. "Yay! I miss Pickles."

Sam rinsed Jake's hair with the bath cup—one of the endless plastic Mardi Gras cups she'd acquired over her lifetime in New Orleans.

Jake raised his hand out of the water. He'd been holding Tony the entire time. "Get Tony."

Sam refilled the cup and rinsed off Tony. "Okay, time for bed."

Drea nearly shot up from her seat. "That's my cue." She walked over to Jake, bent down, and kissed the top of his head. "Good night, little man."

Jake grinned. "Good night, Aunt D."

By the time Sam had put Jake to bed and joined Drea in the kitchen, Drea had already poured them each a glass of Malbec. It was

Sam's favorite wine. Hearty and deep, fruity, sometimes even chocolatey. She was a wine fan, but also spent a good deal of time learning which Argentinian brands tasted decent while staying under $12.

Drea frowned into the sink and lifted the mac and cheese pot Sam had left to soak. "How does one even burn mac and cheese?"

Sam gave her a challenging look. "Shut it." She circled her finger in the air at Drea. "Speaking of ridiculous things, what the hell happened to your hair?"

Drea raised her hands to her curls, trying to tamp them down. "I had the top down."

"In February?"

"Free birds gotta fly, Sam."

Sam rolled her eyes. Drea and Sam had both grown up in Uptown, though they didn't meet until middle school when Drea's family moved there from Baton Rouge. Every neighborhood in New Orleans had character, but Uptown had always been Sam's favorite. It was an eclectic landscape of oak trees, mansions, and creole cottages. Uptown had it all: the historic St. Charles Avenue streetcar, the Audubon Zoo Jake loved, the walking paths through the Park, the beautiful campuses of Tulane and Loyola, and the Mississippi River along its southern border. But a few years ago, Drea had decided to get a swanky apartment downtown. It was less than twenty minutes away by car, but it felt like a huge distance to Sam after having her so close for so long.

They sat at the table as Sam filled Drea in on the Ashley encounter. "I couldn't believe it was her," she added at the end. Sam took another sip of wine and hummed at the smooth taste as she waited for Drea to absorb the information.

"She didn't say why she's back?"

Sam met Drea's piercing blue eyes. Drea was a beauty. Raven hair. Gorgeous eyes. All assets she was aware of and used to her advantage with the ladies . . . a lot. She was also Italian, and most of their quality time together involved food or alcohol. Especially alcohol.

Sam shifted her gaze. "We didn't really get that far . . . I kind of freaked out and barely said hello. I had this fear she would do something to Jake." Sam paused and risked an embarrassed glance at Drea, who was regarding Sam with her usual open, supportive look. "I know it's irrational. I just felt like I was transported back to high school and needed to get away from her and whatever she might be about to do to me or my son. Stupid, I know."

Drea frowned. "We're different people now, Sam. You would never let her treat you or Jake badly. You don't need to fear her anymore." She twirled her wine glass in a circle on the table. "Besides, if you run across her again, don't worry. I've got your back." She waggled her eyebrows and smiled before taking another sip. "And who knows, maybe she had a change of heart, or a lobotomy or something, and is actually a nice person now."

Sam snorted and nearly shot wine out of her nose. "That's hard to imagine."

Sam sipped her wine and gazed at Drea—always the cool, curly-haired beauty who let nothing get to her. Sam never understood why Drea had chosen to be her friend. They were completely different. But in the sixteen years since high school, Drea and Sam had become inseparable. She kept Sam sane and gave her at least one adult to talk with since most of Sam's time was spent being a single mom to Jake. Drea was like the sister Sam never had. The much cooler sister.

Both of them were unusually quiet. People thought of Drea as confident, funny, and beautiful, but Sam had known her long enough to see the characteristics Drea rarely shared with others. When something really bothered her, she either blew up or got quiet. Sam absently wondered if Drea was as shocked by Ashley's return as she had been. Unlike Sam, however, Drea didn't dwell on things. She was good about moving on. Sometimes too good.

"Soooo, anything new with you?" Sam asked to break the silence.

Drea shook her head. "Nothing much lately."

"Whatever happened to that redhead you took home last Friday?"

A slow smile spread across Drea's face. "We had some fun. That's all."

"Mmhmm." Sam nodded knowingly. "Well, I'm glad you had some fun, then."

"Thank you. So am I." Drea smiled and took another sip of wine.

Chapter 2

Wednesday was the pitch session for the marketing campaign Sam's team had created for Julie's Juice Company, a local start-up focusing on natural, locally-sourced ingredients. Sam's team and the three representatives from Julie's sat around the conference table at McGrady Marketing. The firm had been designed with a modern open-space concept in mind, though being surrounded by glass walls and glass tables wasn't always the most practical. Sam had nailed her knee on the sharp edge of pretty much every table and desk in the office in the six years she had worked there.

The representatives from Julie's seemed excited to see what the marketing team had come up with to unveil their new line of juices to the city. Sam didn't know the two women—Ellen, a woman in her late twenties, and Betsy, probably in her early fifties—but she had worked closely with John on the concept for the campaign. He was a friendly, clean-cut, professional guy in his early forties. Sam's understanding was that he had started working for the company as a friend of Julie's and she trusted his decisions when she couldn't be at meetings herself. His lack of business background sometimes made him a bit anxious and quick to doubt his own judgment, something Sam had worked with him on during numerous phone calls leading up to today's meeting.

Pete, the lead on this presentation—and every presentation—was well dressed, as always, in an expensive black suit and red tie that added to the bravado already oozing from his impressively moisturized skin and overly-gelled hair. The rest of the team sat around the table, waiting for Pete to dazzle everyone. Sam sat near the three reps from Julie's, dressed to impress while still being comfortable in stylish wide-leg black pants, black pumps, and a white blouse. She usually went for upscale casual most days, but tried to make an effort on pitch days. Her hair was pulled up into a high ponytail, intending to convey an air of sportiness and competence. She had added turquoise earrings for an extra pop. She crossed her legs under the table and waited for Pete to begin, a notebook and pen laid out before her, in case any changes needed to be made to the designs.

"All right, folks," Pete said, as he clasped his hands in front of his chest. "Let's begin."

Things seemed to be going pretty well as Pete went through the details of the two mock-ups for the campaign. Sam watched Ellen, Betsy, and John out of the corner of her eye, gauging their reactions. They nodded along throughout Pete's speech and flashed a few polite smiles. However, as the presentation came to a close Sam started getting the feeling that the team had missed the mark. John glanced at Ellen and Betsy, who looked hesitant.

"This is really great, Pete," John said and glanced around the table at the team, "and everyone. We really appreciate the time you've put into our campaign." He paused and looked at his colleagues, as if for reassurance, before turning back to Pete. "I just think we had hoped for a more local feel, you know? Something that says we're from New Orleans and proud of it." He turned his gaze to Sam with a half frown.

"What? Like a *fleur de lis* in the background?" Pete scoffed.

John looked down at the table, his leg bouncing nervously as a blush appeared on his neck.

"Something with a bit more soul to it, right?" Sam suggested gently.

John lifted his gaze to meet hers, nodding with recognition. "Yes, exactly."

Pete placed his hands on his hips, staring down at the table in front of him. "Soul, huh?"

John narrowed his eyes at Pete. Sam had to resist the urge to roll her eyes at Pete herself, but pissing off the clients was taking it too far. She jumped in for some damage control.

"How about . . ." Sam coated her tone in sweetness in an effort to diffuse the situation that was about to erupt. She knew from years of experience pacifying Pete that his temper had no boundaries. Everyone turned in Sam's direction. The rest of her team was fidgeting and clearly wanting to escape.

"How about I work with John and Ellen and Betsy for a bit? We can nail down some details to make sure we capture the essence of their product in this campaign. Then our team can make the necessary adjustments and present them next week."

A collective sigh came from everyone as they turned to Pete. "Well, that should be fine. I'll leave you in Sam's hands." He shook the hands of the trio from Julie's and strode out of the room, followed by the rest of the team.

Sam turned to John and the others with an encouraging smile. "How about we order some lunch?"

John took a deep breath and loosened his tie, before looking at her pointedly. "Thank you, Sam."

"Do you have any fours?" Jake asked. He and Sam knelt on the light gray rug around the coffee table, holding cards in their hands. Sam adjusted her position and rubbed her knee, the thin rug not offering much relief from the hardwood floor.

Sam looked at her cards and shook her head. "Nope. Go fish."

Sam's cell phone started vibrating in her back pocket as Jake drew a new card. He flipped the card over, frowning. "Oh, man."

Sam smiled at him. Apparently, he had inherited a bit of her competitive nature. Sam looked at the name on her phone and answered it. "Hi John. How are you?"

"Hi Sam," John said, warmly. "I'm sorry to bother you at home, but I had a couple questions about the ad."

"No problem, John. Let me just grab my laptop." Sam hurried to the kitchen, opened her laptop, and clicked on the mock-up she and John's team had worked on earlier in the day. "Okay, I'm ready. What did you have questions about?"

"Just some minor details, but do you think the royal blue needs to be black on the main text?"

Jake walked into the kitchen. "Hey, Mom?"

"On the main text?" Sam squinted down at the image.

Jake grabbed Sam's hand and yanked it. "Mo-om."

Sam placed her palm over the phone's speaker and held it away from her mouth. "Just a minute, bud."

"I think the royal blue works well. It goes with the color scheme of the rest of the ad, but if you'd prefer black, we can definitely do that," Sam said.

Sam listened as John took a deep breath and slowly exhaled. "Hmm. Okay, let's stick with the blue."

"Okay. What other questions did you have?"

"I was thinking we should make 'Julie's Juice Company' a little larger. I want it to stand out a bit more."

"Okay, no problem." Jake started yanking on Sam's arm and she absentmindedly engaged in a tug-of-war battle to stay in front of her computer. "I can change that tonight and send you the revised design."

"Okay great."

"Anything else?" Sam asked cheerfully. Jake started spinning in circles while holding Sam's hand then began running back and forth to test the limits of her range of motion. Sam stared at the screen, now second-guessing the royal blue.

"Actually, that's it. Thanks Sam."

"Absolutely. I'll make those changes and send you the design within the hour. Feel free to contact me if there are any other changes."

"Great. I really appreciate it. Have a good night, Sam."

"You too, John." Sam ended the call just as Jake yanked her arm hard, causing her to fall toward him.

"Ow, Jake. What in the world?"

A bashful smile formed on his face. "It's your turn."

Sam stared at him for a moment, then pretended to have an eye twitch. Jake giggled and led her back to their game.

"Here's to friends, Fridays, and freakin' tequila," Drea said with a raised glass.

"Oh, hell yeah," Sam said, clinking her glass with Drea's.

They had been coming to Charlie's for years. At first glance, it was the usual dive bar—dim lighting, a couple of pool tables and dart boards in the back—but it was one of the longest-running gay bars in New Orleans. The fact that it was in Uptown was an added bonus. Over the years it had accumulated a loyal group of patrons who kept it in business and supported each other. For Sam, it was a second home, a place where she could relax and be herself. It didn't hurt that Charlie's had some of the best margaritas in town.

"So, how was your week?" Drea asked, after a generous sip from her agave margarita.

"I was ready for this drink on Monday," Sam deadpanned. She licked some salt off the rim of her cocktail glass and took another sip, closing her eyes, savoring it. "Damn, that's good."

"Any other run-ins with your favorite old pal?" Drea flashed a mischievous grin.

Sam rolled her eyes and blew out a breath. "No, thank god. I'm hoping this city is big enough that I won't see her again before she rolls back out of town . . . and I hope that's soon. It was a shock to see her, but with any luck, it will be another twenty years before—" Sam stopped mid-sentence and felt the blood drain from her face.

A very attractive, tall blonde woman in black leather pants that left little to the imagination strode across the room toward the bar, leaving a wave of turning heads in her wake.

Drea turned in her chair to follow Sam's gaze, then looked back at Sam, wide-eyed. "Holy shit! That's not her, is it?" Sam couldn't find words, which gave Drea her answer. "Dammmmnnn," Drea said with raised brows, "time has been good to *her*."

Sam stared at her drink, twirling it absentmindedly, the shock of seeing Ashley again suffocating any thoughts she had held moments prior.

Drea fought to get Sam's attention back by telling her about a prank she had pulled on her new intern at work, but Sam found it almost impossible to be present. Her attention was drawn to the small table across the room where Ashley Valence sat with the blonde woman from the other night.

Why the hell was she here? It had taken Sam so long to let go of her high school memories and Ashley's torment. And they were memories no part of her wanted to relive. She was a different person now—stronger, more aware—and just fine with her current existence, domestic as

14

it was. Jake was all she needed.

When Ashley's gaze met hers, Sam quickly looked away. It was too late though. "Shit, shit, shit, shit," she murmured before downing what was left of her margarita.

"What is it?" Drea asked, with concern.

"Samantha, hi," Ashley said, stopping at their table, smiling down at Sam.

Sam tried to feign a smile, but it came out more like a grimace. She saw Drea smirk at her failed attempt. "Oh, hi, I didn't realize that was you."

Ashley's gaze wandered across the table. "Drea Cordeira. Wow. Long time no see."

"Ashley," Drea replied coolly. "Are you back here for a visit?"

Ashley's smile dimmed. "No, actually, I just moved back a couple weeks ago."

Sam felt like she was going to throw up and knew her face probably wasn't doing much to hide it. Drea just nodded.

"I see you two are still close," Ashley said, glancing between the two women.

"Why mess with perfection?" Drea retorted, but Ashley's attention was already back on Sam.

Drea waited a moment, then reached for Sam's empty glass. "Well, I think I'll grab another round."

Sam lunged for Drea's hand, feeling a surge of panic. "No! Stay. Please. Wait for the waitress."

After Drea managed to pry her hand free, she leaned in and whispered, "You'll be okay. Trust me, you're going to want another drink." She turned and headed for the bar.

Ashley stared at Sam, which made her squirm. "It's really nice to see you again, Samantha. You look great."

Sam's eyes narrowed as she waited for the insult that didn't come. "Um, thanks," she replied hesitantly, wondering what alternate universe she'd entered—one where Ashley played the part of a kind human being.

She braced herself as Ashley opened her mouth to say something, then closed it, and smiled. "Well, I just wanted to say hi. I hope I see you around again."

Sam gave a half-hearted nod as she imagined about a million things she'd prefer to running into Ashley again: being mauled by alligators, sharks, run over by a car—the options were endless. Her gaze lingered on Ashley's retreating form as she headed for the exit. *She does look good in those pants though*, Sam thought lazily, before mentally shaking herself.

Drea returned, drinks in hand. "She certainly was interested in talking to *you*. What did she want?"

Sam shook her head slowly, still staring where Ashley had stood moments before. "No idea. I must be more desperate than I realized if I'm finding Ashley Valence attractive."

Drea gave her a look. "Sam. That . . ." Drea nodded her head at the door, "that woman was hot. Ashley Valence or not." She sipped her drink and puckered her lips at the taste. "That girl can wear the hell out of some leather pants. Damn." She shook her head with a look of reverence.

Sam glared at Drea. As she sat there, Sam felt an eerie calm spread through her body, and she knew with absolute certainty that Ashley's return was significant. She could already feel the stirring of the memories she had spent nearly twenty years pushing out of her mind. She didn't want to revisit them.

Drea's gaze swept over the people in the room before returning to Sam. "You think she realized she was in a gay bar?"

After dropping Ali off at her house, Ash drove aimlessly through the city, trying to come to terms with her encounter at the bar with Samantha and Drea. Neither had seemed particularly happy to see her, but could she blame them? The Ash they had known had been pretty horrible . . . to both of them, but especially to Samantha.

Ash's stomach clenched at the thought of who she had been and how she had treated Samantha back in high school. She slowed to a stop at a light and glanced at the line of people on the sidewalk waiting to get into Tipitina's, one of New Orleans' historic music venues. A guy dressed in a banana suit danced around the crowd. His skinny little legs, clad in yellow tights, protruded from the costume like little toothpicks. The image seemed odd to Ash. She had grown up in this city and became accustomed to ridiculous things—New Orleans was nothing if not accepting of different people letting their freak flag fly. But the fact that this guy seemed a little crazy to her was just one more thing showing her that this place was foreign to her now.

The light turned green and she decided to drive along the river before heading home. The street lamps barely lit the dark, pothole-ridden streets and reflected a soft glow off the white hood of her car.

She thought about earlier and Drea's unmasked disdain. She'd been happy for a moment when Drea left to go to the bar, until she saw the hesitation on Samantha's face.

How could she prove to Samantha she was different now? Would Samantha ever give her a chance? She sighed, glancing at the river as her car rolled by. This was going to be harder than she had anticipated when she decided to move back here. Now, she wasn't sure she'd ever get off Samantha's shit list.

As she steered back toward her house, she let her mind return to the bar. But this time, she didn't think about Samantha or Drea. She thought about how amazing it felt to be in a gay bar for the first time in her hometown. It had taken her years to accept that she was a lesbian, even longer to risk setting foot in a gay bar, and her out life happened after she left New Orleans. Now, it was like two different worlds colliding. Though she still wasn't sure about Ali and whether that relationship would go anywhere—it was way too soon to even consider a future—the fact that she had already taken a huge step to live authentically now that she was back made her proud.

Samantha might never forgive her. And she would be warranted in that. But Ash would never hide herself again.

It felt good to have her glove on again. Sam punched the leather into her palm and flexed it a bit, working the kinks out. It had been sitting on a shelf these past few months. Sam had been waiting all day for tonight. After muddling through another cold, damp New Orleans winter, she saw the beginning of spring finally starting to appear. And the beginning of spring meant one thing: softball.

Sam had never been an athletic kid growing up, but had always wanted to give sports a try. So, when Jake was four, she joined the local recreational women's softball league. She imagined a low-key atmosphere with people socializing on the bench while waiting to bat. That was a speed she could manage for sure. Plus, it would make her feel *active*, and it was much more appealing than actually going to the gym.

After a year and a half on the Lady Lobbers, she was actually in pretty good shape. Their captain, Marci, made sure of that. Sam didn't know if Marci actually believed in Satan, or just had a knack for channeling him, but any rosy images of a team singing kumbaya as players encouraged each other for a good effort after a strikeout or missed catch were long gone following the first practice. After nearly two hours of laps around the bases, push-ups, sit-ups, and sprints, followed by some drills with an actual ball, she had limped to her car, driven home, and collapsed on her sofa until morning.

She probably should have quit then, but didn't want to give up so easily, driven by an urge to make up for lost time. She got in shape—fast—and learned basic ball skills. And mostly learned not to get in Marci's way.

Marci had played softball in college and came to every game with a fervor for winning unrivaled by anyone else on the team. She was captain, mostly because no one else cared enough to dethrone her. And though she ran a tight ship, they were a better team for it. Sam didn't let her ruin the fun of the game for her. Hell, she was looking forward to another season. *Wasn't she?*

Sam jogged out to the field where her teammates were talking and stretching. Lace, short for Lacy, was usually her warm-up partner. At thirty-five, she was only a year older than Sam, and though she had played softball in high school, she lacked Marci's zeal, caring more about having fun than winning. Her name was pretty appropriate. At 5'8", she was elegant and curvy, and even following a game, when she was doused with sweat, she exuded the casual elegance of a lady—a lady who could hit like Babe Ruth. She was often the team's secret weapon since opposing teams prejudged her based on appearance. She also kept Sam in check when Marci got on her nerves and she started talking back.

They had all been playing together for at least a year now, so they just had their weekly Tuesday night games, since no one had time to fit in extra practices. Most of the women had families and full-time jobs. This was a way to get rid of some stress and get out some aggression for most of them.

"Ladies, ladies, gather 'round." Marci's deep voice bellowed across the field from where she stood by first base. If you didn't know Marci and you saw her on the street somewhere, your first guess would be that she was a softball player. She always wore workout clothes and their team cap, and she was the only one on the team who wore legit softball pants to the games.

"I know you're all excited for another season. I know I am." Marci smiled and chuckled as they all waited silently. "Now, we've been a good team the past few seasons, making it to the championships every year. But I'm tired of going home without a trophy."

"Oh, here we go," Sam muttered under her breath as Lace jabbed her elbow into Sam's side. Sam was already imagining what Marci had planned for them, figuring some mandatory weekly practice was about to be enforced.

Marci looked at her, pointedly unimpressed, before gazing back at the rest of the team. "As I was saying . . . I think I've got what we need this season." She turned and gestured over at the bench. "I'd like to introduce you to our new pitcher."

They all turned to see a tall, lean woman walking toward them, hair dangling loosely in a ponytail pulled through the back of their team cap, the bill obscuring her face.

It couldn't be, Sam thought. *Hell, it could.*

The woman settled in beside Marci and turned toward her as Marci placed her hand on the woman's shoulder.

"We're very fortunate to have Ashley Valence here with us. She grew up in New Orleans, but went away for college where she was a Division I pitcher at UCLA. Fortunately for us, she decided to come back to her hometown, and we're so lucky to have her. I'd like you all to welcome Ashley to the team."

Instead of feeling nervous or fearful, Sam felt like she had been kicked in the gut. Her body sagged. Softball was the one thing she had for herself, and now Ashley was here, too.

After the introduction, the team erupted into claps and cheers, most of them breathing a sigh of relief that they weren't being punished with the reinstatement of "lobber liquidation," as they had not so affectionately named their former practice sessions.

Ashley looked around at the team, smiling. "Thanks. And you can just call me Ash." When her eyes finally landed on Sam, they widened and she quickly looked away.

"Hey, you okay?" Lace asked as the rest of the team jogged to the bench.

"Yeah," Sam blew out a breath. "I just got really tired all of a sudden."

"Well, buck up, baby," Lace said as she jogged backwards toward the bench. "We've got some ass to kick!"

They actually won that night's game, by a lot. And Ash was definitely the reason why. She pitched six no-hitter innings. Sam only touched the ball once the entire game, when it shot past Ash's right leg and Sam grabbed it. As second baseman, Sam had to stand behind Ash all night and watch as she dazzled everyone with her pitching skills.

By the time the game ended, Sam felt empty. Ash gave her a tiny smile as they slapped hands at the end of the game with the other team and then their teammates. Sam couldn't bear to return the smile and just looked away. She gathered up her bag and glove, and walked across the gravel parking lot to her unimpressive, ten-year-old Honda. She sat in her car for a while, just thinking about what had transpired.

She watched as many of her teammates crowded around Ash, congratulating her. After a few minutes, Sam draped her arms over the steering wheel and pressed her forehead against it, closing her eyes. Whatever cosmic joke was being pulled, she was clearly its main target. *Universe, why do you hate me?*

At the sound of a car door shutting next to her, she lifted her head and sat up in her seat. Ash sat in the white BMW sedan next to her, her head slightly dipped, looking at Sam through her passenger window. She looked concerned.

Sam met her gaze briefly before looking out her windshield. She scanned the parking lot and field, realizing that everyone else had left. With a deep breath and a slow exhale, she turned her key in the ignition, and pulled away.

Jake was already asleep when she got home.

Lauren, his sitter, was a grad student at Tulane and she'd been watching Jake since he was four. She was reliable, responsible, and most of all, great with Jake. Sam selfishly hoped she never graduated. Lauren met Jake at the bus stop every day after school and watched him until Sam got home from work, except for Tuesdays when she stayed later so Sam could play softball.

"How was he tonight?" Sam asked as she paid Lauren.

"Oh, great! He's been all about the new coloring book." Lauren smiled. "Barely watched cartoons he was so focused on it." She laughed.

Sam warmed. Lauren had brought Jake a Transformers coloring book last week. Sam knew she had hit the babysitter jackpot with this one. She truly cared about Jake and he adored her.

"Thanks Lauren. Have a good night."

After Lauren left, Sam peeked into Jake's room. He looked so peaceful asleep in his bed. It calmed Sam instantly. She tiptoed into the room, picked his dirty clothes up off the wood floor, and slipped back out, tossing the clothes into the hallway bathroom hamper on her way to her room.

After a hot shower, she slipped into bed, thoughts of the game still swirling in her mind. Ever since Ashley had been introduced at the game, Sam felt a weight in her chest. It made it hard to breathe and she absently wondered if her lungs would just cave in on themselves. She could almost hear the shattering of her comfortable existence now that Ashley seemed to be everywhere.

At the thought, Sam felt a small, but consistent, wave of dread. Was this her second version of hell? High school wasn't enough? Ashley had come back for more?

Sam recalled the look on Ashley's face when she had seen Sam tonight. And at the pizza place. They weren't the icy stares she was used to receiving from Ashley. Stares that had haunted her for years. Maybe it wouldn't be as bad as she thought. It had been sixteen years. Surely, that was long enough for a person to change. *Right?*

Eventually, Sam's worry gave way to sleep.

"Hey, Parker!"

Jackie stood with Jessica and Ashley. They pointed and leered as I tried to pass them.

"Nice shirt. Did your mom pick it out for you?"

I kept walking, hoping they would leave me alone.

"Did you hear me, Samantha?" It was Jackie.

I tried to walk faster but it was like my feet were stuck in concrete. My heart pounded.

Jackie stepped in front of me. I stared at my feet. She kept standing there. I started shaking.

"Are you too cool to talk to me, Samantha?"

I didn't answer.

Jackie looked over at Ashley and Jessica. "Looks like Samantha Parker's too cool for us, guys."

"Yeah right." Jessica laughed.

Ashley just stood there. The look on her face made my insides shudder.

"Isn't that right, Samantha?" Jackie shoved my shoulder.

I tried hard not to cry. "No."

"What was that?" Jackie boomed.

"No." I said it louder.

"Well you sure act like it. Why do you walk around with your nose in the air?"

"I don't." I felt humiliated. I wanted to run.

"What was that?"

I made myself look at her. I could see how much she hated me. "I'm sorry."

She leaned down close to my ear. "That's right, you are."

I tried to walk away from them as fast as I could. They didn't follow. I looked back, but Ashley and Jessica were gone. Pete stood there with a wicked grin on his face. John was beside him, nervously tapping his foot.

Pete pointed at me. "Get her Jackie. Get her!"

Sam gasped as she shot up in bed, grasping her chest. *Jackie. Fuck.* Sam hadn't thought of her in years. She could still see Jackie smirking at her with those cold eyes. Ashley and Jessica watching. Sam's entire body was tense. She tried to think back through the nightmare. Piecing it together before it slipped from her memory.

Everyone in school had kept out of Jackie's way. Some thought she was attractive, despite her horrible personality. Most just tried to avoid triggering whatever it was that made her pick on Sam. Jackie made it her personal mission to make Sam's life miserable. It made no sense to Sam. Jackie was popular, athletic, beautiful. Why would she waste her time on someone like Sam? It had taken all of her energy just to survive each day.

It bothered Sam that no one ever stood up to Jackie—well, almost no one. Whenever Drea was around, she went toe-to-toe with her. Jackie would back down then. But Drea usually wasn't there, and Jackie certainly never backed down to Sam.

Jackie was clearly the ringleader, but Ashley and Jessica backed her up. Sometimes they were just as bad. Though Jackie was the leader, she definitely wasn't the brains of the operation. Jessica and Ashley were in Sam's trig class while Jackie was still working her way through geometry. But in Jackie's absence, her two compatriots seemed to find their own footing.

Trig was the only class where the teacher did textbook checks and you lost points if you didn't have yours. Ms. Shepard. She was in her late 60s and stern as they came. Most teachers liked Sam because she was a good student and hard worker, but not Ms. Shepard.

Jessica always seemed to know when a textbook check was coming and would swipe Sam's book off her desk before class started, handing it off to Ashley, as the rest of the class watched. And Ms. Shepard seemed a little too delighted to mark Sam down for not having her book. Sam sometimes wondered if the teacher and the torturers were in cahoots.

Sam and Drea called them the sorority of bitches—S.O.B.'s for short. The name made Sam feel like she still had some power in the situation, little as it may have been. They were all tall and blonde. Jessica was the only non-athlete, but other than that it was often hard to tell them apart. Well, except for Ashley's green eyes. They would have been beautiful if they weren't so cold.

Sam's mind drifted to John and Pete. They'd been in the nightmare too, and it made her uneasy that she was having nightmares about work. She wanted to play it off as a meaningless addition from the events of the day, but deep down she worried it was much more than that.

When her heart finally stopped racing, she laid back down. Mentally exhausted, she fell back to sleep.

Chapter 3

Sam heard Drea answer on the second ring. "Hey, what's the plan for tonight?" Drea asked.

Sam needed a change of scenery, to blow off some steam. "I need the big guns."

"All right, game on."

They met at the Fun Zone, a dreamland for kids and veritable money pit for parents—arcade games, bumper cars, laser tag, batting cages, and most importantly, miniature golf.

They worked through the course at a leisurely pace. Drea was one of those annoying people who was good at most things without even trying. And miniature golf was no exception. There were also very few things she got heated about, which made it hard for her to understand Sam's competitive nature.

Sam loved miniature golf but she wasn't that good at it. For a competitive person, this was a bad combination. As her ball rolled past the hole on her fifth putt, her frustration level rose. Drea effortlessly knocked her ball in on her second putt, and stood nearby watching as Sam's stress level did anything but decrease. Finally, on Sam's sixth putt, the ball dropped into the hole, and she quickly removed the tiny pencil and score card from her back pocket to add up their points— also something Drea couldn't care less about. They were only five holes in, but Drea was already beating her by eight strokes. *Damn it.*

Drea went first on the next hole, placing her ball on the tiny indentation in the green rubber tee-square. She stretched her arms and moved her head from side to side, drawing out the process, as Sam rolled her eyes. When she wiggled her butt before her swing, Sam cracked.

"Would you hit the goddamn ball already?"

Drea chuckled. She loved pushing Sam when she was wound up tight. Despite Drea's annoying tactics, Sam knew she could always count on Drea to get her out of her head. And without taking aim again, Drea launched her ball down the green, narrowly missing a hole in one.

Sam begrudgingly placed her ball on the tee before taking several practice swings. Drea made a show of yawning loudly. Just before Sam swung, two preteen girls ran past them, across the green, and off down the course, chasing each other and giggling.

"Some people are trying to play here!" Sam yelled after them.

"I always forget how much fun it is to play with you," Drea said flatly.

An hour later, Sam and Drea sat on their bench at Riverview Park with the daiquiris they had picked up at the drive-thru. Sam removed the tape securing her straw to the lid and pierced the plastic. Though it was legal to drink in public in New Orleans, drinking and driving were still illegal so the daiquiri places made an attempt, weak as it was, to keep patrons from doing so. As long as the lid wasn't pierced, the cops couldn't charge you. Of course, you didn't need to pierce the lid to drink the contents.

Sam watched barges in the distance glide slowly through the dark along the Mississippi, the sound of waves lapping at the bank a few feet away. It was one of her favorite views in the city and instantly calmed her.

Drea and Sam had started coming here about a year after they met. It was a good walk from their houses, but made them feel like they had escaped to another world. Once they could drive, they came more often. It became their place—where they went when they were sad, stressed, happy. All of it. And when they were old enough to drink, they added daiquiris to the mix.

"Feeling better?" Drea asked, nudging Sam's knee with hers.

"A little."

"Is it Pete? I know the guy's a douche, but you shouldn't let him affect you so much. I thought I was going to have to remove a putter from a teen's rectum for a minute back there."

Sam blew out a breath, knowing Drea was right. She was beyond testy tonight.

Sam felt the chill tonight, despite wearing her puffy black winter jacket. They had just eased into March, a month that was always a crap shoot in terms of predictable weather, especially in southern Louisiana. She was starting to shiver from the frozen drink, but it was worth it.

"Ashley joined my team. She's our new pitcher." As Drea's eyes widened, she added, "She goes by 'Ash' now, by the way."

Drea had a look of disbelief. "What the hell? Do you think she's stalking you?"

Sam took another sip of her daiquiri. "No, I don't think so. She seemed surprised to see me there. I think it was just a really unfortunate coincidence."

Drea made a low whistle and shook her head. "What are you going to do?"

Sam stared at the lights twinkling from the barge passing in the distance, watching their reflections dance along the water.

"I don't think I have much choice. I've invested too much in this team. My friends are there. I don't want to just start over or stop playing altogether."

Drea placed her arm around Sam's shoulder. "Do you want me to come to your next game? For moral support?"

Sam turned and smiled. Regardless of whatever had led Drea to become her friend years ago, Sam was so thankful to have someone she could always count on.

"Thanks, but no. I can handle it."

Deep down though, Sam wasn't sure she could. She'd been thrown ever since Ashley came back to town, and infiltrating Sam's life wasn't helping Sam get back to normal.

Drea chuckled.

"What?" Sam asked.

"I was just remembering that time Jackie and her posse covered your locker with maxi-pads and filled it with tampons."

Sam stared at her. "Yeah, I still fail to see the humor in that."

"Oh, come on. It would've been funny if they weren't such bitches."

Drea laughed again. "I didn't have to buy tampons for months after that." She shook her head. "Dumbasses."

Sam narrowed her eyes at her best friend's huge grin. "Still a little too raw for me. Something about Jackie seeing me buy a tampon in the bathroom and then announcing to the whole school that I was on my period still makes me cringe." She tilted her head and sipped from her straw. "It was horrifying."

Drea had the good sense to drop it. They stared out at the river as Drea slurped the remains of her daiquiri through her straw. She held her cup and proceeded to move her straw in and out of the lid, the plastic reverberations almost as annoying as fingernails on a chalkboard. Sam raised her eyebrows, expressing irritation.

"Pitcher, huh? So, she's bending down in front of you all game long? All hot and sweaty?"

Sam cut her eyes at Drea, wanting to kill her.

"What? I'm just saying. Personality and past aside, it's not a bad view."

Sam stared out at the water, shaking her head. As supportive as Drea could be, her ability to have a one-track mind about women never ceased to amaze Sam.

When Sam got into bed later that night, thanks to the daiquiri, she fell asleep quickly.

> *A small gust of air flew by my ear. I figured it was nothing and continued reading. A wad of paper smacked me in the forehead. I clenched my jaw, knowing it was Jackie and her gang, a few tables away.*
>
> *I tried to pretend it wasn't a big deal, and hoped they'd get bored and stop.*
>
> *Another wad hit my ear. Harder this time.*

Sam awoke with a start. The dreams, they were so real.

She did remember the incident. She could almost feel that wad of paper hit her shoulder. Then one to the cheek. She remembered feeling annoyed, embarrassed, angry, humiliated. And wary. Very wary.

It was like yesterday. She remembered Jackie asking, "Got

something to say, Samantha?"

She stared at Jackie, saying nothing. She could still feel her heart pounding, but pretended to read her book, hoping it would stop.

"That's what I thought," Jackie called in the distance.

Then she felt it. A small, hard, fast thwack to the top of her head. She remembered the panic she felt, looking up to see Jackie, Ashley, and the other kids at their lunch table launching grapes at her. She could still feel them thud against her chest. Another stinging her ear.

The cafeteria had gone silent, with everyone staring but saying nothing. Sam could still feel the emotion—looking at all the faces staring at her and doing nothing. Feeling surrounded and completely alone.

She remembered grabbing her lunch bag and book, trying to get out of there before she started crying in front of everyone. She remembered Ashley staring at her as she rushed out of the cafeteria and went to cry in a bathroom stall.

Sam groaned and rubbed her forehead. All of the details were as vivid as the day it happened. It was bad enough the first time, but reliving it was, in some ways, worse. She laid back down and replayed the scene in her mind until she eventually drifted back to sleep.

When Sam's alarm went off, she was exhausted. She recalled her dream, a nightmare really. Ashley's return was definitely messing with her.

Sam made coffee and showered before driving to her parents' place in Lakeview, about twenty minutes away. Ten years ago, after living in Uptown for decades, Sam's parents had decided to change up the scenery. They wanted a bigger yard and to be close to City Park, where her dad could fish. So, they found a newer home a few blocks from the park and sold Sam the house she had grown up in—for a very reduced price.

Sam loved her house. It was older, and a little larger than the shotgun style typical in most of her neighborhood. She liked the creaky wooden floors, the aged built-ins, the chipping paint. It resonated with her as much as the city did. But, over the past few years, she had grown to love her parents' house too. And as more and more things went on the fritz at her house, she appreciated that her parents didn't have to deal with the issues that came with a 100-year-old-plus house. They could enjoy retirement.

She pulled up to the curb outside her parents' house, painted a cream color with a mix of Cape Cod and French country style. She walked up the concrete sidewalk past the bright green manicured lawn, shrubs, and palm tree skimming the side of the house. She stepped up onto the brick porch and opened the red door, which was left unlocked—something she'd never do in Uptown, even during the day. It wasn't an unsafe area—she had no problem walking around her neighborhood at night—but it was still a city. And enough crime and odd stuff happened for her to know not to tempt fate. Especially not with Jake.

"Good morning, darling," her mom said as Sam entered the kitchen.

"Hi, Mom." Sam leaned in and hugged her. The entire house smelled like bacon and biscuits, causing Sam's stomach to growl.

Sam's parents had been involved grandparents ever since Jake was born, but after Anna's death, they started a weekly tradition of having him over for Friday night sleepovers. It allowed them time to spoil him, but Sam knew the other main reason was to give her some time to herself. She thought it would stop after a few months, that it was just her parents' attempt at helping her get back on her feet, but it continued and became something that they, and Jake, looked forward to each week.

It meant a lot to Sam to have parents that were so involved. It was also nice not to have to worry about finding a babysitter for her own weekly tradition—Friday girls' night with Drea.

"Hey, sis." Sam's brother, Scott, gave her a wet willy as she hugged her mom. Sam quickly let go and swung out her leg to kick him in the butt, but he hopped away too fast.

Their mom rolled her eyes and grinned. "Maybe when you two are eighty, you'll quit acting like children."

Scott was four years older than Sam, and he was the proverbial bachelor. Because of the age difference their relationship mostly consisted of a playful rivalry. Sam had spent her early childhood trying to hang out with him and his friends, which he easily avoided. He had already left for college by the time she started high school and spent much of his time afterward traveling and exploring the world. When he moved back to New Orleans a few years ago, he tried to stop by their parents' place occasionally on Saturdays for brunch with Sam and Jake.

Jake and Sam's dad came in from the backyard.

"Mom!" Jake yelled as he ran over and hugged her waist.

"Hey, bud. Did you have a good night?"

He nodded as Sam's dad gave her a one-armed hug. "Hi, honey."

"Hi, Dad."

They sat around the large dining room table, relaxed, enjoying each other's company. Sam's mom was an excellent cook, something she didn't inherit at all, and Sam often went home feeling stuffed for the rest of the day. The warm, flaky biscuits slathered with melting butter were a meal in themselves, but along with the bacon, scrambled eggs, and sausage, it was a veritable feast.

Scott was telling them about a leak under his kitchen sink that had started innocently enough but after he returned from his latest trip had grown into a serious issue.

"What you need to do . . ." their dad said as he chewed.

Scott caught Sam's eye across the table and mouthed the words with him as Sam smothered Jake's biscuit with strawberry jam.

"Here you go, hon," Sam said, handing the fully loaded biscuit to Jake.

Jake's eyes went wide at the jam as he smiled.

"Is go to the dollar store . . . what are you two laughing about?"

Sam's dad was very frugal, which always amazed her because her mom was not. Her mom elevated his life in every way. She wasn't careless with money, by any means, but she did believe that you get what you pay for.

And so, she let Sam's dad buy most basic things at the dollar store, while she spent a bit more on things that mattered and would last. At first glance, they were an odd pairing. Sam's mom always had her long, blonde—now silver—hair perfectly coiffed, wrapped smoothly in the back around an elegant comb that held it up off her neck. She always wore a blouse and slacks, the epitome of elegance. Sam's dad always wore T-shirts and cargo shorts with the same faded ball cap covering his hair, which was rapidly turning white. They seemed like complete opposites, but it was this delicate balance between two very different people that was the backbone of their forty-year marriage.

"Dad, I hardly think some duct tape is going to solve a major plumbing problem."

"Scott, maybe if you had tried the duct tape sooner, it wouldn't have become a major plumbing problem." Sam's dad shook his head, continuing to eat. He had tried hard to instill his frugal ways into his two children, but they had clearly failed him, choosing to shop at regular grocery stores for toilet paper and condiments. Such a disgrace.

"Well, isn't this lovely?" Sam's mom said with a glimmer in her eye, used to the usual lighthearted bickering.

It was, though. There had always been a steadfastness to Sam's family. They were solid. A constant. Though a lot had happened in her life, it meant everything to know her family was there if she needed them. She wasn't always good about asking for help, but she felt comfort knowing they were there. Sam looked around the table. Even when they were bickering, it was with love. When her gaze landed on Jake, she stifled a laugh. His face was covered in jam.

After they finished breakfast, Sam took Jake to the bathroom to wash off the jam residue, then her dad took him into the backyard to play catch. Sam stayed inside to help her mom with the dishes.

"Are you all right, honey? You look tired."

Her mom didn't miss much, but Sam wasn't up for telling her about Ashley or the nightmares keeping her up at night. Not yet, anyway.

"Yeah, I just haven't been sleeping well lately."

Sam could tell from her mom's lingering gaze that she knew there was more to it. Thankfully she let it go.

Sam was still a little bothered by how nonchalant Drea had been the night before about the bullying. It wasn't like Drea didn't know how bad it had been. She had been there to comfort Sam every time Jackie and her posse did something.

Sam pinched the bridge of her nose and rubbed her forehead, not wanting those memories back in her life. But Ashley's return had awakened so many things she thought were behind her. Especially one specific incident.

After months of convincing, Sam had agreed to go to Senior Prom with Drea, who had a crush on AJ, the star soccer player. Drea had decided to come out to her at prom and ask her out.

Sam had been a little surprised that the prom evening didn't completely suck. She wore a brown satin halter dress that was pretty flattering and Drea looked great in a skin-tight, black strappy number. She definitely had her eye on the prize.

Drea finally worked up the courage to talk to AJ. But Sam was worried. She wasn't sure AJ was gay, and she didn't want Drea's night to be ruined if things didn't work out.

Sam went to get punch for both of them while Drea made her move. On her way back, Sam saw Ashley standing with Jessica, who was leering at Sam. There was something different about Ashley that night. It was the first time Sam had seen her in a dress—very different from her normal grunge look of T-shirts and flannels. Her hair was up, but not in the usual ponytail. It was actually styled. Sam wasn't sure if it was the hunter green dress that brought out her eyes, or if it was something else, but Ashley looked different that night. Pretty. No, beautiful.

Maybe if Ashley had looked like her usual self, Sam wouldn't have stared so long. Maybe she would have looked where she was walking. But she wasn't looking and she tripped over something that sent her flying. One punch cup went up, then down, dousing her hair and dress with sticky red liquid. Her tight grip split the other cup open and the sharp plastic cut her palm.

Everything went silent except for Natalie Merchant's melodious voice singing "These Are Days." That is, until a lone cackle filled the room. Sam, sprawled on her belly, propped herself on her elbow and saw Jackie.

Jackie had tripped her. *Of course.*

Sam looked at the blood dripping from her palm onto the wood gymnasium floor.

"Samantha."

Ashley bent down beside her. Sam couldn't read her expression—fear, panic, concern?

"Get the fuck out of here!" Drea grabbed Ashley's arm and pushed her away. "Come on, Sam." Drea helped Sam to her feet, Sam cradling her hand, as everyone stood and watched them leave.

It was the last time she ever remembered seeing Ashley or Jackie. There had still been a few weeks between prom and graduation, but she had blocked them out. There was just that terrible night.

Ash stared at the plate full of greens, covered in beets, with goat cheese sprinkled on top. Ali had been talking for a while, but Ash had stopped listening at some point along the way. When Ali said she was starving and knew a great seafood place for their date, this was not what Ash had envisioned.

Was she on a diet? Did she not like seafood?

When Ash was starving, a pickled beet salad wouldn't cut it. She stuffed another forkful of fried catfish in her mouth and tried to hide a look of suspicion as she met Ali's eyes.

Ali was attractive, there was no doubt about that. She knew how to dress well. She carried herself with confidence. Both attributes Ash figured served her well in her job. She was fit and curvy in all the right places. But there was just something . . . off.

They had only been on a few dates over the past weeks, so Ash tried to tell herself she was just being too picky. She needed to give Ali a chance.

Still, there was just something. A nagging feeling she couldn't get rid of.

Ali's sudden silence snagged her from her thoughts. Her body stilled as if she had been caught daydreaming in school.

Ali stared at her, expectantly.

"Sorry, what?"

"What about you?"

Ash hesitated. She had no idea what Ali had been talking about, not enough to even attempt an answer that might work. She held Ali's gaze, feeling nervous.

Ali sighed. "Do you want kids?"

Ash blinked in surprise. *Jesus. How long had she been daydreaming?* "Um . . ." She reached for her glass of ice water, trying to buy some time. Ash wasn't a private person, necessarily, but there were certain things that were a bit more personal to her. Some that were harder to talk about. Not things she wanted to tell just anyone over a meal. Having kids was a challenging topic for her as it brought up deeper issues she didn't usually talk about. At least not until she deemed the person worthy of that conversation.

She tilted her head and tried to act nonchalant. "I've never really thought too seriously about it." Well, that was partly true. She held her breath, hoping Ali didn't push. Something she seemed to be good at doing in the little bit of time Ash had known her.

Ali's brow wrinkled. "How old are you again?"

Ash hid her shock. She was learning that Ali was a straight shooter, but it took some practice not to be offended by it. "Thirty-four."

"Ash. You need to think about these things. You don't have a lot of time left."

It took a lot for Ash to swallow a snarky response—to try to think of Ali as caring and not bossy. But she managed, and didn't say anything.

Ali looked at her fancy silver watch—an accessory Ash figured was just another status sign for her.

Ash knew appearances mattered. You couldn't show up to a client meeting in a wrinkled T-shirt or a car that announced its presence from a block away, but there was a difference between looking professional and broadcasting your wealth. Ali seemed to be in the latter camp.

"It's not too late. Do you want to go get a drink?" Ali asked with a hopeful look.

Ash sighed internally. She was being too judgmental. Ali was a nice person. Just because she knew what she wanted and went for it didn't make her a jerk. And it was Saturday night after all. Might as well enjoy it. "Sure. Let's go."

She grabbed her lightweight bomber jacket from the back of her chair and waited as Ali put on her beige Burberry coat.

They walked down Magazine Street for less than a block before a quaint outdoor patio caught Ash's eye. "Let's go here."

After eyeing the multitude of beers on tap inside the dark tavern, Ash finally chose an IPA. Ali asked for the same. To Ash's delight, they found one vacant table out on the patio. The round metal table was big enough for the two of them and teetered to one side as they placed their drinks on it, which made Ali frown. Ash grabbed a couple sugar packets off the table and stuffed them under one table leg to balance it.

As Ash took in the trees above them wrapped in white lights and the laughter and smiles of the people around them, she exhaled for what felt like the first time that night. This place was more her speed. She sipped her beer and smiled at its slightly bitter, hoppy taste.

Ali scooched her chair closer to the heat lamp nearby and tightened the scarf around her neck. "Brrr. Let's finish this drink and go somewhere warm."

Ash's smile faded as she took a large gulp of her drink. The joy of the evening turned to that nagging feeling again. As she set her glass down, she absently wondered what Sam was doing tonight. A surge of panic spread through her body.

"You okay?" Ali asked.

Ash rubbed her arms, pretending she was just cold. "Yeah. Let's go."

"Here's a good spot." Sam stopped at a small area along the sidewalk that the crowd hadn't filled yet. She started unfolding the two camp chairs she had carried from her house as her mom and Jake peered down Magazine Street, trying to see the start of the Thoth parade. The sound of a high school band played in the distance, the drum beats and brassy trombones pumping up the crowd.

"I see them," Jake pointed as he jumped up and down.

Sam's mom took his hand and led him back to the chairs. "Okay, let's get settled before they come." She unzipped the red cooler she'd carried, pulled out two plastic champagne flutes and proceeded to fill them from a thermos filled with an orange liquid. She handed a flute to Sam and they raised their glasses in a salute before taking a sip.

Everyone had their Mardi Gras traditions. Mimosas during the Thoth parade was one Sam and her mom shared.

"Can I have some orange juice?" Jake asked.

"Now how are you going to catch the good throws if you're holding juice? Don't be silly." Sam's mom smiled and ruffled Jake's hair to take any harshness out of the words. Sam couldn't help but marvel at her mom's ability to diffuse a situation effortlessly. She also couldn't help but wonder how many times her mom had used that skill on her.

To many people, Mardi Gras was a big parade in New Orleans

one day a year where people got drunk, women flashed their boobs for beads, and general debauchery was sanctioned, if not celebrated.

But to anyone who had ever lived in New Orleans for any amount of time, Mardi Gras was the beating heart of a city that was as alive as any other organism on the planet. It was tradition. Community. Joy. Family.

Mardi Gras was a month full of parades, not just the culmination on Fat Tuesday. In the week leading up to Tuesday, there were parades every day. Having lived in New Orleans her entire life, Sam had learned to pace herself. There were certain parades she went to each year. Mostly the ones with routes by her house—the ones locals went to. Sure, people drank and danced and celebrated, but it wasn't the Bourbon Street level that the tourists attended.

Each parade had its own krewe—a social group that had its own theme. Often, the members of the krewe had to receive a special invitation to join. They were the ones who rode the floats and tossed throws—beads and other goodies—to the people in the crowd. It was a privilege to be a member of a krewe, kind of like a secret society forming the lifeblood of the city.

Twenty years ago, when Sam started high school, her dad had been invited to join the Krewe of Thoth. Thoth was the Egyptian patron of wisdom and the inventor of science, art, and letters, so most of the floats centered around Egyptian and mythological themes related to those fields. The Thoth parade was also unique because it had an unusual route, taking it by a number of institutions serving sick and injured people who didn't normally get to see the parades. Sam's dad worked as a physician at the Children's Hospital in Uptown, one of the institutions along the parade route, and was very involved with service to the community, so the krewe was a natural fit for him. Every Sunday morning before Fat Tuesday for the past twenty years, Sam and her mom had walked down to Magazine Street to cheer her dad on.

"Keep your eye out for the Egyptian float," Sam's mom called after them as she got comfortable in her chair. All of the men in the Krewe of Thoth wore masks during the parade and were assigned costumes and float positions at the start of the route, so Sam's dad had texted to let them know which float he'd be on.

As the floats rolled by, Sam and Jake ran alongside to get beads and cheer them on. It was joyous chaos. Everyone was happy. People tried to catch beads, but they were kind about it, letting the kids get up close to the floats and helping them catch the stuffed animal throws, while saving the nicer beads for themselves. The massive floats full of bold colors and intricate sculptures that had been built over the course of the year were always impressive. Purples, greens, and golds—the colors of Mardi Gras—were everywhere: on flags, floats, and costumes, even the clothes of the crowd. Nearly every balcony and fence along the parade route and throughout the city was draped in beads.

"Mom! Egyptian float," Jake yelled, pointing.

Sam looked to the rear of the approaching float and saw her dad. Though he was masked and hard to pick out from the others, there was one telltale sign: a satin rainbow sash across his chest. When Sam came out to her parents at the end of college, she wasn't sure how they'd take it. She knew they were open-minded people. They lived in New Orleans after all. But she wasn't sure if they'd feel differently when it was their own kid. She didn't want to disappoint them. Like all things in her life, they had supported her without hesitation. Something she had always been grateful for. But they didn't discuss it much.

Sam was always pretty private about her personal life and was still coming to terms with being gay. She didn't want it to be the only thing that defined her, but at the time, it felt all-encompassing. And she couldn't help but wonder if back in high school, Jackie's posse bullied her because they suspected something she hadn't yet discovered.

The spring after she had come out to her parents, the week before the Thoth parade, her dad pulled her aside. He grabbed a plastic bag off the living-room bookcase and pulled out the rainbow sash—a big grin on his face. "I bought this to wear on the float. Now, you'll always know which one is me." At Sam's stunned silence, he hugged her. "I love you, Sam."

Whenever Sam saw her dad on the float, she felt a sense of pride, in him, in her community. It was a strong connection to this place they called home. Seeing him wearing the sash each year gave her a sense of belonging and acceptance greater than anything she had ever known.

It took many years before Sam felt confident enough to fully accept and love that she was gay; to know it was one of the best things about her. But Ashley's return shook that confidence. She felt vulnerable. Wary. But of what?

"Mom!"

Jake's yell brought Sam back to the present. She lifted Jake under his arms so he could almost reach the float. Her dad bent down and handed him a stuffed polar bear as the float rolled on.

Chapter 4

Once Tuesday rolled around, Sam was ready to get some aggression out on the ball field. It had been another rough week at work. Nothing had happened per se, but she was finding it harder and harder to put up with Pete.

They were playing one of their main rivals, the Metairie Mavens, and Sam's competitive nature had been building the tension all day. She was hopeful they might have this in the bag thanks to Ash's skills, but she was also still grappling with her feelings about Ash's addition to the team. The nightmares last week had thrown her, but not seeing Ashley for a week was a nice reprieve. Maybe she could handle her presence, as long as she didn't have to see her more than once a week, nightmares aside.

After a short warm-up with Lace, the team took the field. Sam was pumped.

Three innings later, the Metairie Mavens were still a challenge, though much less so with Ash's fastballs and strikes. The few times someone did manage to contact the ball, Ash rarely let the ball get past her. And after nearly an hour of staring at Ashley on the mound, the feelings from Sam's nightmare resurfaced. *Damn it. I do not want to feel this way.*

The batter hit a pop ball in Sam's direction and she jogged backwards a little before catching it in her glove. Her teammates cheered.

Ash smiled at Sam as she tossed the ball back to her. "Nice job, Samantha."

Sam glared at her. "I go by Sam." *Shit.* She hadn't meant to sound so snarky, but Ash had a way of pulling that side out of her really easily.

Ash's smile faltered as she turned back to home plate.

By the top of the last inning, they were leading by two runs. The Metairie Mavens had a runner on second and their best batter was up. Sam moved back a few feet in anticipation of a hit. The batter didn't disappoint, knocking the ball past the bases, but not far enough to reach Amy in right outfield. Sam scrambled toward the ball, grabbed it, and leaning on her back foot for leverage got ready to throw it home before the runner scored.

"Sam, here!" Ash held out her glove for Sam's throw but Sam knew they wouldn't get the runner out if she threw it to Ash first.

"I got this!" Sam yelled before letting the ball fly directly toward home.

But Ash jumped up and caught the ball midair before spinning on her heel, firing to Janet, the catcher. The runner sprinted toward home with Sam watching as the ball pounded into Janet's glove with a loud thud, followed by a puff of dirt just before the runner crossed home plate. Sam's team erupted into cheers with the final out as Sam stood staring at Ash, anger spreading throughout her body.

The Lady Lobbers lined up to slap hands with the Metairie Mavens before congratulating each other. Marci was hooting and hollering, probably already having visions of championship trophies in their future.

Lace slapped Sam on her back and grinned. "Nice job, Sam."

Sam barely heard her as she watched with an icy expression as Ash approached.

"Great throw, Sam." Ash smiled.

"It would have been a great throw if you hadn't caught it and risked us the game," Sam said with an edge. Ash's smile disappeared.

"You can't stop being the ace, can you? Let some of the rest of us play?" Sam added.

"Sam . . ."

"Don't bother. I wouldn't want to get in the way of the Ashley show." *Whoa. Where did all this anger come from?*

Actually, it was clear: from years of being tormented by Jackie and her posse. Made to feel like nothing. Sam realized, even in her angry haze, this was not the appropriate venue to rectify years of pain.

But she couldn't help it. She stared at Ash, still seething. She couldn't read the emotions in Ash's eyes. Regret, guilt, pity? *Oh, hell no. Ashley Valence is not going to pity me.*

Sam looked around, as her teammates stood around them, watching with unbridled interest. Marci's jaw hung open. A shudder passed through Sam at the thought of retaliation from her. Ash was her golden goose. Sam was sure Marci would kick her off the team in a heartbeat if it suited her.

Lace put her arm around Sam's shoulders and walked with her toward the bench. "Sam, what the hell was that about?"

Sam rolled her eyes. "It's a long story."

"Well, you can't just go off on a teammate like that. We won. You should be jumping for joy."

"I had it, Lace. If she'd left it alone, my throw would have made it."

Lace gazed at Sam with concern. "Sam. We won. This is a team effort. Let it go."

Sam blew out a breath as she bent over and rummaged through her duffel bag, searching for her car keys. She found them and met Lace's eyes, then watched Lace look at someone behind her.

"Sam . . ." It was Ash. She cleared her throat. "Could we talk for a minute?"

Sam turned to face her, ice turning to tears in her eyes. "There's nothing to say," she managed to choke out, swinging her bag over her shoulder and walking with determination toward her car.

It took a long time for Sam to fall asleep that night. She mentally replayed her verbal jabs with Ash, reliving the anger, yet also feeling embarrassed for acting like a child. Eventually, exhausted from replaying the loop, she fell asleep.

> *"Man, I've got to pee! Sam, can you grab me a soda and I'll meet you by the bleachers?"*
>
> *"Sure." I headed toward the concession area as Drea sprinted toward the ladies' room. My stomach growled. Luckily, the line for food wasn't long.*
>
> *I walked back to the bleachers, balancing nachos and two cokes. Jackie and Ashley walked in*

*my direction. I looked for an escape route, but there
was none. Students pushed past me. I took a deep
breath and continued on.*

*"Hey, Samantha," Jackie said in an overly
sweet tone, making me wary. "Those nachos look
really good."*

I watched her cautiously.

"Can I have them?"

I sighed and handed them to her.

"Thanks!" Jackie said, a little too cheerful.

I tried to walk away.

"How about a drink?"

*I stopped and stared at the bleachers ahead of
me. The football team marched by in lockstep, like
Marines.*

*"Samantha . . . I asked you for your drink." The
familiar threatening tone was back.*

*I turned back to her and handed the soda
over. There was an evil smile on Jackie's face.
I looked at Ashley. She stared at me like a
zombie.*

I tried to walk away again.

"Hey, Samantha."

*I glanced back at them, but Jackie wasn't there.
Only Ashley. Adult Ashley.*

"Enjoy the game." Ashley smiled at me.

Sam's eyes flashed open and she gasped, in a panic, before realizing
she was safe in her bed. *God. This is just getting worse. It's like she's here to
bully me all over again. Except now, I'm doing the work for her.*

Sam leaned over and turned on the small lamp on her bedside
table. The light cast a soft glow on a silver-framed picture. She picked
it up and held it in her lap. The photograph was of Jake and her wife
Anna, not long before Anna passed away. They had all spent the day at
City Park having a picnic and laughing. Jake, only two then, had been
obsessed with the ducks in the nearby pond and was delighted when
they had come close for him to feed them bread crumbs. A rather

43

territorial goose joined the pack and started to waddle onto the bank to get closer to Jake. Anna swept Jake up in her arms before he realized he was in danger, which earned her a nip in the leg from the obstinate goose. Sam had taken the picture of Anna holding Jake, both of them laughing. Anna's million-dollar smile and sparkling blue eyes emanated warmth as she held Jake on her hip. Jake's head was tilted toward her, a wide grin on his face.

Sam stared at the image of her late wife for a few minutes, feeling the hard lump in her throat that always appeared when she thought of Anna. "I wish you were here, baby. I miss you so fucking much." Tears ran down her face. After a few moments, Sam leaned over and switched off the lamp. She lay back down, clutching the frame to her chest, and drifted off to sleep.

Ash had been staring at the same paint chip for the last hour. She groaned and rubbed her eyes. This was usually one of her favorite parts of her job, but there was no joy in it tonight. She sat at her kitchen table with an assortment of fabric swatches and paint chips strewn in front of her, working on a room design for a new client. Tried to, at least. She put her pen down on the sketchpad where she had drawn the room layout and sighed. Picking up the bottle of IPA she had been drinking, which was now room temperature, she took a swig.

Goose, the little brown terrier mix she had adopted from the shelter the day after she found this rental home, had been sleeping by her feet. He lifted his head at Ash's movement and then let it fall back against the hardwood floor when he realized she wasn't getting up.

Ash propped her elbow on the large walnut table—much too large for a house with only one person—and rested her chin in her palm. Ever since she had come home from the softball game, she hadn't been able to get Sam out of her mind.

She knew it would take a while for Sam to give her the time of day and knew she deserved that. And she'd been trying to be patient and stay positive around Sam—for everyone's sake. But the amount of anger Sam had shown her tonight made her wonder if Sam would ever forgive her.

Sam hated her.

Hated. Her.

Ash knew she was a different person now. She had put in the time—a lot of time—to work on herself. To face who she was as a person—the good, the bad, and the ugly. She knew why she'd acted so horribly to Sam in high school. It didn't excuse it, but it wasn't as black and white as it seemed. She'd spent the majority of her life hating herself after being shown only hate from those supposed to love her. People couldn't just flip a switch and become okay after years of verbal abuse, no matter how much they wanted to change. It took time.

It had taken everything in Ash to move back here, to face the girl she once was. But this was her home, she wanted to create a life here, a real life. And she finally cared enough about herself to follow her heart.

She reached across the table and picked up the purple silk carnation. She brought it to her chest and twirled it in her fingers. A woman covered in beads had been handing them out at the Krewe of Muses parade on Thursday night. This was the only Mardi Gras parade she had ever gone to in New Orleans. Her mom had taken Ash their first year here. Her mom had been so excited because it was an all-female krewe and they gave away elaborately decorated shoes as their signature throw. It had been magical.

On that night long ago, as the warm glow of dusk turned to night, colorful wands and lights lit up in the crowd. It felt intimate—like a big block party of friends. It was the first time Ash had seen her mom smile in months.

Her mom left later that year. Ash had gone back alone every year before she moved away, trying to recapture a semblance of that night, but mostly she just felt sadness.

This year, she had wanted to face that parade, not wanting the bad memories haunting her new life. She was happily surprised when she only felt a tinge of sadness. She saw the parade with fresh eyes and it gave her hope that she'd made the right decision in coming back.

Ash twirled the flower in her fingers again. The image of Sam's hazel eyes, filled with anger, flashed through her mind again. Ash loved softball, but she didn't like being the villain. And she didn't want to bring pain to anyone anymore, most of all Sam.

What should she do?

She let out a deep sigh, causing Goose to scurry up from the floor. He watched her with soulful brown eyes, his cute little ears flopped over.

He was adorable. One look at that face and she was a goner. "You know, just because I move doesn't mean we're going somewhere."

His tail wagged at her voice, causing his whole body to wriggle. His eyes somehow managed to be even more pleading than the moment before.

"I'm trying to figure out something important here."

He tilted his head to the side.

She sighed. "All right. Let's go for a walk."

Goose was at the back door before she'd even finished the sentence.

"All I'm saying is think about it," said Sam's brother, Scott.

"Don't be ridiculous, son. Why would I waste money on some fancy car when mine runs just fine?"

"It might run fine, but half of it is held together with duct tape. I worry about you and mom. You need to have a safer vehicle. You know, one with airbags for starters. Then you'd only be a few decades behind the rest of the world."

Sam's dad rolled his eyes. "That's the problem with your generation. You don't invest in anything. First sign of trouble, you just toss it in the trash."

Scott and his dad had been reprising the same conversation in different forms for the last thirty years. Sam had learned not to waste her energy by joining in. Being frugal was the essence of who her dad was—born of a childhood of struggle that he rarely discussed.

Sam's mom followed her out onto the deck to have some iced tea while they watched Jake play in the grass. They sat at the black wrought-iron patio table watching him for a few moments.

"Honey..."

Sam heard the hesitation in her mom's voice and turned toward her. Then she saw the frown on her lips. *Oh boy.*

"I tried to keep out of it, but I'm getting worried about you. You look exhausted. Would you please tell me what's going on?"

Sam saw the concern in her eyes and knew she had to come clean. She sighed. "Do you remember Ashley Valence?"

At the sound of the name, her mom sat up straight, bristling with anger. *Okay, I guess she does remember her, about as fondly as I did.*

"Well . . . she moved back to town recently. And now she's on my softball team, as our pitcher." Sam braced herself, not sure what reaction this new revelation would bring.

Her mom stared off toward Jake for a few moments, silent.

Sam wasn't sure if she should continue. Her mom seemed upset and Sam didn't think she needed to mention the nightmares and make her more concerned.

Her mom finally turned back to Sam with a look of determination in her eyes. "Those girls were horrible to you. If I could have slapped them silly, I would have, but there are laws against that sort of thing." She shook her head. "Unfortunately."

Sam was surprised. Her mom was usually the epitome of calm and collected, but she was clearly agitated now.

"I didn't...I didn't know you knew about that," Sam said quietly, looking down at the table. Drea had always been the one Sam confided in about the bullying. She had been too ashamed to tell her parents. It was humiliating enough without needing to worry them, too.

"I didn't at first. I just noticed you became really sad and withdrawn. I thought it was just normal teenage hormones and angst at first, but something told me it was more."

Sam met her mom's gaze. "So how did you figure it out?"

Her mom's mouth crooked up into a mischievous smile. "I cornered Drea when she was over here one evening and threatened to tell her parents about that little soirée you two had at her place when they went to Mobile that one weekend. She spilled the beans pretty quickly after that."

Sam's mouth gaped as she stared at her mom.

Jesus.

"But what does that little shit's return have to do with you being exhausted?"

Sam looked around, wide-eyed. *Am I on Punk'd or something?* She had no idea who this woman was sitting next to her.

"Honey." Her mom placed a hand on Sam's knee, grabbing her attention. "Answer the question."

"I, um, I've been having nightmares . . . about high school. And all of these memories are coming up." Sam felt embarrassed just saying it.

A pained expression filled her mom's eyes. She withdrew her hand and stared at her iced tea for a long moment. When she finally spoke, her voice was small. "I've thought about that situation so many times over the years. Whether I should have handled it differently. Done something, anything, to stop it." She shook her head slowly, still staring absently at her glass. "I was trying to let you be independent. I tried to trust that you'd come to me if it got bad. But you never did. When I finally realized how much it affected you, it was too late."

She shook her head again and looked at Sam with wet eyes. "I'm so sorry, Sam. I think I'll regret that decision forever."

Sam leaned toward her mom and wrapped her in a hug, inhaling hints of jasmine and biscuits—a mixture she always identified with her mom. She felt her mom shake with silent tears. "It's okay, Mom. You didn't know."

After a few moments, Sam's mom chuckled and they both sniffed and wiped at their tears before pulling apart. "Oh enough of that," her mom said cheerfully.

She clucked her tongue and looked out at Jake. After a few moments, she turned to Sam with an intensity in her eyes Sam hadn't seen in a long time. "We can't always choose who's in our life, honey. But we can choose how we let them affect us. You are an incredibly strong, intelligent, and beautiful woman, Samantha. Don't you *ever* let anyone make you feel anything different, you hear me?"

Sam nodded. "Yes, ma'am."

She raised an eyebrow. "I'd still like to slap her. I think the laws are a bit more lax once the victim isn't a minor."

"Mom!"

She tilted her head toward Sam, raising her eyebrows innocently. "I'm just saying."

The revelation from her mom stayed with Sam for the rest of the afternoon. She had known all of these years. And she had never said anything.

Now that Sam was a mom herself, she couldn't imagine not doing something if Jake was ever bullied. Sure, she was older than Jake when it happened to her, but still. How could her mom have just trusted her to handle it? She was a teenager for fuck's sake.

The next morning, Jake had a little extra pep in his step as he and Sam explored the Insectarium. It was one of Jake's favorite places in the city, and Sam enjoyed it as well—when she wasn't busy being creeped out by massive spiders and insects with way too many legs for her comfort level.

Jake giggled as they wandered through a darkened cave and came across the hissing cockroaches, repeatedly putting his finger close to their plexiglass enclosure trying to elicit their defense mechanism.

Sam felt a little bad, even for them. She read the information placard next to the enclosure. The bugs were native to Madagascar. That was quite a difference in locale. Well, maybe not in terms of humidity. Even as someone who grew up here, Sam often wondered if it was healthy to live in a place that became so humid it could be hard to breathe.

Jake giggled again, tearing her attention back to his undeterred fascination with the creatures. She smiled at the giggling sound, her favorite sound in the whole world. Unabashed happiness. Sam figured as long as she heard that at least a few times a week, maybe she wasn't doing too badly at this whole motherhood thing.

She took his hand and tugged gently. "Come on, bud. Let's go harass some other creepy crawlies."

They wandered past the Bug Appétit where actual chefs made gourmet delicacies out of insects for people to sample. Sam knew there were many countries where insects were a diet staple, or at least a solid addition of protein. But unless she was actually in those countries, experiencing their culture and food, she tried, as a rule, to abstain from consuming insects. But as a mom with a five-year-old, she found herself doing a lot of things she wouldn't normally do.

"Come on, Mom," Jake said, pulling her hand, as he leaned his entire body weight toward the entrance to the kitchen of horrors. He glanced back at her hesitation and rolled his eyes. *Wow, only five, and already rolling his eyes at his mom.* "Mo-om," he said stretching the word out for several seconds. Sam had the distinct feeling she was getting a sobering glimpse into what his teenage years might be like, but allowed him to pull her forward anyway.

A middle-aged man in a white chef's coat stood behind a small table with the three sampling options. Sam pondered for a moment what might have transpired in his life to lead him to a job where he used his culinary skills to sauté mealworms in garlic and bake crickets with cinnamon.

Jake bounced in his sneakers as he took an insect out of one of the rather classy white porcelain bowls and tasted it. Sam watched as he scrunched his nose at the garlic mealworm. "Blah," he said, sticking his tongue out. Sam's stomach turned at the sight of mealworm bits on it.

She grabbed a napkin and wiped his tongue off, then turned her head and gagged a little.

Jake was unfazed. He grabbed a cricket coated in cinnamon and eagerly tossed it into his mouth. "Mmm." His brown eyes danced. He moved down the counter to the final bowl. The label read "Chocolate-covered crickets." His face lit up at the word chocolate. His reading vocabulary was still burgeoning, but Sam had taught him the important stuff. He snatched two of the crickets and eagerly chewed. Sam laughed as he jumped up and down. "These are really good, Mom."

Sam eyed the bowl warily.

"Try one, Mom. Don't be a baby."

Sam raised her eyebrows at him and he tucked his chin with a bashful smile and giggled.

She took a deep breath and reached for one of the chocolate-covered crickets. She held it in front of her face, which was a bad idea, as she saw all of the legs and antennae protruding from its body. Battling her internal resistance, she closed her eyes and took a small bite. She mostly tasted the sweetness of the milk chocolate, and tried not to focus on the crunchy bits. She figured the chef probably wouldn't appreciate her throwing up his creation.

"Come on, Mom. Take a real bite."

She took another deep breath—it was almost worse knowing what to expect—and tossed the remaining cricket into her mouth, closing her eyes as she chewed rapidly and shaking her hand as if it would speed up the process. Thankfully once it was finally over, the only aftertaste was of chocolate.

Jake clapped his hands, and Sam smiled at him. "All right. Now can we move on?"

He nodded with a grin.

Sam's favorite part of the Insectarium was the butterfly room. Though she realized butterflies were insects, they were much less horrifying for some reason. Maybe it was the way the beautifully colored creatures drifted gracefully in the air, completely different from a cockroach, which thrived in New Orleans.

Jake started to get restless, so they walked quickly through the butterfly room, crossing a short wooden bridge through a plethora of plants as butterflies floated in the air all around them. It was so peaceful. Sam would have loved to stay longer, reading a good book, nestled amongst the calming surroundings, but Jake pulled her hand to keep moving.

"Hey Mom?" Jake said as they strolled hand in hand amidst the palm trees and street lamps scattered along the brick sidewalk outside the Insectarium. There were a lot of people out and the honking from the heavy traffic along Canal Street made the city feel alive. Sam felt the warmth of the sun against her face and smiled at the thought of spring arriving.

"Yes, honey?"

"Can I sleep over at Max's on Saturday?"

Max was Jake's closest friend in his kindergarten class. He was a bit more outgoing than Jake, which Sam viewed as a good thing. She figured he could help Jake move past his shyness at certain things. However, Max was also remarkably precocious for his young age in terms of his use of curse words and penchant for being a bit of a troublemaker. So, Sam was also a bit hesitant about her son spending too much time with him.

"Will it just be you spending the night?" she asked tentatively.

"Yeah."

She frowned and searched the ground as she tried to figure out how to deal with this. She didn't have a good feeling about Max, but she didn't want to be one of those overprotective moms who realized the error of her ways when her forty-year-old son was still living at home. It was times like this she wished she wasn't the one solely responsible for all of the parenting decisions.

"Pleeease, Mom. I promise I'll be good."

She met her son's eyes, large and hopeful. He was holding his hands clasped in front of him in classic begging fashion. There was no way she could say no.

"All right."

He jumped up and down and squealed. Okay, that was her second favorite sound.

Chapter 5

Sam's team buzzed around the office all morning on Tuesday as Bill McGrady had scheduled a staff meeting in the conference room at two o'clock. Bill was known primarily as a hands-off CEO—he had built McGrady Marketing from the ground up thirty years ago—preferring to have behind-closed-door meetings with the main managers and little to do with the rest of the staff.

Sam wasn't quite sure what to think and her mind drifted back and forth from positive to negative outcomes, dwelling for a bit on the catastrophic. Was the company going under and they'd all be jobless, with no severance package, by the end of the day? Had Bill fallen in love with a Russian supermodel and was running away to Bali, gifting his precious company to Pete, whom he adored like a son? What was this about?

As a project leader, Sam was one of the second-tier staff, concerned primarily with the fun parts of creating marketing campaigns and working directly with clients. So, she wasn't too surprised she had no idea what was about to transpire. However, when she had spoken with Audrey—the diligent, driven, and very serious woman in her late fifties who had been Sam's boss for the past six years—and she had no idea either, Sam grew concerned.

She ate a salad at her desk and tried to focus on the team's current campaign, set to pitch at the end of the week. After forty-five minutes of failing miserably, she typed in the web address of a local job search company to peruse what, if any, options might be available in her field.

Just in case.

At 1:50 p.m., she headed toward the conference room, feeling slightly nauseous. Everyone crowded in, talking nervously about what could be going on. Sam stood silently against the wall, arms crossed over her chest, and glanced across the room at Audrey, who met her gaze with a mirrored expression of calm guardedness.

At exactly two o'clock, Bill McGrady entered the room, all conversations ceasing immediately. The anticipation was palpable.

"Thank you all for being here," he said with no expression. He remained standing, like most of the occupants of the room. Sam searched his round, blank face for some sign of impending doom, but saw nothing. He was professional and detached as usual.

"Well . . ." He placed his hands on his hips, cinching up the sides of his open black suit jacket. Sam glanced at his big belly stretching the seams of his light blue shirt, threatening to shoot buttons across the room at everyone like death missiles. At this point, she was beginning to think that might be an easier fate than whatever was about to come out of his mouth. He gazed down at the table. Sam sent a worried glance at Audrey, but her face remained calm—stony, but calm.

Bill raised his head and Sam's heart stopped momentarily as she saw something she had never seen before. He was smiling. A huge, beaming smile that even elicited a subtle twinkle in his usually vapid gray eyes. *It's the Russian supermodel.*

"I have some great news. Our firm has been short-listed for an Adrian Award for our drone imagery campaign of Frenchmen Street for the New Orleans Tourism Bureau. While we've been fortunate to win a number of awards over the years, this award is the most prestigious at the international level—a true feather in our cap. So please put your hands together for the campaign lead, Pete Marks."

Bill gestured to Pete and summoned him to his side, as hesitant applause trickled through the room. Bill draped his arm over Pete's shoulders, a fairly monumental feat given that Pete towered over his portly boss by about six inches. "Pete, you continue to raise the bar for this company and set an example of true success."

Pete wore a Cheshire grin on his smug face.

Sam watched, willing him to give credit to their team who had done all of the design and multi-media content on this particular campaign.

"Thank you, Bill. It's an honor to work for you, and I truly appreciate you noticing my efforts."

Sam sighed. What did she expect? This was Pete, after all.

"Absolutely, absolutely!" Bill continued enthusiastically. "And that's not all. *New Orleans Magazine* would like to schedule an interview with you to highlight our company in their next issue." He leaned closer to Pete, but didn't lower his voice at all. "And I wouldn't be surprised if you find a hefty bonus coming your way." He winked up at Pete conspiratorially.

Sam tried to cement a polite smile on her face, despite the soul-crushing blow she felt deep inside. She glanced around the room to see a similar expression on most peoples' faces. They clapped again without much gusto, and a few snuck a glance at Sam, revealing sympathetic smiles. Sam smiled warmly back at them and nodded, trying to remain encouraging.

Though it was never verbalized directly between Sam and her team, they all knew the standard protocol at McGrady Marketing was to work as a team to create awe-inspiring campaigns rivaled by no one, and then to sit idly back as Pete claimed all of the credit for their efforts. He was the figurehead. It might have been less demoralizing had he tried to extend some of his success to the others, even a simple compliment or 'thank you'. It might also have been more acceptable if his very attitude and general personality, which easily rubbed most clients the wrong way, didn't nearly cost them every campaign they worked on.

The news stuck with Sam for the rest of the afternoon. Audrey left around four-thirty to squeeze in a dental appointment. And so, Sam decided to take a risk, small as it might seem, to stand up for her team.

She knocked on Bill's solid oak door and waited.

"Come in," he said after a few moments.

She opened the door and walked toward his desk, trying to hold her head up and exude the confidence she wasn't feeling.

His expression conveyed surprise at seeing her. Sam had never met with him privately before. Even when she was hired, Audrey was the point person. In hindsight, that should have been a red flag about his managerial style.

"Hi, sir." Sam stood deferentially in front of his desk as he gazed up at her. "I'm sorry to bother you, but I was hoping to have a brief moment of your time, if I may."

"Please," he said warily, motioning with an upturned palm to one of the two brown leather chairs in front of his massive oak desk—a stark contrast to the contemporary design of the rest of the firm's furniture.

"Thank you," Sam said quietly as she sat. Bill met her gaze with a look of interest. "Sir…" Her nerves rattled and she kept her hands clasped in her lap so he wouldn't see them shaking. Sam steadied her breath and continued. "In light of the recent accomplishments of our team, I was hoping you would be amenable to permitting me to throw a small celebration for them tomorrow … to let them know their hard work is appreciated."

He narrowed his eyes and steepled his hands in front of his chest.

Seeing prospects of a pink slip, Sam rambled on. "Nothing too fancy … just some snack platters and maybe a few pralines."

His brow furrowed. "Have you run this by Audrey?"

"No, sir. I didn't get a chance before she left." Sam paused. "I'll be sure to run it by her in the morning though."

"Hmm, well, okay. As long as Audrey approves and the cost is minimal. I suppose we can do that."

Sam nodded, before forcing a smile. "Thank you. I know the team will greatly appreciate your generosity."

He nodded, but his gaze lingered on Sam, an unreadable expression on his face. "I appreciate you being a team player, Ms. Parker."

Sam's eyes widened slightly. Had she been wrong all this time and maybe Bill McGrady did realize how much effort the team had put in for Pete to be honored? "Thank you, sir."

"I'm sure it must be challenging working in the shadow of an all-star like Pete, but you're right, it is good to acknowledge the little people occasionally as well. Keep morale up." He grinned and Sam wasn't sure if he even realized what a colossal douchebag he was.

She looked down into her lap and nodded slowly. "Have a good evening, sir."

By the time Sam arrived at the softball field that night, following her conversation with Bill, she had mentally kicked herself about a thousand times for not correcting him, not standing up to him.

"Everything okay?" Lace asked hesitantly as Sam rocketed the ball into her glove during warm-ups.

For six years, she'd let an arrogant child-of-a-man get all of the credit for efforts that were largely not his own. When she first joined the team, she trusted that her work ethic and skills with both design and clients would make her reputation. But as time went on, she realized it was just another boys' club. Pete could do no wrong in Bill's eyes, even though he rarely did anything at all. But Sam also blamed herself. The exact qualities she valued and that made her good at her job—building solid relationships with clients, being a great team member, smoothing over crises—were what kept her from fighting for more. More acknowledgment. More money. And more respect. It pissed her off to be treated unfairly time and time again when she gave so much of herself to her team and the company. But it enraged her to know she might have been complicit.

"Yeah. Just some work stuff. I'll be fine once the game starts."

"All right." Lace didn't bother trying to mask the doubt in her voice.

Sam was wrong, though. As the game wore on, she became increasingly agitated. First, by recurring thoughts of Pete's smug face and Bill's inability to see through the shallow veneer of Pete's bravado. True, Pete was a talented designer, but so were most of the people on their team. It didn't make up for all of the negatives that accompanied his presence.

Finally, those thoughts faded as Sam became more aware of the game around her and how Ash was once again busy being the one-woman team. Yes, Sam wanted to play on a successful team, even make it to the championships, and hopefully win, for once. But she also wanted to actually play ball, not just stand in the middle of the field watching somebody else do it all. She couldn't speak for her teammates, but their bored expressions suggested she wasn't the only one torn about the addition of their new pitcher.

The crack of bat against ball pulled her attention back to home plate. The batter stared high into the sky at the ball she had just popped up rather than out. She began a run to first base, just in case. The ball, on its downward arc, was set to land between the pitcher's mound and Sam's position.

"I got it!" Sam yelled, focused and running forward a few feet to get her glove underneath it. At first, she didn't register the other person calling for the ball at the same time.

As the ball came down within a couple inches of Sam's glove, almost as if in slow motion, another glove landed atop hers, pushing her glove down.

Sam's eyes widened as she watched the ball come down in the other glove, as a forearm painfully slammed against her face, followed by a hard body crashing into her chest, knocking the wind out of her.

Sam landed with a thud, and she couldn't breathe for a few seconds. She tried to sit up, gasping for air, but there was a body on top of her, pinning her down. Then, she realized it was *Ashley fucking Valence* who had used Sam's body as an inflatable mattress to buffer her impact with the ground, letting Sam take the full brunt of the hit.

"Get off of me!" Sam pushed Ash off her chest and sat up.

"Hey! Don't *push* me." Ash pushed Sam's hand away as she sat up, a bit stunned herself.

Sam's eyes went wide. "Don't push *me*." The seriousness of Sam's tone was as subtle as a dagger.

Ash slowly turned her head toward Sam, a mixture of challenge and wariness flickering through her eyes as she met Sam's gaze. "You." She looked at Sam pointedly. "Started it."

Sam didn't appreciate her condescending tone. "Oh, that's it." Sam lunged forward, Ash's eyes widening just before Sam's hands landed on her shoulders, knocking her backward onto the ground. Sam used as much force as she could muster from a seated position, but her rage made up for what physics prevented.

Ash was in shock and it took a moment for her to realize Sam was pinning her down in the dirt. Well, a brief moment, before absolute rage filled her eyes, too.

Sam was pretty sure she flinched at the sudden shift, but this had been a long time coming. It was now or never. Running was not an option.

"What the hell is your problem?" Before Sam could answer, Ash flipped Sam onto her back, pinning her down with her arms.

Sam let out a growl and responded in turn as they wrestled for dominant position, continuing to flip each other over in the dirt. Ash was taller and stronger than Sam, but nearly twenty years of built-up anger created surprising power, making them more evenly matched.

After what was probably only a few seconds, Sam was nearly exhausted—enough for Ash to get the upper hand and pin her down for good. Sam lay there, Ash's long legs sprawled on top of hers, Ash's hands pinning Sam's arms against the ground beside her face. Their faces were inches apart as they both let out ragged breaths. Staring at each other. Sam saw anger in Ash's eyes, but in an instant, the anger vanished and Sam felt a calm through her body as she and Ash held each other's gaze.

"Ladies! Get on your feet now!" Marci's booming voice jolted them back to reality.

Ash looked up at Marci, who was standing over them. Then she gazed at Sam, and slowly loosened her grip on Sam's arms, placing her knees on the ground to get up, effectively straddling Sam's hips.

Ash closed her eyes as her face dipped toward Sam's for a brief moment. Sam's breath hitched at the closeness, just as Ash's eyes snapped open, and she quickly scrambled to her feet.

Sam quickly followed her up, still stunned. *What the hell had just happened?*

Marci looked from Sam to Ash and back to Sam.

"Have you two lost your damn minds?"

They both looked at the ground.

"I'm sorry, Marci."

"Me too." Ash quickly added.

"You are acting like children out here. It's embarrassing."

Sam and Ash both nodded, still staring at the ground.

"Sarah! Take over as pitcher. Margot! Cover second."

Sarah and Margot scurried off the bench and out to the field.

"You two. Come with me."

Marci marched off the field toward the parking lot, followed by Ash, then Sam. When she reached the edge of the gravel lot, out of hearing distance from the rest of the team, she stopped and turned around, hands on her hips.

"I don't know what your history is, but it's clear that you have some. Sam, you've been an absolute asshole to Ash ever since she joined this team. I tried to let you both work it out. I mean, Jesus, we *are* all adults here. But it's clear things aren't getting any better and it's affecting the whole team."

"Sorry, Marci," Sam said, embarrassed.

"Yeah, I'm sorry," Ash added, genuinely.

"I don't want to lose either of you, but I will if you can't get it together. I want you to both go home and really think about your actions. If you decide to stay on the team and come back next week, this is over. I don't want to hear another peep out of either of you, unless it's something positive. Do you hear me?"

They both nodded a "yes," then turned to walk toward their cars.

"Oh, and ladies . . ."

They both gazed back at Marci. "Before you go, I want you to apologize to each other. If you come back here, it's going to be with a fresh start."

Sam closed her eyes, steeling herself. She stared at the ground as she turned toward Ash. They met each other's gaze with hesitation. Sam glanced back at Marci, who gestured for her to speak.

"I'm sorry, Ash," Sam said meekly.

"Yeah . . . me too."

Marci nodded and headed back to the field. Sam and Ash headed in opposite directions across the parking lot.

Having driven home in a stupor, Ash stood emotionless by the open back door as Goose did his business in the yard along the fence, then bounded back to her. Then they both collapsed into the sofa.

Goose seemed to know something was wrong and toned down his usual out-of-body excitement at her presence. Instead, he jumped up onto her chest, licked her face as she stared at the ceiling, and curled up beside her.

There had been only one concrete thought circling in Ash's mind since she left the game. *What the hell just happened?*

As she stared at the empty white ceiling, she worked to process things. She had been trying so hard to be adult about all of this, to be polite to Sam no matter how Sam treated her. And in an instant, it had all gone to hell.

Was it the tension between them the past few weeks? The excitement of the game? She wasn't sure. What she did know was that she and Sam had a fight—something she was very ashamed of. Being physical with someone like that, even in a game situation, was not okay. It made her uncomfortable even thinking about it.

She wasn't even sure how it happened, as everything was still a little fuzzy. She remembered going for the ball, the impact, Sam pushing her. She recalled the rage in Sam's eyes. And then . . . the lack of rage. Something else entirely.

Oh fuck. She had almost kissed Samantha Parker. Ash covered her eyes with her hand and groaned. It had been so intimate, being that close to Sam, with Sam's breath on her face. She recalled the feel of Sam's body against hers. Then, when she ended up straddling Sam. *Well, damn.* That was a surprise. Thankfully, Sam's sharp intake of breath had shaken Ash back to reality.

Ash groaned again, because clearly, the way Sam had looked at her left no doubt that Sam knew what she had been thinking. *Fuck.*

Ash had known about her feelings for Sam since she saw her at the pizza place. Before that, if she was being honest. It was her feelings for Sam so very long ago that made her realize she was, well, different. She didn't know what it was at first, but she finally figured it out. College had a way of helping sort out those kinds of things.

But Sam now? Sam was beautiful. When she walked into the restaurant, time had seemed to stop. Even thinking about it now made Ash swallow hard.

It was ridiculous though. Sam hated her. She made that abundantly clear. And she was probably straight anyway. Ash had a knack for falling for straight girls. Put her in a room full of lesbians and one straight girl, and guess which one she wanted to hit on? Her therapist would say that to protect herself, it was her subconscious preventing her from pursuing a real commitment by going for someone unattainable. Ash wasn't sure about all that. But it happened often enough to wonder.

Ash thought about Sam. The feel of Sam's body underneath her, how her eyes changed from anger to . . . what? Lust? There had been something there.

She shook her head, trying to dislodge the thoughts tormenting her. "Enough," she said to the empty room. She heard Goose snoring quietly beside her and she focused on the gentle cadence, finally allowing her to fall asleep.

When Ash woke up, her back ached. She sat up, realizing she had slept on the sofa in her clothes. She grimaced and rubbed her back. The heather gray sofa had been a stylistic choice to complement the blues and creams in her living room, but damn, it wasn't very comfortable.

Light streamed through the living-room windows and she glanced at her watch to see it was just after seven o'clock. She stood up, slowly, and stretched, realizing Goose had been beside her all night. He was still curled in a ball, watching her.

"You want to go for a walk?"

He slowly got to his feet and took his time stretching his front legs, then back legs, before letting out a loud yawn.

"Did you turn into an old man overnight?"

He licked his nose and jumped off the sofa. Ash wondered if he had been as uncomfortable as she had been.

She walked Goose through the neighborhood, taking in the Southern charm of quaint cottages, wraparound porches, and people who waved and said 'good morning,' whether they had seen you before or not. Goose pulled on the leash a little, but was being pretty obedient for a puppy.

They turned down an unfamiliar street and the smell of bread had Ash and Goose both sniffing the air. A few patio tables and chairs were placed along the sidewalk and Ash glanced in the open doorway to see a bakery there in the middle of a residential area.

A woman behind the counter smiled and waved.

Ash waved back and looked at the sign hanging above the door. Daily Bread. She made a mental note to come back and try it out.

As they walked back to the house, Ash thought about the game, Marci's words, and Sam. Ash liked it here. She liked the team. She liked the neighborhood. She liked all of it. She wasn't going to let things with Sam derail her from creating a life here.

Sam would have to make up her own mind about things. But Ash wasn't going anywhere.

"You didn't deck her?" Drea asked as they sat down at their usual table at Charlie's.

"No, but I held my own."

Drea shook her head. "Man, that's some restraint. I'd have decked her."

Sam rolled her eyes. "There was no restraint involved. That's the problem. I acted like a child."

"Sam, she totally deserved it . . . and so much more."

"Maybe, but I'm still not proud. Well . . . I'm proud that I didn't back down to her, but I should've handled it differently. I think just the crap at work and the unresolved stuff from high school hit a boiling point."

"Hi, ladies. What can I get you to drink?"

Drea and Sam both turned to regard the perky, brunette waitress.

"The house margarita, please."

She nodded quickly before turning her gaze to Drea—a gaze that Drea met and held for several seconds as a slow smile spread across her lips.

"Same for me . . . thanks."

"Absolutely," the waitress said with a smile before heading toward the bar.

Sam raised an eyebrow at Drea and gave her a knowing look. Drea chuckled.

"Anyway . . . it's over. From here on out, I am going to focus on the game and act like an adult."

"That's no fun."

"Here you go, ladies." The waitress placed the margaritas on the table. "Can I get you anything else?" She looked adoringly at Drea.

"Thank you, honey. Not *right* now." Drea smiled.

A blush crept up the waitress's neck. Beaming, she walked away.

Sam raised both brows at Drea. "Really?"

Drea chuckled. "It's a blessing and a curse."

"Is it me or does your Southern drawl tend to get much thicker when you talk to attractive women?"

Drea just smiled and winked.

"Always the charmer . . ." Sam sighed.

Sam had decided not to tell Drea everything about the scuffle with Ash. She'd gone over it a million times in her head since Tuesday night. Initially, she focused on working through the anger. That was fairly easy to understand. She tried to ignore the rest of it, but eventually let herself face it. A little. She had felt something. When Ash was on top of her, Sam's body responded. And not in the way you'd ever want your body to respond with the person who used to be a merciless bully. At first, Sam chalked it up merely to the intimate position, her body responding in kind. While she could admit—if forced—that Ash wasn't too hard on the eyes, she was sure her body would have responded the same way to any mildly attractive woman lying on top of her. She was even a little thankful to know her body still could respond. She hadn't been in a situation even bordering intimate since Anna, so it was nice to know everything still worked. That's all it was, wasn't it?

But if she was being honest, she knew it was more. Sam felt like her body had betrayed her by responding to something her mind hadn't yet recognized. Or something she wasn't willing to recognize. Not yet anyway. But what did that mean? It scared her. She didn't like not understanding things. And this—*this*—had her really fucking confused.

When she allowed herself to remember how she felt, well, that wasn't scary. The way Ash looked at her calmed her entire body. Instantly. She'd never felt that kind of release before. It pulled at her heart and she felt curious to explore it. She remembered the way Ash dipped toward her as if she was about to kiss her. Sam reacted with shock in the moment. But afterward, was there regret?

"You okay?"

Sam blinked and realized Drea was staring at her. She let out a small laugh. "Yeah, sorry. Must have dazed out for a second." She sipped her margarita as she collected herself. "I had an interesting conversation with my mom the other day."

"Oh yeah?" Drea sipped her drink and began fidgeting with her napkin.

"Very."

Drea met Sam's eyes with an anxious look.

"Anything you'd like to tell your old best friend?" Sam asked.

Drea's face began to color as she avoided eye contact. "I don't think so."

"Interesting . . . because it seems you had no problem telling her all kinds of secret information from years ago."

That got her. "Sam, I've wanted to tell you forever, but I didn't know how."

"Seriously? You told my mother about Jackie's posse, about the bullying, and never told me?"

"I'm sorry! Truly." Her eyes looked pained. "She was going to tell my parents about that weekend we got smashed when they were out of town. I had no choice. They would have kicked my ass."

Sam stared, unmoved.

"Please forgive me." Drea's pleading eyes were too much to bear.

Sam rolled her eyes, shaking her head. "It's fine. I just wish you had told me."

"I know, I'm sorry." She blew out a breath and sipped her drink. "Sam, your mom is really intimidating. You don't even know." Drea shook her head with a look of fear in her eyes.

Sam nodded. "I'm beginning to think you're right."

Saturday night came too soon for Sam. Jake was supposed to sleep over at Max's house and Sam regretted saying yes. It was Jake's first sleepover and she'd expected him to be nervous, scared to sleep in a strange place. *Wasn't that a normal reaction for a kid?* But Jake was excited— really excited—about tonight. She was the only one freaking out.

As five o'clock approached, she grabbed his blue Transformers backpack which matched his comforter, sheets, and curtains and knelt down in front of her son.

"Okay, honey, you've got your toothbrush here, your PJs and clothes for tomorrow here." She pointed out the contents of each compartment as she spoke. "I put some animal crackers in here, just in case you get hungry."

"Mom."

Sam looked up from the bag and saw Jake's smile, instantly relaxing her.

He put a hand on her shoulder. "It's going to be okay."

She pulled him into a hug. "I'm so proud of you." She released him and let out an embarrassed chuckle at how emotional she was being as she fought tears.

"I love you, Mom."

"I love you, too, sweetie."

After Sam dropped Jake off, she intended to relax at home, watch some shows that weren't cartoons for once, and be ready in case Jake called with any issues. By the time eight o'clock rolled around, she'd checked her watch at least twenty times. Still no call. She turned off the television and sat there in deafening silence. It felt so foreign to be completely alone and not be doing something for Jake. She didn't like it.

She shook her head and tried to laugh at herself. She should be proud of her son for being so brave and not needing her. *Ouch*. That was not a thought she was ready for yet. He was only five. Of course, he still needed her. He just maybe didn't need her *right* now.

Sam grabbed a beer to turn down her anxiety. On her way back to the couch, she stopped suddenly as a hot pain shot up through her foot. "Son of a—" She lifted her leg, resting her foot against her knee to see what it was, fully expecting a huge splinter from the old hardwood floor.

She shook her head and smiled when she saw the red plastic LEGO embedded in the soft skin of her arch. She sat down on the sofa and rubbed at the impression the toy had left in her skin. Normally she'd be annoyed at Jake leaving out his toys, but tonight, it was comforting.

Sam tried to just enjoy the quiet, but her mind started spinning. She went through a mental checklist of things she should do—laundry, dishes, vacuuming—realizing one by one, that everything was done. Well, not the vacuuming. But it could wait another day.

She took another sip of her beer, laid down on the sofa, and closed her eyes, trying to force herself to relax. It was less than another minute before her mind wandered to Ash. Her eyes. Her body—she *was* in really good shape. Sam could admit that. It was an observable fact. Her lips . . . what it might feel like to kiss—

"Nope." Sam sat up abruptly. "Nope, nope, nope."

She turned on the television and took another sip of beer. She knew what she had to do, she just wasn't looking forward to it.

Chapter 6

"Thanks for seeing me on such short notice."

Allison smiled. "Of course. I had a last-minute cancellation, so it worked out perfectly. It's great to see you, Sam. How are you?"

Sam felt a bit nervous as she sunk down into the brown leather couch in Allison's office. Allison Eckhart was an interesting mix of professional woman and spiritual healer, right down to her clothes, which were always stylish and classy while also being free-spirited. She had her curly auburn hair up with a few strands hanging down along her neck. A magenta blouse, loose but tailored, accented a tan pencil skirt. Bright yellow heels sat on the carpeted floor beside her chair. She managed to exude just the right amount of warmth while maintaining a professional distance.

After Anna's death three years ago, Sam had really struggled with the loss. Drea and Sam's parents tried to be patient, but after a month, they encouraged her—strongly—to find a therapist to work through her grief. Sam fought the idea at first, wanting to deal with things on her own and at her own pace. Finally, though, she had to face the fact that not only wasn't she getting better with time, she was getting worse.

She took some time looking for the right person. She wanted a woman with experience working with the LGBTQ community. Though there were a few options, it was Allison's experience as a grief counselor which stood out the most. Sam also liked that they were about the same age. And though Allison rarely talked about her own life, she did disclose she was a lesbian, making Sam feel less alone.

Sam knew she hadn't been an easy client. She was angry, pretty resistant to therapy, and severely depressed. But Allison never gave up on her or made her feel bad for needing to go slowly. They worked together for about a year before Sam felt like she could do things on her own again. While the focus had been grief recovery, it brought up the persistent bullying memories of the past, so they had worked a bit on her recovery from that trauma.

Sam took a deep breath, trying to calm herself. "I'm good." She looked at the wooden side table next to her, where one large white crystal and a smaller pink crystal sat on a hot pink and orange scarf serving as a tablecloth. She nodded toward them. "I see you've still got the crystals."

Allison gave a light laugh. "I do."

Sam hadn't known what to expect when she first started seeing Allison. But the moment she stepped into her office and saw the crystals, she was a little put off. She explained that she wasn't into spells or sorcery or any of that shit. Had Sam been in a better place emotionally, she probably would have exercised a bit more tact. At the time, Allison nodded politely with a slightly amused look on her face and assured Sam she didn't need to worry about any of that *shit*. It turned out that Allison did utilize lots of tools with clients—crystals, shamanism, animal medicine—but she and Sam stuck with traditional talk therapy.

"How's Jake?"

"He's doing well. Great, actually."

"Good. I'm happy to hear that." They sat nodding and smiling politely for a few moments before Allison took the initiative. "So, what can I help you with?"

Sam took a deep breath. "Well, you remember the bullying I dealt with in high school?"

"I do."

"I thought I was good with that. But, well, one of the girls just moved back here and it's brought things up again."

Allison nodded. "I see. Well, I'm proud of you for reaching out, Sam. That takes a lot of courage."

"I tried to deal with it on my own for a bit, but I keep having these nightmares and they've really been messing with me." She clasped her hands in her lap. "I was hoping you could help me get a handle on things."

"Okay, why don't you tell me what's been going on."

Sam filled Allison in on Ash, the nightmares, the softball team, and the fight—well, some aspects of the fight. Allison listened intently as Sam spoke.

"I think what's throwing me, even more than the nightmares, is how angry I get. I'm usually able to cope pretty well, but the stuff with Ash just takes me back to high school. It's like a switch flips and I become someone else, all filled with anxiety and fear. I'm right back there. Even though I know I'm safe now, my body still reacts like when I was a teenager. And I find myself lashing out. Why can't I just let it go?" The weight of the last words pulled at Sam and tears filled her eyes. She quickly looked at her lap and bit the inside of her cheek until she could blink back the tears.

Allison uncrossed her legs and leaned forward in her chair. "Well, I think the most important thing to realize is that you're in control, Sam. You might feel like this stuff is happening to you, and it is to some degree, but you're in control now of how you let it affect you."

"Okaaay. Even the nightmares though?" Sam was skeptical.

Allison nodded. "I suspect the shock of Ash being back in your life has awakened those old memories of being bullied and tormented and not having control over that situation. This was traumatic for you, especially because it happened during an already hard time in a girl's development. It happened as you were trying to figure out who you were. And while you've gone on to be a successful adult who has done some truly amazing things, you've never really dealt with that past trauma. It's still with you. Ignoring it doesn't make it go away. Sometimes when we try to ignore something with our conscious mind, our subconscious has a way of making us address it."

Sam frowned. She knew what Allison was saying was true, knew she'd done pretty much anything possible to keep from facing that part of her past. She had really hoped she could just move on and it would go away eventually. "Sometimes I feel like a failure for letting it affect me back then, and even now."

Allison's eyes showed concern. "Why?" she asked gently.

"Because back then everything else was really good in my life.

70

I had a supportive family, a good friend. I know I was ashamed and tried to hide the bullying from my parents because I didn't want to disappoint them. But I still struggle with how much it affected me. All these years later, I still struggle with my self-worth and self-confidence because of those fucking girls in high school. Why couldn't I just overlook it?"

"First, you're not a failure, Sam. Not in any sense of the word. Having a supportive family is a great thing, but it doesn't prevent you from being hurt or having insecurities when awful things happen to you. And you kept a lot of that experience to yourself. You internalized the bullying and believed it. That can take a lot of time and attention to get over."

Sam nodded, trying to absorb the information. "So, what do I do? I mean, even if it is only once a week, I have to see Ash regularly for the next few months."

"Have you been using any of your coping skills?"

Sam looked down at the floor. "No."

Allison laughed. "It's okay, Sam. You're not in trouble."

Sam met her gaze.

"When you're in the moment and feeling overwhelmed or anxious, try to focus on your breathing. As your body calms, remind yourself that you're in control. You can make it into a mantra to repeat to yourself until you feel your body and mind calm. This takes practice, but as you work on it, relief should come naturally."

Allison watched Sam for a moment, making Sam aware that she looked tense as she tried to imagine a mantra. She quickly relaxed as Allison smiled.

"What about your artwork? That used to help you a bit, right?"

Sam nodded, then frowned. Drawing had really helped her work through her emotions before, but she hadn't created anything of her own, that wasn't for work, in a long time. She couldn't even remember why she had stopped. "I haven't kept up with that."

"Well, maybe that's worth starting up again."

Sam nodded and looked away. She knew she had one more truth to discuss. The nightmares were relatively easy to talk about, but in order to move forward, no matter how uncomfortable the conversation would be, she knew she had to put everything out there.

But knowing you need to do something and actually doing it are two different things.

Sam closed her eyes and rubbed her fingers up and down along her forehead, as if trying to massage away the truth. *How do I say this?* When she opened her eyes, Allison was watching her, calmly.

"There's one more thing," she blurted. "I think there might be a part of me… a very small part," she added quickly, "but still a part of me that is attracted to Ash." She winced at her own words. "I mean, I don't like her. I hate her, really, for what she and her posse did to me. I don't like her. At all." She blew out a breath and rolled her eyes for emphasis. "But my body betrays me when I'm around her. That doesn't mean anything though, right?" She laughed nervously.

Allison nodded, her silence escalating Sam's already high anxiety. Sam felt actual fear grip her, dreading whatever Allison was about to say.

"It's hard to know at this point what is behind that, Sam, but maybe it shows that, at least to some degree, you are seeing Ash for the woman she is now, not just the girl from high school. And I think that's a big step. I would try not to worry too much about what it means and focus instead on just getting to know her for who she is now. Then we can see how that affects what you're feeling toward her."

Sam crossed her arms over her chest. "Okay, none of that was comforting."

Allison laughed. "Sorry. Life isn't black and white. This probably will take time to figure out."

Sam glanced at the clock on the side table. Time was up. She felt a little sad to have to leave already.

"Sam."

Sam looked at Allison and was met with her usual warm smile. "These kinds of issues can take time to work through. You're not alone in this. And you're definitely not expected to be over it after one therapy session. If you want, I'd be happy to keep seeing you to work through this."

Sam took a deep breath, letting it out slowly. Talking to Allison today helped, but she knew there was much more work to do. She didn't want to keep running and have it keep showing up in her life in different ways, especially now that Ash was back in town. She needed to face it. Finally. It was time.

She looked up at Allison. "Okay. I'd like that."

As worried as Sam was about Jake's sleepover, things seemed to have gone well and as far as she could tell, Jake hadn't picked up any bad habits or four-letter words at Max's house. Though seeing her son grow up made Sam a little sad—wanting to keep him young and protected for as long as she could—she also felt a sense of relief that he could spend the night at a friend's house without any issues.

Over the next few weeks, Ash and Sam were the epitome of polite to each other at games. The few times Sam got the ball, she tossed it back to Ash like she was any other teammate. They even shared a joke or two on the bench.

Thankfully, Marci seemed to notice how bored the rest of the team was when Ash was pitching. She started rotating Sarah in when they were winning, and while Sarah was pretty good, she wasn't Ash. And Ash, apparently feeling less pressure to prove herself to the team, seemed to ease up and trust her teammates more. The increase in ball time, along with the lack of snarky comments and all-out brawling by Sam and Ash, seemed to raise team morale.

Sam's nightmares had also stopped, *thank god*, which meant she was more rested and a generally happier person. The act of standing up to Ash during their fight seemed to have convinced her subconscious she didn't need to fear her anymore. And the weekly sessions with Allison had helped her better understand her responses to Ash. Sam even started drawing again after putting Jake to bed and had really been enjoying it. It reminded her how much she enjoyed the process of creating something just for her.

As the midpoint of the softball season approached, Marci decided to throw a team party to celebrate their as yet undefeated season. She went all out and even rented an event space in a newly renovated high-rise downtown.

Since the party fell on a Saturday night, Sam's parents offered to keep Jake for two nights so Sam didn't have to worry about a babysitter. Sam argued that she only planned to make a brief appearance, an hour at most, but they insisted.

Well, maybe she'd stay two hours. She went so far as to put a little makeup on, not remembering the last time she had gone out beyond her casual Fridays with Drea.

The sun had just set as Sam walked along the street downtown. She took a deep breath, marveling at the beauty of the pinks and purples reflecting off nearby shop windows. It left a soft, almost magical air amid the vibrant storefronts. The air was still a little cool for early April, but Sam wasn't ready yet for the sticky humidity of summer, so a little cool air was just fine with her. She reached the high-rise and took in the vibrant teal wooden shutters offsetting each window against the light gray brick. New Orleans was never dull. Every aspect of the city—its food, architecture, cultural heritage—was infused with life. It was what Sam loved most about her hometown.

As she strolled across the updated lobby, she noticed the mix of old and new décor and was glad that the traces of the past hadn't been completely erased in the remodel. Inside the elevator, she pressed the button for the eighth floor and let out a contented sigh as she watched the doors start to close.

"Hold the elevator, please," a faint voice called.

Sam grabbed the half-closed metal door and strained to push it open, just as Ash appeared in the opening.

They both stood a little straighter when their eyes met. Ash took a half step backward before clenching her jaw, forcing a small smile, and stepping into the elevator.

Sam forced a return smile as the doors closed again. They stood silently beside each other against the back wall as it passed the second floor. Sam stared forward and noticed Ash's reflection in the shiny door. She was dressed up for the party, wearing dark jeans, black heeled boots, and a shimmering silver shell under a black leather jacket. Her hair was even down for once. She looked good . . . really good. Sam started to feel slightly underdressed in her faded jeans, Pumas, and purple V-neck sweater, makeup aside. Feeling less confident than before she'd entered the elevator, it bothered her that she even cared what Ash looked like or how she might look to Ash. She sighed internally, noticing for the first time that Ash's head was raised toward the ceiling and her eyes were closed. *Wow, does she really hate being around me that much?*

Just after they crept past the third floor, a loud metallic screech filled the car, followed by a mechanical grinding sound no one ever wants to hear while suspended a few stories in the air. The elevator stopped abruptly, jolting both women forward.

Sam's eyes widened as she stared at the control panel. "You've got to be kidding me." She moved toward the panel and pressed the 'open door' button. Nothing. She pressed the button for the third floor. Nothing. Fourth floor. Nothing.

She leaned over and tried to pry the door open with her fingertips. No luck. As annoyance and anxiety spread through her body, she moved back to the control panel and pressed the emergency button. She stared up at the perforations above the buttons where an intercom theoretically was connected. Was there anyone there at all? Anyone? She pressed the button a second time, and waited. Still nothing. She punched it three times rapidly—just for good measure—before blowing out a frustrated breath.

"Well, that's not a good sign."

Sam had forgotten Ash was still in the car with her, and turned to meet her eyes.

"Um, yeah. You'd think things would actually work after a renovation."

"Well, it is still New Orleans." Ash shrugged.

"True." Sam grabbed her cell phone, hoping for a signal despite being in an elevator shaft. There was one bar. "I'll try to text Lace and let her know the elevator is stuck. Hopefully, she can get help." After a few attempts, her message finally went through. A few seconds later, her phone vibrated in her hand.

The screen read: *We're trying to reach maintenance right now.*

"Oh, thank god. They're trying to reach maintenance."

Ash nodded, her expression unreadable. They stood silently, avoiding eye contact for a few moments, until Sam's phone vibrated again.

It looks like it might be a little while. There was a water line break in another building. They'll try to get somebody here as fast as they can.

"Oh, man. It might be a while."

The phone buzzed again. *Is it just you?*

No. Ash is here too.

Okay, just try to relax. We'll get you out as soon as we can. And Sam?
Yeah?
Don't kill each other.

Sam glanced up at Ash, who met her gaze with a curious expression. "What did she say?"

"To try to relax."

Ash leaned her head against the wall, and slowly slid down it to a seated position. At least there was a clean, new, albeit thin, carpet beneath her rather than just a concrete floor.

Sam walked to the side wall and leaned her back against it. "Well, at least we're not claustrophobic. That would suck," she joked, trying to lighten the mood.

"I am . . . actually," Ash said softly, before exhaling slowly.

Sam gazed down at her, realizing for the first time that she did seem a bit uneasy. "Oh, um, sorry."

Ash could feel Sam's eyes on her. When a few moments had passed and she still felt the weight of them, she turned her head to meet Sam's gaze. "What?"

Sam seemed in a daze, staring at her blankly. Ash's words startled her back to reality. "Oh, sorry. I just . . . I didn't think you were afraid of anything."

Ash laughed quietly, staring ahead at the door. "Well, maybe you don't know me that well."

"I don't know you at all, Ash." The lightness in Sam's tone was gone.

Ash wrapped her arms around her bent knees, trying to feel more secure. She glanced at the control panel, felt a tightness in her chest, and her anxiety and body temperature rose. *Damm it.* She'd considered taking the stairs, but eight floors was a hike. She had seen the elevator doors closing and made a split-second decision. Knowing she wouldn't be alone in the cramped space made it more conquerable, until she had realized who the other occupant was.

Stuck in an elevator with Sam. *This was some next level shit.* She almost laughed out loud. Was the universe determined to throw them together? As much as Ash tried to move on, everything seemed to be forcing her and Sam to figure out their stuff.

After a couple moments, she looked up at Sam with an open expression. "What would you like to know? About me. You said you don't know me."

Sam's eyebrows shot up. "Are we really doing this, now?"

"It seems like as good a time as any. I've tried to talk to you, but apparently forced seclusion does the trick." She gave Sam a small smile, hoping it would take any sting out of her words.

Sam stayed silent. Ash watched her at first, but then turned her attention to the space in front of her, tightening her grip around her legs. She wasn't sure what was worse, the anticipation of Sam's words or the fear clutching her body in the tiny space.

Finally, she heard Sam take a deep breath, letting it out slowly. Ash braced herself.

"Why were you so horrible to me in high school?"

Ash met Sam's eyes. "Wow, you're really going for it, aren't you?"

"I never did anything to you, but you made my life a living hell. It was torture. Why?"

Ash looked at the space in front of her, stretched out her legs, and rested her clasped hands on them. She sighed before looking up.

"Sam, I will answer whatever you ask me tonight. I owe that to you." She paused. "I came back to this city for two reasons. To make a home here, and, if I ever saw you again, to try to make things right between us. I don't know if you can ever forgive me, but please believe me when I tell you that I regret nothing more than how I treated you back then. It's worn on me for such a long, long time." She held Sam's gaze for a long moment.

Sam seemed stunned and a little cautious. "Okaaay," she said hesitantly.

"I've thought about that question a lot over the years, and I think I went along with our posse, those horrible girls, because, well, it comes down to the fact that I was jealous of you."

"Look, if you're not going to be honest, then just forget it." Sam folded her arms across her chest, anger flashing in her eyes.

"Sam, I *am* being honest. I need you to believe me."

"Why in the world would you have been jealous of me? You were the star athlete, popular, smart . . . beautiful . . ."

Ash tilted her head at the last word, a tiny smile forming at the corners of her mouth. She hoped Sam hadn't noticed and quickly cleared her throat before speaking again. "Things weren't exactly what they seemed back then," she said softly.

"What do you mean?"

Ash looked down at her hands again. She'd thought about this conversation so many times over the years. How it would go. What she would say. How Sam would react. But all of that fell away in the moment and she couldn't remember any plan. She could only feel Sam's presence next to her. Nothing else mattered in this moment, but the truth. And all of it. The whole truth was her only hope if she was ever going to get Sam to even consider forgiving her.

She met Sam's eyes, hoping her sincerity was obvious. "You had everything I felt like I was missing. Your friendship with Drea—a real friendship, not just flaky acquaintances. Parents who supported you. Plus, you were really smart, always reading, and not afraid to go your own way. Do your own thing. I envied you. You were so completely yourself."

Sam stared at her with a look of absolute shock, mixed with something else—anger, disbelief, confusion? She wasn't sure.

Ash shook her head. "Really. I felt like I was barely surviving all of the expectations and pressure. I put on some façade to not disappoint anyone. But, I was completely alone." Her voice turned cold. "No one really knew me or what was going on."

"What do you mean 'what was going on'?" Sam asked, cautiously.

Ash stared at her hands. It had been a long time since she'd talked to anyone about her past, having spent years in therapy trying to work through it all and put it behind her. She'd learned the hard way that ignoring it didn't make it go away. She had kept seeing the same patterns year after year and finally decided to face it. But no matter how much she'd accepted it and moved on, she still felt a little vulnerable discussing it.

She steeled herself. "My parents and I moved here from California when I was twelve because my father got a job here. Things seemed okay for the first year. My mom was trying to give it a chance, but it was clear that she missed California, where she had grown up. When

I was in eighth grade, I came home from softball practice to find a note on the kitchen table. She had decided to move back to California. Alone."

"Ash." There was warmth to Sam's voice. "I'm so sorry. I had no idea."

Ash nodded but continued to stare at her hands. "My father and I had never been that close. At first, we just kept to ourselves, both heartbroken that she'd left us so easily. My father started drinking a lot and then he started picking fights with me."

Ash paused and scratched her nails along the outside of her knee. She didn't want to cry right now, not in front of Sam. "It was just yelling and name calling at first. But then he got physical." She dug her nails deeper into her leg. "I tried to stand up to him, but he was a lot bigger than me." She shrugged. "I just blamed the bruises on softball."

She paused for a moment, then kept talking. "I used to pray my mom would come back for me, but, after a few years . . . I stopped praying and decided to save myself."

There was silence. After a few moments, Sam closed the short distance between them and sat down next to Ash, only a couple of inches apart.

"I'm so sorry, Ash," she said quietly.

With her gaze still fixed on her hands, Ash nodded and gave a small shrug. "It is what it is."

When she finally looked up, she saw Sam's eyes glistening. Ash had to look away quickly before she started crying. It took a few seconds before she could find her voice again and risk another glance at Sam.

"I felt so alone back then," Ash began. "When Jackie and Jessica welcomed me into their group—the cool kids...," she laughed bitterly and shook her head. "I just needed to not feel so alone. I was so happy to be included someplace, anyplace, I let myself ignore how they treated you, how *I* treated you."

She held Sam's gaze. "I am so very sorry, Sam. And I'm sorry I never tried to stop Jackie. I should have done *something*, not just gone along with it. I just felt so powerless. Against my father. Against Jackie." She shook her head. "When the people who are supposed to love you the most tell you you're worthless, day after day after day, you start to believe it. No matter how strong you think you are."

Sam stared at the floor. Ash continued, "It took me a long time to be able to face what I had done. It was only when I admitted what had happened to me and what I had done to you that I realized I was just as bad as the person I hated most. That was really hard to face. I had convinced myself that Jackie was the bully and I was just a bystander. But I wasn't. Even when I saw how much it hurt you."

Ash felt the tightening in her chest, making it hard to breathe. But it wasn't from fear. Or anxiety. It was sadness—utter remorse—for what she had done to Sam. The only thing that mattered was taking that pain away from Sam.

Sam stayed quiet. She was still staring at the space in front of her, but Ash could see the tears running down her face.

Ash placed a hand on Sam's forearm. "Sam . . ." she said as gently as she could.

Sam turned around and the sadness in her eyes hit Ash like a punch in the gut.

"Sam, I am so incredibly sorry for hurting you. There is nothing I regret more." She squeezed Sam's forearm slightly.

Sam gave a small nod and they sat side by side in silence for a few minutes.

"I know this is a lot. You probably need time to process it." Ash shook her head. "I never thought I'd run into you so soon or that we'd be thrown together like we have. I'm sure it hasn't been easy for you. But, I'd really like a chance to start over with you . . . if you'd let me."

Sam turned away and stared at the floor again.

Ash wasn't sure if she should keep going, but she needed Sam to know all of it. She didn't know if she'd ever get a chance to say this to her again. "I'm not a horrible person, Sam. It's important to me that you know that. And it would mean a lot to me to prove that to you. I wish I could change how I acted back then . . ." She shook her head. "But I can't. I can only hope that you'll give me a chance to make a different future." Her eyes were pleading as Sam turned to her.

Sam held her gaze before speaking. "Ash, I'm sorry you went through all of that, but you really hurt me. It messed me up for a long time. Sometimes it surfaces even now. Now that I know what was going on with you, I'm not going to hold it over your head, because frankly, I need to move on and lay it to rest too . . . I guess, I just need you to understand it might take some time. I can't just flip a switch and say we're all good."

Ash nodded, looking down at her lap. She'd done the best she could.

"But," Sam continued, and Ashley looked up, "I'm willing to give it a try. Just . . . baby steps, okay?" Sam gave her a small smile.

A huge grin spread across Ash's face. "Yes! I mean, okay." Her smile dimmed slightly as her tone became more serious. "Thank you, Sam."

Sam nodded shyly and looked back at the floor. They sat beside each other, shoulders grazing for a bit. "How are you feeling . . . with the claustrophobia and all?"

Ash shrugged. "It's not that bad. I think I was drained by our conversation, so there isn't much energy left to be afraid."

Sam nodded. "So . . ."

Ash's curiosity got the best of her. "What?"

"Is that why you closed your eyes when you got on the elevator? Because you're claustrophobic?"

"Yeah. Ali thinks I should take anxiety medication for it."

"Ali?"

"Yeah, my girlfriend."

"Like your girlfriend or your girlfriend, girlfriend?"

Ash laughed. "Girlfriend, girlfriend." Sam looked stunned. "Sorry, I thought you knew when you saw us at Charlie's that time."

"Oh, of course. No, I didn't . . . but, I mean, it's fine. It's cool."

"Good." Ash laughed. *Well, I was right. Sam is straight. No lesbian would react like that. Right?* But something still nagged at her, so Ash decided to ask. "Actually, I wasn't sure if you and Drea were there . . . together," she said hesitantly.

Sam gave her an incredulous look. "Drea! And . . . me?" She laughed heartily for a few seconds. Ash would have enjoyed the sound of it more if disappointment and embarrassment weren't crushing her.

When Sam finally finished laughing, she spoke. "Um, no, we've always been just friends."

"Oh." Ash hoped Sam didn't notice the blush she felt creep up her neck. "I just . . . I always wondered if there was more to it."

Sam nodded, and gave her an odd look. "No. Not me and Drea."

Ash noticed the wording of Sam's response. She nodded, but felt more confused than before.

Fifteen minutes after they had stepped into the elevator, the car finally jerked back to life.

Sam got to her feet and held out a hand to help Ash up.

The elevator stopped on the eighth floor and they exchanged a shy smile as the doors began to open. So much had transpired in that tiny space that part of Sam felt sad to leave it. Everything was different now, but only to them. Everything around them was the same as it always had been.

Sam stepped out of the elevator into the arms of a frenzied Lace. "Oh, my god! I was so worried about you both. Are you okay?"

Sam and Ash exchanged a knowing smile. "Yeah, we're good."

"Do you want to get a drink?" Lace asked hesitantly.

"Yes," Sam and Ash said in unison.

Lace laughed. "Alrighty then."

Sam stayed for a little while, laughing and joking with her teammates, but the few times she caught Ash's eye, there was a weight to it. Something told her things would never be the same between them.

When Sam got home, she was exhausted. Mentally, emotionally, physically. She fell asleep as soon as her head hit the pillow.

> *The bell went off. I felt relief. Lunch was over. Soon, I could go home and cry about the cafeteria incident. I closed my book and headed to math class.*
>
> *I avoided people's faces—afraid to see pity. I was already too humiliated.*
>
> *A girl stood alone at the end of the row of lockers. It was Ashley. I made eye contact. Her eyes were sad. Her lips lifted into a small smile. I looked away and walked faster.*

When Sam woke the next morning, the image from her dream came back. She thought about the look in Ash's eyes and wondered if it *had* really happened. And for the first time, Sam wondered, if it had been real, what else she might have missed.

Chapter 7

Over the next few games, it was like a dam had been breached, and Sam and Ash could finally just be themselves when they were around each other. Sam had to admit, Ash was an amazing pitcher. She thought about that a lot, as well as other positive attributes, as she stood behind her on the field.

Sam resolved not to spend any more time dwelling on the past and who Ash had been back in high school. It wasn't easy at first—trying to give Ash the benefit of the doubt—but she was getting better at it. In the absence of the past, Sam's mind was flooded by the woman she saw before her. Ash had always been attractive. Sam knew that, deep down. But it was hard to be attracted to someone with a horrible personality. Now that she was beginning to know the real Ash, Sam realized how incredibly beautiful she was . . . even in softball gear. She had a classic, natural beauty—medium-length dirty blonde hair, striking green eyes, lean, strong arms, and legs that went on and on. The girl next door with a killer fastball.

When Sam wasn't busy appreciating Ash's looks, she was developing a friendly camaraderie with her on the field. The few times the ball reached her, Sam would toss it back to Ash with a smile. At first, Ash just smiled back, but over time, the smile turned into a wink.

Sam was a bit stunned the first time it happened, and quickly turned to jog back to her position, hoping Ash didn't see the surprised look on her face. As it kept happening, Sam started to play along, challenging her with a raised eyebrow. Ash stopped in her tracks the first time Sam did it, but as they continued flirting, they both became more comfortable. Sam assumed it was all in good fun—Ash had a girlfriend and they were just teammates, after all. But deep down, she didn't mind the rush Ash's attention gave her—the jolt that ran through her body every time Ash held her gaze for more than a brief moment. And that sexy wink—well, that kept her up on more than one restless night.

Apparently, the rest of the team noticed the change as well.

"If I had known being locked in an elevator together would have made y'all friends, I would've suggested it weeks ago," Marci quipped after one game. Sam looked away to hide her eye roll.

"Seriously though," Lace said quietly as they walked toward the bench to grab their stuff. "What *happened* in that elevator?"

Sam shrugged. "We just talked through some stuff. No biggie."

Lace raised an eyebrow. "I'd say it was a biggie. Anyway, I'm just glad you worked out whatever it was. I was afraid I was going to lose my warm-up partner." She smiled sweetly at Sam.

"Never," Sam said, returning the smile.

"Hey, everyone!" They turned to look at Sarah. "A few of us want to grab a drink. Anyone else interested?"

"I'm game. Let me just let my babysitter know I'll be a little longer," Sam said, then turned to Ash. "You coming?"

Ash tilted her head from side to side as she thought about it.

"Come on, come have some fun with us," Sam said, smiling.

Ash held her gaze for a moment before smiling broadly. "All right. I'm in."

About eight team members ended up crowded around a long, wooden table at the sports bar down the street. Televisions mounted on the walls played various sporting events, but none of the women paid them any attention. Sarah and Lace carried over two pitchers of beer and a stack of pint glasses for the table.

"Here you go, ladies," Sarah said, pouring beer for the women at her end of the table.

Sam held out a glass for Lace to fill and handed it over to Janet, a stout brunette in her forties who had been their catcher long before Sam ever joined the team. "Thanks, Sam," she said.

Lace handed Sam another glass just as Ash joined them, taking the open seat next to Sam.

Sam handed the glass to Ash. "Here you go."

"Thanks."

As Lace handed her another beer, she gave Sam an odd look. Sam felt her cheeks heat up and she looked away quickly. *Could Lace sense something between her and Ash?*

They listened as Janet filled them in on her recent weight loss journey. Sam doubted the value of a diet plan that seemed to encourage red meat at every meal, but decided not to rain on her parade. A couple more women showed up, making them squeeze together at the table.

Sam tried to pay attention to the conversations around her, drifting from one to the other, but she only managed a smile and occasional nod. The only thing her brain focused on was the heat of Ash's leg pressed up against hers underneath the table. The slight bit of contact enveloped all of her senses and rendered her speechless. She absently wondered if Ash noticed it as well—if her body reacted the same way to Sam's touch. Sam angled her head so she could take her in without being too obvious.

Ash laughed occasionally and smiled while listening to Lace, but Sam noticed she wasn't saying anything herself. As if feeling her watching, Ash slowly turned to Sam. The look in her eyes caused Sam's stomach to flip in surprise, and in that moment, she had no doubt Ash was feeling exactly what she was feeling. She glanced down at Ash's full lips, slightly parted, and had the sudden urge to kiss them. Ash seemed to read her mind as a blush spread across her face and her breathing seemed to deepen.

Her vibrating phone jerked Sam back to reality. She grabbed it, realizing it was the alarm she had set so she didn't keep Lauren waiting too long.

"Sorry, guys. I need to get home and relieve the babysitter," Sam said to the table. "This was really fun. Thanks for suggesting it."

As a chorus of goodbyes sounded, she risked a glance back at Ash. "Good night," Sam said quietly, still feeling the weight of the air between them.

Ash nodded, an almost pained smile on her face. "Good night, Sam."

When Sam got home, Lauren told her Jake was having a hard time falling asleep. Sam thanked her and walked her to the door, before creeping down the hallway and peeking in on Jake. He was lying in bed, his blue Transformers comforter pulled up to his chin—his eyes wide open in the soft glow of the bedside lamp.

"Hey, honey. How come you're still awake?"

He glanced over at Sam. "I couldn't sleep."

"Why not?" she asked as she sat down beside him.

"I wanted to see you when you got home. I missed you." *Dagger to heart.*

"Aw, honey. I missed you too," Sam said, rubbing his arm.

"You did?"

"Of course, silly. You're the most important person in my life." She ran her hand through his shaggy hair. He was going to need a haircut soon. "Is everything okay?" She touched the back of her palm to his forehead. "Are you feeling all right?"

Though they had a close relationship, when Jake got extra needy, it usually meant he was sick. His temperature seemed normal though, which almost concerned Sam more. Something just felt off. She tried not to dwell on the sinking feeling in her gut, as she was working hard to be more open and positive, not letting anxiety control her.

He nodded unenthusiastically, looking down at the comforter.

Sam frowned, trying to figure out what might be wrong. "Hey, how about I lay down with you until you fall asleep?"

Jake grinned, his brown eyes twinkling. "Yay!"

He scooted his little body up against Sam as she lay down beside him. She turned on her side and wrapped her arm across his chest, as he snuggled in closer. She leaned down and kissed the top of his head. "Good night, bud. I love you."

"Night, Mom. I love you, too."

Within a few minutes, she felt his breath deepen, the tell-tale rise and fall of his chest beneath her arm.

She lay beside him, still anxious about what had him upset. She knew there was more to it than he had let on, but hoped he'd tell her in his own time. As she reassured herself, her mind wandered back to the sports bar and the feel of Ash next to her. Up until tonight, she had played off her body's reaction to Ash during the fight as coincidental, a by-product of being on her own for so many years. Her reaction tonight, however, and the look in Ash's eyes was making it harder to ignore. There was something there. But she wasn't ready to ponder what it meant. How could she be attracted to the person who had made her teenage existence unbearable?

Sam was working through her past with Ash in therapy, but she hadn't worked up to discussing the attraction. Maybe it was just her body tricked by the mental gymnastics of revising her entire view of Ash. Maybe it was just acknowledging a beautiful woman . . . who just happened to be gay.

Even if there was something between her and Ash, she was sure it was temporary—she had a girlfriend, anyway. So, it wasn't worth even thinking about. Maybe it was just a clue that it might be time to consider dating again, and had nothing to do with Ash at all. Yeah, that was probably it. The realization made Sam feel lighter as she gave in to sleep.

It was almost ten o'clock when Ash got home from the sports bar. She let Goose out to pee and closed the door. She bent over and placed her hands on her knees, staring at the linoleum kitchen floor. *What. The. Fuck.*

She didn't even know where to begin with what had just happened. Normally she didn't like to use the treadmill after a couple beers, but she was still wearing her softball gear, and needed to think through this.

She let Goose back in, but when he saw her walk to the treadmill in the guest bedroom, he stayed in the hallway. She'd tried to see if he liked running on the treadmill one day. He didn't.

Ash started at a slow jog, trying to warm up a bit and work through the haziness from the beer. The image of Sam smiling at her, inviting her to the bar passed through her mind.

She increased the speed and started a slow run. She had seen the empty seat next to Sam. There were other empty seats. But she had wanted to sit next to Sam. She had looked so cute with her light brown hair up in a ponytail and her gray Tulane T-shirt over her pink shorts.

She raised the incline and increased the speed a little more. She started to breathe harder. It had been light and fun, like a real fresh start between them. She wondered if that was what a friendship with Sam could be like. But Sam's bare leg pressed against her own—the warmth turning to heat, had dimmed everything else. The voices around her sounded like they were underwater—distorted, slow. She had tried to keep a smile on her face, to pretend everything was normal.

She increased the speed more, the incline higher.

She'd felt a fire between her and Sam. She had never felt so connected to anyone before. And just when she could almost feel Sam's lips on her own, the phone sliced through them, cutting them loose.

Ash realized she was effectively sprinting up a mountain as she gasped for air. She lowered the incline and went back to a normal run, her breathing slowly returning to its usual cadence.

Okay, she knew she was attracted to Sam. She had accepted that a long time ago. What she hadn't let herself acknowledge was how things had been developing between them. The night in the elevator. When Sam sat next to her, the anxiety from the small space had vanished.

The flirting on the field. She meant it as playful, matching Sam's challenges. A small part of her felt guilty about Ali though. Because Ash knew that, at least for her, there was more to it.

She had really tried to give Ali a chance, but the more time they spent together, the stronger Ash felt that it wasn't working. They were too different. They didn't like the same things. And they definitely didn't value the same things. They looked good on paper, and maybe even in public, but that's where it ended. There was no connection. Nothing deeper.

Ash thought about Sam again. She couldn't help but smile when she saw Sam now. She looked forward to it. It felt good. The chemistry tonight though, that was another level. Ash felt a renewed tightness in her chest just picturing the look in Sam's eyes.

She pressed the red stop button on the treadmill, hopped out onto the side rails, and grasped the handrails until the belt stopped moving. She smoothed the sweat-drenched strands of hair that had escaped her ponytail back in place and blew out a breath.

Ash didn't know if she and Sam would ever become anything, but it was clear she couldn't be with Ali. It wasn't fair to keep pretending when she felt so much more for someone else. She had to break it off.

"All I'm saying is if you don't want to be duct-taped to a chair, at least put up a fight. Don't just go all limp and accept your fate."

Sam stared blankly as Drea detailed her latest office shenanigans. She couldn't move past the image of a helpless twenty-year-old kid taped to a chair, and wondered how Drea hadn't been fired already.

"So how are things at your work?"

The question snapped her back to reality. She shrugged and took a sip of her drink, once again thankful for Charlie's, Friday nights with Drea, and the healing powers of a strong margarita. "Actually, some pretty big changes. Audrey was promoted to CEO and old Bill McGrady has left the building." She gestured her hand toward the exit. "Of course, he did it in typical McGrady fashion, behind closed doors with top-level management, before sneaking away into retirement."

Drea's eyes were wide. "Wow. I didn't think he'd ever retire, wasn't he like, seventy-five?"

Sam shook her head. "Seventy."

"Well, that should be a good thing though, right?" She glanced at Sam with curiosity.

"I think so. Audrey's been in the business for a couple decades. She knows her stuff, but also has some social skills, unlike Bill. And she's aware of the issues with Pete. So, I'm hopeful things might get better over time."

Drea nodded. "Sounds great, then. Cheers!" They clinked glasses. "And things with Ash?"

Sam focused on her drink for a moment, licking the salt rim before the acid of the margarita hit her tongue. Sam hadn't told Drea anything about the shift in her relationship with Ash. She wasn't ready to. She felt a little guilty keeping it a secret, but Drea had been by her side through all of the school bullying, and Sam didn't expect her to give Ash a second chance easily. Plus, there really was nothing to tell. They were getting along. That's all. The playful flirting wasn't important. It was all just in fun. Completely harmless.

"Nothing to report."

Drea watched her and Sam worried maybe she sensed something, but then a cute girl walked by, grabbing her attention, and saving Sam.

Chapter 8

The following week, Sam stood on the orange clay of the softball diamond, the occasional bead of sweat running down the side of her face. For late April, the temperature was warm, and the humidity forced the air to hang around like a wet blanket, making it all the more unpleasant. They had skipped right over spring it seemed, heading straight into a humid summer that would last until October. As Sam stood waiting for something to do, she couldn't help but notice the enticing expanse of Ash's legs, the lean muscles that rippled as she launched each pitch, the way her shorts clung to the curve of her hips, and the tight butt that filled them.

Had she not been ogling Ash's ass, lost in her own fantasies, maybe she would have noticed when Ash moved abruptly to the side. She heard Janet yell, "Sam, heads up!"

Sam blinked, saw Ash, wide-eyed, staring at her, just before she felt the ball slam into her forehead, instantly knocking her off her feet. She felt the impact of the ground against her back before everything went black.

"Sam. Sam, open your eyes."

She slowly opened her eyes, and blinked away the blurriness, taking in a bunch of faces peering down at her.

"Sam, can you hear me?" Ash was kneeling over her, her face hovering a few inches above Sam's. The concern in her eyes was obvious.

Sam blinked again.

"Sam?"

"I'm," she coughed—her throat suddenly parched. "I'm okay." As she became suddenly aware of a screaming pain in her forehead, she raised her hand to the spot. There was a huge knot where the ball had hit her and the pressure of her fingers against it made her wince.

"Do you think you can stand up?" Ash asked.

Sam nodded, noticing the intense dizziness for the first time. She closed her eyes, hoping the spinning would stop. When she opened them again, Ash was watching her with even more concern.

Ash held two fingers in front of her face. "How many?"

Sam tried to roll her eyes, but felt woozy and closed them. "Two."

"I think you need to see a doctor, Sam. You took a hard hit to the head."

"No, I'm fine. Just help me up."

Ash tried to argue, but Sam held up her palm, stopping her. "Please."

As Ash helped her to her feet, Sam stumbled and Ash grabbed her arm to steady her. "Okay, that's it. I'm taking you to a doctor."

Sam bent over at the waist, placing her hand on her knee, willing the spinning and nausea to stop. "Okay."

After more than an hour at Ochsner Urgent Care, Sam was released into Ash's care, diagnosed with a mild concussion. Ash had called Lauren when they arrived to let her know what was going on.

"If you can just drop me at home, I'll be fine," Sam said as Ash helped her down the brick steps to the small parking lot.

Ash looked at her. The swelling on Sam's forehead had gone down a little, but almost looked worse now that the blue and purple bruising had set in.

"Thank you for bringing me here, Ash. You didn't need to do that."

"Don't worry about it. I just wanted to make sure it wasn't serious." Ash pressed the key fob to unlock her car and opened the passenger door for Sam.

Sam slowly lowered herself into the car, still a bit unstable, then Ash hurried to the driver's side and got in.

Sam held the ice pack the nurse had given her against her forehead as they meandered through late-evening traffic along Magazine

Street. They were silent except for Sam's occasional directions to her house.

When Ash pulled into the graveled parking area in front of Sam's house, she was pleasantly surprised. Most of the houses in this area were one-story duplexes with the porch divided into two front entryways. But Sam's porch had a single entry, with large windows where a second door probably once existed. It was getting dark, but Ash could tell the house was a shade of gray with elegant, dark plantation shutters framing the windows and a good-sized porch. It was classic—understated—in a city filled with bold colors. Ash turned off the car and turned to Sam.

Sam lowered the ice pack with a slight wince, before turning to Ash. "Thanks again for everything. I guess I'll see you next week." She gave Ash a half-hearted smile and got out of the car.

Ash watched Sam slowly climb the front steps, but felt wrong leaving her alone. She got out of the car and jogged up to Sam, who stopped and stared at her with a curious expression.

Ash smiled shyly. "I'd like to make sure you get settled."

"Ash, you really don't need to do that."

"I insist."

Sam started to argue, but then let out a sigh and continued to the front door.

As Sam said good night to Lauren, Ash took in the room. The house had clearly been renovated to make it into a single-family dwelling and, as a result, was really spacious inside. The rich oak floors and archway into the kitchen added an element of history, but the buttery yellow walls, comfortable-looking furniture, and abundance of pictures and artwork made it inviting and warm. It was calming.

Ash glanced at Sam as she closed the front door. She looked pale and uncertain.

"I think I need to lie down," Sam said.

Ash followed her down the hallway.

Sam stopped at the first bedroom, peeking in at a little boy sleeping. *That must be Jake.*

Sam closed the door softly and continued toward the last bedroom.

As Ash entered behind her, she felt an awkwardness at being in a place as intimate as Sam's bedroom—like she was invading Sam's space.

Sam stood looking at her from the middle of the room. Ash could tell she felt awkward.

Ash smiled at her, trying to make them both relax. "Where do you keep your Tylenol? I'll grab it for you while you get settled in bed."

"In the medicine cabinet, above the sink," Sam said, pointing toward the bathroom.

When Ash returned, Sam was beneath the fluffy white duvet. It looked like a cloud against the light blue walls. Ash walked to the side of the bed, next to the small nightstand. "I'll leave the Tylenol here, okay?" As she placed the bottle in front of the lamp on the nightstand, she saw a framed photograph of a striking, red-haired woman with bright blue eyes. She was holding Jake. They both looked so happy. She stared at the image for a moment, trying to piece it together, before her heart sank.

She turned to Sam. "Are you alone tonight?" she asked hesitantly.

Sam looked confused.

Ash nodded slightly toward the photograph.

"Oh . . . yes, I'm alone." Sam looked sad, closing her eyes for a moment.

Ash sensed the weight of what had just happened immediately. She quickly changed the subject. "How are you feeling? Still dizzy?"

Sam started to nod and quickly stopped. She raised her hand to her temple and closed her eyes again. "Yes. It's not as bad as earlier though."

"Okay, good." Ash glanced at the Tylenol bottle. "I'm going to go get you some water in case you need to take some pills later. Do you need anything else?" Ash met Sam's eyes and smiled.

Sam shook her head slightly and as Ash glanced at the door, Sam said, "Ash?"

"Yes?" She turned back to Sam.

"Thank you."

Ash gave her a small smile. "Get some rest."

Walking out to the living room, Ash was worried. She knew Sam shouldn't be alone after suffering a concussion. She needed someone to wake her every few hours during her first night to make sure she was all right. She turned around and sat down on the charcoal gray sofa. She'd stay. The comfortable sofa practically wrapped itself around her like a big hug. She'd have to set an alarm for herself to avoid nodding off.

This is so surreal. I'm in Sam's house and it feels wrong to be here when Sam isn't awake. Normally, you get to know someone, friends or otherwise, they invite you over, maybe one day you see their bedroom. Not like this. It just feels weird.

Ash thought about the photograph. *Who is that woman in the picture?* She didn't expect to be bothered by the thought of another woman with Sam. But, that meant Sam was gay. *Right?* Ash felt relief at that idea, but wondered again who the woman was, why she wasn't here, and what it all meant.

A few hours later, Ash went to check on Sam. She was sound asleep and Ash felt bad waking her, but it was important to make sure her condition hadn't worsened. Ash sat on the edge of the bed and brushed her hand over Sam's arm, but she didn't respond. So Ash tried gently shaking her arm.

Sam's eyes fluttered open, just staring at Ash. She didn't seem fully awake.

"Hey," Ash whispered as she looked into Sam's eyes, trying to gauge her responsiveness.

Sam smiled at her. "I love your eyes."

"What?" She couldn't help but chuckle.

"Coconuts are too cold for supper." Sam's eyes closed and she was asleep before Ash could think of a response.

For a brief moment, Ash felt like they were sharing something important. But clearly, Sam was just suffering from mild head trauma. She shook Sam's arm a little harder now, worried that her injury could be getting more serious.

Sam's eyes opened. "What?" she asked groggily.

Ash held two fingers in front of Sam's face. "How many fingers am I holding?"

Sam squinted. "Two."

"What day is it?"

"The day my motherfucking head got smashed in." Sam groaned, rolling onto her side, and fell back asleep.

The glorious aroma of pancakes and coffee roused Sam from her sleep. The early morning light streamed in and she blinked a few times, trying to get her bearings. A piercing pain shot through her skull as she tried to focus on the room around her. She raised her hand to her forehead, feeling the raised bump, and recalling the events of the previous night. At least the bump didn't seem as large or as painful as last night.

She reached for the water glass on her nightstand. At the sight of the Tylenol bottle, she smiled, remembering how sweet Ash had been to her last night. She took a couple of pills, hoping they'd help lessen the searing pain in her brain, and headed toward the inviting smells. *What is my crazy kid up to?*

As she reached the kitchen doorway, she stopped in her tracks, not sure of what she was seeing in front of her. She placed her hand against the doorway to brace herself.

Jake was perched on a step stool leaning over the stove. He was wrapped in the "Kiss the Chef" apron she had given Anna. It was about two feet too long for his tiny frame. He watched with intense fascination as pancakes sizzled in a frying pan. On the counter in front of him was a glass bowl filled with batter, and he held a measuring cup at his chest, batter dripping off it onto the tile floor.

Sam stared in confusion, seeing someone standing next to him, flipping the pancakes out of the pan onto a stack resting beside the stove. "Okay, hit me," the woman said as Jake filled the measuring cup with batter and poured two circles in the pan.

A lump formed in Sam's throat as tears welled in her eyes. *Anna?* Then the woman turned to see Sam in the doorway and Sam smiled.

"Sam? Sam, are you okay?"

Sam blinked back the tears blurring her vision, suddenly realizing it wasn't Anna, it was Ash standing with Jake. She stared down at the floor in confusion.

Ash walked over and placed a hand on her arm. "Sam, are you okay?"

Sam met her gaze, still stunned. "Sorry, I just . . . I wasn't expecting you to be here."

Ash stepped closer and Sam felt butterflies from her standing so close and the sincerity in her eyes.

"I hope it's okay," Ash said softly so only Sam could hear. "I didn't want to leave you here alone . . . in case you needed anything."

"You stayed all night?" Sam asked, surprised.

She nodded, smiling, then stepped back and spoke louder. "I wanted to make you a nice breakfast to get you back on your feet, and I found the most amazing helper." She winked at Jake, who beamed from his step stool.

"Yeah, Mom! Ash taught me to make pancakes! She said it might make your boo-boo feel better." He was nearly vibrating with excitement.

"I see that. You two are quite the team." Sam eyed the heap of pancakes on the counter.

"Wait til you try them. My pancakes have been known to have restorative powers," Ash said with a wink. The butterflies ratcheted up a notch.

Sam raised an eyebrow and lowered her voice into a sexy tone. "I bet that's how you get all the ladies." Ash burst out laughing and Sam felt her face heat up from embarrassment. "I'm going to sit down now." And die. *What the hell came over me?*

After stuffing themselves with pancakes, and coffee for the grown-ups, Sam hurried Jake along to get ready for school. He was clearly sad to leave, looking at Ash as Sam walked him to the front door.

"Don't worry, honey. Maybe Ash can come hang out another time."

"Really?" His eyes glowed with excitement.

"I'd love to," Ash said, smiling as she joined them by the door. "Where else am I going to find such an excellent sous chef?" She grinned down at him.

"Soup chef?" Jake asked, baffled.

Ash laughed and kneeled down so they were eye to eye. "*Sous chef.* It's just a fancy word for assistant chef."

Jake's eyes lit up. "I'm your assistant chef?" Wonder filled his voice at the special title.

"If you don't mind. I could really use the help."

He squealed and jumped up and down as Ash laughed and stood up.

"All right bud, say goodbye to Ash. We need to get you to school."

"Bye, Ash," he said with a bashful grin. Clearly, he was taken with her. *Get in line, bud.*

"Bye, Jake." Ash tousled his hair.

"I'm just going to take him to the corner to wait for the bus. I'll be right back." Sam took Jake's hand and headed out.

When she returned, the kitchen was spotless, and Ash was wiping down the counter with a wet rag.

"I can't thank you enough for breakfast. It was amazing."

Ash tossed the rag on the sink ledge and turned to her. "My pleasure. It was fun cooking with Jake." She held Sam's gaze for a beat. "I hope you didn't mind. He snuck up on me and asked to help. I figured it would keep him busy until you woke up."

Sam nodded. "I appreciated it. He did too, clearly." She laughed. "I haven't seen him cook in a long time."

"You don't cook?"

Sam laughed. "Only enough to keep us alive. Pasta and fish sticks are about all I manage, and fairly poorly." She couldn't help but frown.

Ash nodded, then squinted with confusion. "But you used to cook with him?"

"No . . . my wife did. She was an amazing cook."

Ash suddenly understood. "The woman in the photograph by your bed?"

Sam nodded.

"You're . . . you're not together anymore?" she asked hesitantly.

Sam looked away and swallowed. Pain still infused her body every time she thought back to that day.

"I'm sorry. That was nosy. It's none of my business. Sorry."

Sam shook her head. "It's fine." She took a steadying breath, still avoiding Ash's eyes. "She died a little over three years ago. Brain aneurysm. She died instantly."

"Oh, god, Sam. I'm so sorry."

Sam shrugged and nodded, trying to force a small smile. "Thanks." There was an awkward silence.

"So how are you feeling?" Ash asked. "Dizzy? Nauseous?"

"All of the above." Sam laughed, thankful for the change of topic. "But the nausea is just from stuffing myself with amazing pancakes."

Ash smiled.

"I am still a bit dizzy. Not as bad as last night, but too much to focus on anything beyond just breathing. I'm going to have to call in sick, unfortunately."

Ash nodded. "Would you like some company?"

"Thanks, but you've done way too much already. Besides, your girlfriend is probably worried sick by now."

Ash looked away. "We broke up."

"Oh, I'm sorry."

She met Sam's eyes. "Don't be. It just wasn't right."

Sam nodded. "Okay, but don't you have a job? People that might be unhappy if you don't show up?"

She shrugged. "I work for myself."

Sam took a moment with the information. "I don't even know what you do for a living."

"Interior design. I started my own firm when I moved back here."

"Wow. That's impressive."

Ash appeared shy at the compliment. "What do you do?"

Sam looked down, thinking of the stress and problems at work, then looked up and met Ash's gaze. "I'm in marketing."

"You don't like it?"

"Why do you say that?"

"Your face . . . did something when I asked what you do."

"Oh. It's been a bit stressful lately." Sam blew out a breath. "It's complicated." She changed the subject. "Why do you want to waste your free time taking care of an invalid? I'm probably just going to sleep most of the day anyway. I can't focus on much else right now."

Ash shrugged. "I just want to make sure you're okay. You shouldn't be by yourself after a concussion. I can work on my laptop down here—it's in the car—and check on you occasionally."

Sam's eyes narrowed, a vague memory pulling at the edges of her mind. "Did you check on me last night?"

"I woke you up a couple of times to make sure you were still conscious. The first twenty-four hours after a head injury like yours can be dangerous."

Sam was touched she cared. Then she remembered Anna used to tell her she talked in her sleep when she was really exhausted. She narrowed her eyes, almost afraid to ask. "Did I say anything . . . when you woke me up?"

A huge grin broke out across Ash's face.

Sam closed her eyes. "Great."

When Sam woke up from her nap, the room was filled with muted sunlight. She grabbed her phone off the nightstand and realized it was already afternoon. She walked down the hallway and stopped at the entrance to the living room when she saw Ash sitting on the sofa.

It was the most comfortable sofa Sam had ever owned. Sometimes she even slept on it when she was too tired to get into bed. Now Ash was perched there, her long legs crossed at the ankle on top of the wooden coffee table. Sam realized Ash still wore her clothes from the softball game the night before.

Ash's laptop rested on her knees and her stylish black-rimmed glasses nicely accented the blonde hair tied up in a loose ponytail. She frowned at the screen, clicking the mouse. *She is so cute.*

When Ash looked up and saw Sam, a warm smile broke out across her face. Sam couldn't help but return it. "Hey, sleepyhead. Feeling better?"

Sam blushed at the warmth of her words, suddenly feeling shy. Sam joined her on the sofa and nodded at her screen. "I hope you've been able to get some work done so this day isn't a total waste."

"Well, I didn't have a lot of time after I snooped through all of your belongings . . ."

Sam's eyes widened.

"Relax," she laughed, placing her hand on Sam's upper arm. "Kidding. Your house is really peaceful, actually. And this sofa is just—" she spread her arms out across the top of the cushions, "amazing."

A flutter shot through Sam's body at the closeness of Ash's fingers to her shoulder. Ash dropped her head back on the cushion and sighed. It was incredibly sensual, and Sam sat, taking her in for a moment . . . the length of her exposed neck. The full lips she now wanted to kiss. The beautiful eyes staring back at her.

Sam realized too late that Ash had caught her staring. No. *Ogling.*

There was nothing subtle about the way she'd been looking at Ash or what she was thinking. Ash's eyes told Sam she knew exactly what she was thinking.

Sam turned away abruptly as heat spread through her body. She jumped to her feet. "I should really take a shower before Jake gets home."

Ash slowly closed her laptop, set it on the coffee table, and slid her feet to the floor.

Sam braced herself. *Is she going to call me out for mentally undressing her?* She felt sick at the thought. Ash stood and faced Sam.

"I have an idea." She smiled. "How about I go home and get cleaned up?" She pulled at her shirt and made a face. "I'm still wearing the same outfit from the game. Yuck. And then I can stop by the store and pick up some stuff to make us dinner. Jake and I can have another cooking lesson and both of you can eat something tastier than fish sticks. What do you think?"

Relief washed over Sam. "I *think* you've already done way too much for me and you should go home and enjoy yourself."

"Sam . . ." Ash's tone seemed sincere. "I want to. I rarely get to cook for someone else. Let someone take care of you for a change."

Sam paused a moment before giving in with a sigh. "Fine." She smiled. "You win."

Ash smiled broadly. "I *really* love hearing those words come out of your mouth. Can you say them again?"

Sam rolled her eyes and pointed to the front door. "Get out of here."

Chapter 9

Well damn. Maybe Sam's half-asleep, half-concussed comment wasn't nothing. Except the coconut one. That was just crazy talk.

The way Sam had looked at her on the couch . . . Ash couldn't remember the last time anyone had looked at her with such desire. Maybe never. That was kind of sad.

Ash, carrying the grocery bags up Sam's steps, was hit with a robust lemony scent. She'd know it anywhere. She turned around, searching for the source, to find a huge magnolia tree nestled beside Sam's front porch, providing a bit of shade and privacy. Ash closed her eyes and breathed in the floral aroma, one of her favorite scents and almost overwhelming at close range. There weren't many magnolias near her place in Los Angeles. It felt like home.

She rang the doorbell and a moment later Sam opened the oak door. Her hair was down and the ends were still a little damp on her shoulders. She looked cute in her white Saints T-shirt, faded jeans, and bare feet. There was an intimacy to her look—what she'd wear around the house—and Ash felt both calmed by the familiarity and a little nervous.

"Hey," Sam said with a lazy grin.

"Hey."

They stood there, grinning like idiots, before Jake's laughter shook them.

"We've been watching cartoons. Come in."

Ash's eyes were drawn to the worn edge of Sam's back pocket—

a small hole forming amidst the tattered threads. Ash swallowed hard.

Sam watched as Ash unloaded the contents of the paper bags onto the beige Formica counter. Mozzarella cheese, canned tomatoes, pizza dough, flour, basil, garlic. "You didn't have to buy us a week's worth of groceries you know."

Holding a pineapple, Ash said, "This is just for tonight."

At Sam's incredulous look, she added, "I'm very serious about pizza."

"I can see that."

Sam sat down at the small, cute kitchen table, much more appropriately sized than her own table. It was a semicircle with the flat edge against the wall and three chairs placed around it. Sam watched as Ash started to orchestrate dinner, assigning tasks to Jake.

She decided to deal with some of the more challenging steps and give Jake the fun and messy parts. Jake stood on the step stool and smashed tomatoes in a bowl with his fists, giggling the whole time, while Ash made quick work of chopping garlic. After a couple minutes, she glanced at Sam, whose head was resting on her fist, fighting a losing battle with unconsciousness.

"Why don't you lie down on the sofa until dinner is ready?" Sam didn't reply.

"Sam?"

"What?" Sam blinked her eyes open.

"Why don't you lie down until we're done?"

"All right," she said sleepily and slowly headed toward the living room.

Jake watched her leave, then looked at Ash. "What's wrong with my mom?"

What do I say? Ash kneaded the dough. She wasn't used to kids, but knew she might need to filter her answer. "She got hit with a softball last night. So, she's a little extra tired from that."

"Oh." Ash braced herself for further inquiry, but got none. Instead, Jake started squealing at the tomato juice he was getting everywhere and Ash exhaled.

She glanced at the little blue Transformer on the counter next to Jake. "I see you brought an assistant." Jake stopped for a moment and looked at Ash, confusion on his face. She pointed at the toy. "What's his name again?"

Jake burst into a huge grin, almost jumping with joy on the step stool. "Tony!"

"Right, Tony." Ash smiled. "Is he your favorite toy?"

"Yeah." Jake focused on the tomatoes. "My Momma gave him to me."

Ash was struck by how tiny and sad his voice seemed, not like the happy kid from before. She panicked, fearing she didn't have the skills for this "mom" stuff. She didn't want to say the wrong thing and screw him up for life.

"Wanna throw some dough?" *Please work, please work, please work.*

Jake's face lit up.

Oh, thank god.

Sam awoke to someone gently shaking her arm. Ash leaned over her, a twinkle in her green eyes. They smiled at each other, holding each other's gaze.

"Dinner's ready. Are you hungry?"

Sam nodded.

"Come on, then." She reached out a hand to help Sam up.

Dinner was amazing. Ash, with Jake's help, had made several pizzas—pineapple, pepperoni, and margherita. They sampled each of them, but when Sam bit into the margherita one, she closed her eyes and moaned. The sweetness of the tomato and garlic sauce, along with the basil and melted fresh mozzarella made it the best meal she'd had in a long time. Simple ingredients played off of each other, creating a symphony of taste. She opened her eyes to see Ash watching her intently.

"Oh, my god, this is one of the best pizzas I've ever had," Sam said.

Ash chuckled. "I'm glad you like it."

"Like doesn't even begin to describe how I feel about this pizza." She took another bite and held her hand to her chest.

"Oh yeah?" Ash leaned in, placing her elbow on the table and her chin in her palm without breaking eye contact. "Tell me about it," she whispered.

Sam stared blankly at her, mid-chew, with every neuron in her body firing. *When did Ash become so damn sexy? And how could she turn it on in an instant?* Sam glanced at Jake, before meeting Ash's eyes again. She tilted her head toward Jake. "I would, but little ears."

Ash straightened in her chair as if suddenly realizing they weren't alone. "Well, looks like the customer is pleased with our creation," she said to Jake, before high-fiving him.

He grinned, bouncing in his chair as he chewed. "Mom, Ash taught me how to throw the dough," he said excitedly.

"Really? That's pretty awesome." Sam smiled.

Ash grinned at Jake. "There were a few casualties . . ."

Jake grinned back at her.

After they cleaned the dishes, Sam sent Jake to get ready for bed. "I'll be right behind you," she called.

He began to run, then stopped abruptly, turning around. "Good night, Ash."

"Good night, Jake," Ash said, smiling.

Grinning, he took off.

"Hey, this should just take a few minutes. Are you good here?"

"Absolutely."

Jake was already in his batman PJs when Sam got to his room. As he crawled into bed, she pulled back his sheets and handed him Tony.

He briefly fidgeted with Tony's arms, then clutched him to his chest. "Mom?" he said, looking up at Sam as she sat on the edge of his bed.

"Yes, honey?"

"Today was really fun." He grinned.

"It was, wasn't it? I'm really proud of you. You're such a great helper in the kitchen."

"Soup chef," he corrected. Sam let that one slide.

"I thought for a minute you might go home with Ash," she teased.

His eyes widened. "Can I?"

Sam's jaw hung open. "Only if you want your dear, old mom to be heartbroken forever."

He made a show out of thinking.

Sam frowned. "Your hesitation is truly disappointing, son."

"I'm just *kidding*," he giggled. Sam shook her head at him, a smile playing on her lips.

"All right, honey. Get some sleep." She leaned down and kissed his forehead. "Sweet dreams."

She left his door open a crack and headed back to the kitchen.

Ash looked up as she entered. She was wiping down the counter again.

"You know . . . the chef isn't supposed to do the cleaning as well."

She smiled. "This is only while you're an invalid. You're totally cleaning next time." *Next time.* Sam liked the sound of that.

"Are you up for dessert?"

Sam's mind quickly flipped through a montage of dirty thoughts that comment inspired. She coughed, hoping Ash wouldn't notice the blush she knew was spreading across her face. "I think I have a little room left."

"I would have brought some wine, but I figured we should wait until you're feeling better."

The tiramisu was amazing. Sam couldn't remember the last time she had eaten so well. As they sat on the sofa, the empty dessert plates abandoned on the coffee table, Sam began to feel like this was a date.

Maybe it was being alone with Ash at night after a nice dinner. Or the fact that neither of them wore sweaty softball clothes. Ash had changed into something casual—dark jeans and a sage green crewneck sweater over a light blue button-down—but she still looked incredible. The sweater made her green eyes look even more ridiculously intense than usual. It was almost annoying how good she looked in everything.

As the silence stretched on, Sam became increasingly anxious about what to say. Thankfully, Ash spoke up.

"I meant to ask earlier, did you draw those?" Ash nodded toward the sketches on the coffee table.

Sam hadn't realized she had left them there and felt a little exposed. They were just basic sketches of Jake and places in New Orleans, but Sam hadn't planned on sharing them with anyone. "Um, yeah."

"They're really good Sam. I'm impressed." Ash picked up the one of Jake that was resting on top. "Really. I have to sketch a bit for my work, but it's nothing like this."

"Thanks." Sam smiled. Ash seemed genuine enough.

"So, you're feeling better now?" Ash asked.

"I am. Apparently, a good meal helps." Sam smiled at her. "The dizziness is pretty minimal, so I'll head back to work tomorrow."

Ash nodded. "Well . . . I guess I should head out so you can get some sleep." She stood slowly.

"I'll walk you out." They walked awkwardly to the door, before turning to each other. Sam wasn't sure how to say thank you. Ash had gone out of her way to take care of her and Jake. She was still a bit stunned by the level of her generosity. "Ash, I can't thank you enough for everything. It was really kind of you. I hope somehow I can return the favor."

"You don't owe me anything," Ash said warmly.

"You have a fan for life now," Sam said, jerking her thumb toward Jake's room.

Ash held her gaze. "Is he the only one?"

Sam's pulse quickened as they looked into each other's eyes. It felt like something big had happened between them and she didn't want Ash to go. She didn't want whatever was happening to end. She bit her bottom lip and looked at the ground, barely shaking her head.

When Sam looked back up, Ash was smiling at her.

Ash opened her mouth, and then, as if deciding against it, closed it again. "I'll see you Tuesday, Sam." She opened the door. "Good night."

"Good night," Sam said, so soft it was almost a whisper.

Ash turned and walked out the door and Sam felt the loss immediately.

By the time Tuesday night arrived, Sam was almost giddy at the thought of seeing Ash. The past week had been a slog of normalcy, made all the more depressing and notable in contrast to the joy and fun Ash had brought into Sam's home.

She saw Ash stretching by the bench with the rest of the team and strode confidently toward her. "Hi," Sam said, unable to contain her grin.

Ash turned to her as a slow smile spread across her face. There was such warmth in her eyes and her eye contact so intense, Sam could only stare. They both stood there, just grinning at each other.

"Sam!"

Sam's body jerked. Nothing could end a private moment like the sound of Marci's voice bellowing across the field. She walked toward Marci, who jogged her way, clipboard in hand.

"Glad to see you back, Sam. Unfortunately, I can't let you play for another week."

"What?" Sam almost yelled.

Marci held out placating hands. "Now, now, there's nothing I can do. It's a league rule. But you can sit on the bench and root for your teammates."

Sam glared at her, and she quickly backed away to go talk to the umpire.

"You've got to be kidding me," Sam said to no one in particular. She caught Ash giving her a half-smile from a few feet away before the majority of their teammates ran out onto the field.

Sam walked over to the bench where her bag was resting, picked it up and dropped it on the ground. She sat down with a huff. *This sucks.*

Lace sat beside her when their team was at bat. After two innings, Sam's anger had dissipated and she focused on just enjoying the game. They were playing a mediocre team, so it wasn't a nail-biter by any stretch, but she appreciated the different vantage point of her teammates. They really were a good team, she had to admit, working seamlessly together, like a well-oiled machine. Of course, there was one teammate who dominated most of her attention.

Ash snuck a few sly smiles at Sam when she caught her staring at her. At first, Sam quickly looked away, and then just started smiling back. Ash was pretty cocky when she pitched—she knew she was good, and she knew Sam was watching.

At the bottom of the sixth inning, Ash sat beside Sam. She bumped her shoulder into Sam's and grinned at her. Sam grinned back, and tried to hide a look of horror when she felt her cheeks heat up. *Real smooth, Sam.* Apparently, she was operating at a kindergarten level when it came to her dating game. *Maybe I should ask Jake for advice?*

They sat silently together on the bench and watched their teammates bat, clapping when someone hit the ball; clapping slightly less enthusiastically when they missed.

At the final out of the inning, Ash leaned against Sam, her breath hot against Sam's ear. "Are you going to stay until the end?"

Sam gulped and managed to commandeer her few functioning

brain cells to nod in response.

Ash got up and jogged backwards as she pointed at Sam with a sexy smile. "Don't go anywhere."

Sam nodded again, glad Ash didn't realize she would do anything Ash told her to do with her body pressed against her like that.

At the end of the game, Ash grabbed her bag and walked over. "Can I walk you to your car?"

Sam nodded, trying to tamp down her curiosity about why Ash wanted her to stay. They walked in silence across the gravel lot, anticipation increasing as they got closer to Sam's car.

Sam unlocked the door and tossed her bag in the back, next to Jake's booster seat, before turning her attention back to Ash. They both leaned against the side of the car, facing each other. Sam wondered if Ash could tell how nervous she was, but Ash seemed a bit nervous herself, as she held Sam's gaze and then looked away, biting the inside of her cheek. The bravado from the field was completely gone.

Sam steeled herself. "Did you want to talk to me about something?" she asked gently.

Ash looked at her and nodded, but didn't say anything.

Okaay. "What . . . would you like to talk to me about?" The fact that Ash wasn't saying anything made Sam increasingly nervous.

Ash took a deep breath and smiled, shaking her head. "I'm sorry. I'm just nervous."

Sam was lost. "About what?"

Ash closed her eyes.

"Ash." Sam placed her hand on Ash's arm, growing concern replacing her nervousness. "What is it?"

Ash opened her eyes. They were intense and several shades darker than a moment before.

When she placed her palm gently against Sam's cheek, Sam felt her knees weaken. "Ash," Sam whispered, leaning into her palm.

That was all Ash needed. She closed the distance between them as her warm lips took Sam's. It wasn't hurried or forceful, just confident and sure.

Sam reached behind her neck and pulled her closer, deepening the kiss. Every inch of her body was on fire, the jolt of energy from Ash's lips shooting straight through her. Just as Sam realized she couldn't get enough of this kiss, Ash gently pulled away.

She leaned her forehead against Sam's as their ragged breaths filled the silence. "That's what," she whispered. "I've been wanting to do that for so long."

Sam had thought about kissing Ash all week. But nothing had come close to how good it actually felt. "I'm glad you did."

Ash stepped back slightly as a shy smile spread across her lips. "I actually had just planned to ask if you'd go on a date with me." Her smile widened. "That probably should have happened before the kiss."

Sam was stunned by how beautiful Ash looked when she smiled.

"I'm not a stickler for order." Sam pulled Ash into a searing kiss.

When they finally broke apart, Ash gave Sam an amused look. "So, is that a yes?"

"Yes." Sam couldn't hide the grin on her face. And she didn't want to.

Chapter 10

Sam agreed to meet Ash on Saturday at the entrance to the Audubon Zoo. The end of the work week hadn't come fast enough and on Friday night, Sam was careful to avoid divulging anything to Drea. Sam's dad wanted to take Jake fishing for the day now that it was warm outside, so she arranged to pick Jake up after dinner.

As Sam pulled into the large parking lot, nearly full of cars—people excited to be outside in the warm weather now that winter was behind them—she felt a burst of nervous energy at the thought of going on a date with Ash. She also felt woefully unprepared. She hadn't dated anyone in so long, she didn't know if the rules had changed. Though she was nervous at the prospect of spending time with Ash—definitely an unexpected and new aspect for their relationship—she was also excited to feel like a woman who someone desired.

Sam parked and took a deep breath. *Well, regardless of whatever happens, this will be an experience.* She stepped out of her car and headed toward the entrance. She had gone with casual for today, figuring she didn't need to be too fancy to walk around the zoo. Along with faded jeans and her nice sneakers, she wore a dark gray, thin sweater and some small silver earrings. She probably didn't need to smell too nice either, given the venue, but she had still put on her favorite perfume—a soft, floral scent. She wanted to make some effort.

Ash was easy to spot. Tall, beautiful, blonde watching Sam walk up. Ash's smile grew as Sam got closer. Apparently, she had the same style ideas, as she wore a pair of dark jeans, black low-heeled ankle boots, and a forest green long-sleeve shirt that accented her eyes perfectly. Her hair was pulled into a loose ponytail, and she looked casually elegant.

"Hi," she said cheerfully.

"Hi," Sam replied, feeling suddenly shy.

Ash stepped forward hesitantly and gave Sam a brief, awkward embrace. They both chuckled and avoided eye contact as they broke apart.

"So, I'm hoping you like animals." Ash eyed Sam hesitantly.

"Love them. Well, the furry ones mostly." Sam flashed back to her childhood and her brother scaring the bejesus out of her with rubber snakes and fake spiders. It had left an impression.

Ash smiled. "I'll keep that in mind."

Inside the zoo, they meandered past the Bengal tigers. Sam tried to remind herself that they could kill her with one swift bite, and thus should be revered. But as she watched them yawn and stretch out in the grass, she couldn't help but compare them to Pickles. A very large, very strong Pickles. They headed toward the Elephant Pavilion and watched the giant beasts for a while.

"What?" Ash asked as Sam shook her head.

"Oh, I'm just always so amazed by elephants. I think they're my favorite animal."

"They're not that furry though," Ash teased.

"Yeah, but they're big enough you see them coming."

They continued on until they reached the Giraffe Overlook. Sam stood, mesmerized, as a giraffe bent down to eat a leaf off of the tree in front of her. She was taken by its long, dark eyelashes.

"I'm going to call this one Fiona," she announced. Ash watched her with a grin.

"Should I be jealous?" Ash asked teasingly.

Sam tilted her head. "Maybe a little."

"Uh-oh. I didn't even make it through a whole date." She leaned against the wooden railing and read the placard about the giraffes, before looking up with a smug grin.

"What?"

"Apparently this group of giraffes is all male." She laughed at Sam's frown.

"So, no Fiona?"

"Nope. Say hello to Fred." They both laughed.

"Well, I guess you still have a chance then . . . for now." Sam flashed a mischievous grin as Ash raised an eyebrow. *Flirting, just like riding a bike.*

Ash stood tall. "I accept the challenge."

Sam gestured her forward. "Lead on."

At the Louisiana Swamp area, Sam couldn't decide if the all-white alligator with blue eyes was more horrifying than the original or just as bad.

"Not a fan?" Ash asked at her involuntary shiver.

"A healthy respect, I'd say."

"Fair enough."

"Are there any animals you're afraid of? You seem fine with everything we've seen today."

Ash thought for a moment. "I think mostly just the usual culprits—snakes, the occasional spider."

"That's it. This will never work out between us." Sam placed her hands on her hips and looked at the ground, shaking her head.

Ash seemed shocked at the declaration. "Why not?"

Sam had to stop herself from smiling at the unfiltered sincerity and sadness in Ash's voice. It reminded her of Jake.

"Who would kill the spiders? I certainly won't do it."

Ash's whole body seemed to relax.

Wow. She seems genuinely interested in this working out between us. Cool.

As they walked through the South America Pampas, along the elevated boardwalk with their footsteps reverberating through the wood, the late morning sun gleamed off of the flamingos standing in the lagoon.

"God, it's so beautiful," Sam said in awe.

"It is." Sam turned to see Ash looking at her intently. She reached for Sam's hand, a question in her eyes. Sam smiled and rubbed her thumb over Ash's knuckles in response. They walked on to the next exhibit, hand in hand, the rest of Sam's body tingling.

"One last stop?" Sam asked.

"Sure. Where do you want to go?"

Sam pulled Ash toward the mesh-roofed aviary, until she felt her suddenly resist. She turned back in confusion. "What's wrong?"

Ash glanced at the aviary, then back at Sam, before shaking her head. "Nothing, let's go."

Sam opened the wooden screened door and held it for Ash. Just as she entered, a small bird flew down by her ear. Ash ducked and spun on her heel, heading swiftly out the door.

Sam had to hustle to catch up with her. "So . . . snakes, spiders, *and* birds?"

Ash glanced at her with an embarrassed look. "Um, yeah."

Sam smiled, taking her hand. "Come on, silly." They walked back toward the entrance, slowing slightly as Sam noticed the sign for the Häagen-Dazs stand. She looked at Ash.

"One last stop?" Ash asked, smiling.

They sat on a metal bench around the water fountain near the entrance enjoying their ice cream. It was a nice relief to the sweat trickling down Sam's back. The trip to the zoo had been amazing and Sam felt a slight sadness that it was about to end. Being with Ash had been so easy and fun. Sam felt like she could just be herself, with no pressure to impress Ash or say the right thing. Ash seemed lost in her own thoughts as well as they sat in silence, watching the water cascade down the fountain.

"Jake's going to be so jealous if I tell him about today. Though I'm not sure if he'll be more jealous that I went to the zoo or that I went with you."

Ash looked surprised.

"Oh, come on. You must know he adores you."

She chuckled. "Well, I think he's pretty amazing himself."

Sam nodded. "Good, because he is."

Ash eyed Sam for a moment. "Do you need to be back soon or would you be up for spending a bit more time together?" She added, "Unless you and Fred the Giraffe already have plans, that is?"

Sam laughed, relieved they didn't have to say goodbye just yet. "He's playing hard to get. I think he's stuck on the height difference."

Ash nudged Sam's shoulder. "Lucky for you, I'm very accepting of short people."

"Hey! I'm only a few inches shorter than you . . . and if I recall, it didn't create any problems last time we were together."

Ash blushed.

"Did you have anything in particular in mind?"

Ash looked at her, wide-eyed.

"I meant to do next ... if we spent more time together ... in public," Sam stammered.

"I do, actually. Does that mean you're in?"

"I've got some time," Sam said, trying to play it cool to make up for her blunder a minute before.

"All right, come with me."

Sam followed her out the main entrance.

"It's not far, but do you want to leave your car here and ride with me?" Ash asked.

"Sure."

Sam followed Ash to her car, remembering the last time she had ridden with her, after her concussion. She was looking forward to a better memory.

Ash turned onto Magazine Street and then kept turning as if they were headed back to the zoo. Sam wondered if she had changed her mind about hanging out longer. Just as Sam was about to say something, Ash turned down a tree-lined street that almost seemed like a park. Sam had never seen it before.

Ash pulled over and smiled. "Follow me." She grabbed a blanket and medium-sized cooler out of the trunk and they walked across the grass a short distance before Sam stopped suddenly, gaping at the sight before her. She had never seen anything more beautiful.

A massive live oak tree stood in the middle of the field, its branches draped in Spanish moss, blowing lazily in the breeze. Sam had never seen an oak tree so large. She walked over to it, taking in the colossal limbs winding, in every direction, from the trunk. She rubbed her hand along a limb, feeling the roughness of the bark against her fingertips.

Ash joined her, having dropped the blanket and cooler on the ground nearby. "Pretty impressive, huh?"

Sam looked up at her with wonder, still rubbing the bark. "Ash, this is amazing. How did you know it was here?"

She shrugged. "I used to drive out here when I was a teenager. When I needed to get away." Sam's heart sank a little for her, knowing what she was referring to. "This tree, this place, reminded me there were still amazing things in this world. Things bigger than me."

Sam nodded. She was touched that Ash had shared something so personal. "Thank you for showing it to me."

Ash flashed a smile, a challenge in her voice as she asked, "Want to climb it?"

"Yes!"

She reached her hand out. "Come on."

Sam took her hand and stepped onto a limb that had grown down to the ground. Ash stayed on the ground and kept hold of her hand, steadying Sam as she wobbled along the limb. "This is so huge!" Sam laughed. "Come up here with me."

"Okay, stay there." Ash let go of her hand and walked back to the lower portion of the limb, before easily walking up it, arms outstretched for balance. She stopped in front of Sam, smiling.

"Show-off."

"Well, how else am I going to impress you?"

Sam held her gaze for a beat. "I'm sure you'll think of something," she whispered.

Ash's smile faded as she leaned down and kissed Sam.

Sam felt it through her entire body. She tried to deepen the kiss, but swayed slightly as her footing became uncertain.

Ash broke the kiss and grabbed Sam's arm to steady her. "Easy there, tiger," she said with a wink, before hopping down to the ground. She held out her hand and walked Sam down the limb a few feet before holding out her arms for Sam to jump.

Sam barely felt her feet hit the ground before Ash took her in her arms in a passionate kiss that left Sam's head spinning when Ash pulled away. They stared at each other for a moment, catching their breath.

"Hungry?" Ash said.

It took all of Sam's willpower not to leap across the blanket and continue that kiss as they ate the food Ash had packed. Thankfully, the food was so amazing, it helped pull Sam's focus away from those thoughts. They sat together—stuffed with potato salad, fried chicken, and green beans—sipping Riesling from plastic wineglasses as the warm breeze caressed their skin.

"Well, you certainly know how to woo a girl. I'm impressed."

Ash's eyes twinkled as a slow smile spread across her lips. "There is one more thing," she said hesitantly. "Though I'm not sure if I should show it to you."

"Why not?"

Ash tilted her head and bit her lip. "It might ruin my chances with you."

"Ash, trust me. You do *not* need to worry about that."

"Promise?"

"Promise."

"Okay, then." She smiled. "Turn around."

Sam spun around, expecting something to jump out at her, but there was nothing there. "Ash, there's nothing here."

"Keep looking."

Sam watched the grassy field, scanning it, by habit, for snakes, before she noticed movement in the distance. She raised her eyes to a fence covered by dark green mesh at the perimeter of the field with a bunch of trees on the other side of it. Above the fence, two giraffe heads floated among the trees. Sam spun back to Ash, her jaw gaping.

Ash laughed. "That's the edge of the zoo. I think that's your boyfriend right there."

Sam turned to watch the giraffes, taking in the beauty of the moment, before turning back, shaking her head. "Ash. This is incredible."

She beamed. "I told you it was an amazing place."

"Hey, I just realized you never told me what your favorite animal is."

"It *was* giraffes." She frowned. "But Fred is making me rethink my choice."

Sam gave her a sly grin before leaning over and kissing her. "Lucky for you, Fred's not really my type."

Ash pulled her BMW into the empty space beside Sam's car.

As she turned off the engine, Sam turned to face her. "Ash, this has been one of the best days I've had in a really long time. Thank you."

Ash smiled. "You're welcome. And me too."

Sam shook her head. "I can't believe you showed me something entirely new about the place I've lived all of my life. You don't even know how much time I've spent right around here and never went down that street. I can't wait to show the tree to Jake." Sam laughed. "He's going to lose his mind."

Ash looked down for a moment, feeling suddenly unsure. She wanted to see Sam again, to feel this way again as soon as possible, but she didn't know how Sam felt. She felt really vulnerable about putting herself out there. She wasn't sure if it was just because of their past, but she realized that everything about this situation felt different. That scared her, but she also knew that the times she had felt this kind of fear before—whether it was softball, traveling, or moving to a new place—those risks ended up being her biggest joys.

The difference was that all of those risks had been her choice. This time, it was up to Sam.

She took a deep breath, looking at Sam, trying hard not to look as terrified as she felt. "So, do you think you'd like to do this again sometime?"

Sam's face relaxed. She took Ash's hand and squeezed it gently as she smiled at her. "I would love to."

Ash's face lit up. There was something comforting about Sam. Ash wasn't sure if it was because she was a mom, but Sam seemed to be able to see Ash's vulnerability and calm her without even trying.

Sam still held Ash's hand. Ash didn't want the date to end, but she knew Sam needed to go soon.

Almost on cue, Sam's phone rang, seeming unusually loud in the quiet car.

"Sorry," Sam said with a frown, grabbing it from her back pocket. "Hello?"

Ash could make out a woman's voice on the other end.

"Oh good. Okay, do you want me to help you cook the fish?"

There was a pause before a flurry of words. Sam rolled her eyes and shook her head.

"Okay, then. I'll head on over. Thanks, Mom."

Sam looked at Ash with a half frown. "I'm sorry. I've gotta go. My mom's cooking the fish Jake and my dad caught." She laughed. "She won't admit she thinks I'm a bad cook. She tried to reject my help by blaming it on the small size of the fish Jake caught."

Ash laughed. "She's just trying to protect your feelings."

"I suppose." Sam turned serious. "I'll see you soon?"

Ash nodded as Sam leaned over and kissed her gently. Sam looked a little sad when she pulled away.

"Bye, Ash."

After dinner with her parents, Sam took Jake home for a meticulous bath to get all of the worm guts and fish smell off. She dried him and told him to brush his teeth while she put his clothes in the laundry. She was careful not to let him see her grin.

Sam grabbed the Nerf gun from her closet—set aside for sneak attacks—and waited in her bedroom doorway for Jake to finish in the bathroom. When he stepped into the hallway, she pulled the trigger, sending an orange foam dart sailing past his chest. He stopped and looked at her for a moment before sprinting into his bedroom, laughing. Sam ran down the hallway, sending another dart flying as she passed his room. He was ready for her. He crouched in his doorway and nailed her three times in the back before she could turn the corner. A little while later, after they had exhausted themselves, both of them still panting, they cuddled up together on the sofa to watch a Transformers cartoon before bed.

It wasn't long before Sam's thoughts wandered back to Ash and their amazing date. She marveled at the turn their relationship had taken and the twists and turns life takes. Just a few months ago, she had despised Ash, stuck on the teenage girl who had put her through such pain. And now, well now, she was lusting after the same woman like a horny teenager . . . or a sex-deprived thirty-four-year-old adult.

That night trapped in the elevator had changed things. That, and some pretty deep soul-searching about who she wanted to be as a person—someone who held onto old pain despite all else, or someone who could give a person a second chance. It didn't excuse how Ash had treated her, but understanding the pain she had endured and how truly alone she had been opened Sam's eyes. It wasn't black and white. Plus, with a bit of time between then and now, Sam was more able to look at it objectively. Or at least try to.

Sometimes she felt a wave of panic. What was she thinking? This was Ashley Valence, her tormentor. But the Ash she knew now had done nothing but show her kindness and generosity. She wasn't the same person. And neither was Sam. Even when Sam let her doubts get the best of her, holding back with Ash, when they were together, something else took over. It felt comfortable and easy. And good. Really good. It was almost like there was a force pulling them together. Sam couldn't help but give in.

Today's surprise was hands down one of the best dates Sam had ever been on. And there was a softness to Ash that Sam had never seen before. Part of it was opening up about her past, but there was something else, almost an insecurity. Could Ash be doubting herself with Sam?

It was weird. Sam was so used to seeing the overly confident, all-star pitcher side of Ash. It was nice to see a different side, but it also made Sam a little sad. Ash had gone through a lot with her family. Sam couldn't imagine what that must feel like—to be treated so horribly or left, completely, by your own parents. She knew she was lucky for the family she had, but getting to know Ash better made her good fortune that much more apparent. Sam wasn't sure if there was anything she could do to take away some of Ash's pain, but she knew she wanted to try.

As the cartoon credits rolled across the screen, Sam looked down at Jake nuzzled against her side, fast asleep. She turned off the television, scooped up her son, and carried him to bed.

Chapter 11

"You know, I didn't say anything last week when you were clearly hiding something. But canceling on me? Now I *know* something's up, missy. Don't think I won't get it out of you," said a lovingly irritated Drea.

Sam rolled her eyes and sighed. She and Ash planned their second date for Friday night and Sam waited until Wednesday to tell Drea. Sam knew she wouldn't let it go easily and would hunt down the truth like a hound dog chasing a scent.

There were four things Drea was relentless about—having a good drink, pranking interns, sniffing out a lie, and sleeping with the entire lesbian population of New Orleans.

She never had to make much of an effort with the last challenge—women flocked to her. Sam marveled at how Drea managed to sleep with so many people and not have any of them coming for her afterward. It was probably the Southern charm, and one of the sexiest drawls this side of the Mississippi.

As for sniffing out a lie, Drea had her in her sights.

"I promise I will fill you in soon. I just really need you to give me a little time on this one first, okay?"

"Okay . . ." Sam could hear the skepticism in her voice. "But whatever it is, you make sure it doesn't start interfering with our Friday nights. One cancellation is forgivable. But two and I'm coming after you."

Sam wanted to say that it shouldn't affect Drea's usual routine of taking some wide-eyed baby dyke home to blow her mind after she and Sam hung out on Friday nights, but she bit her tongue. It didn't bother Sam how Drea was with women. She just wondered why Drea chose that route rather than looking for someone she wanted to see a second time, or more. But Drea never talked about that, and Sam had never pressed.

As close as they were, there were things Drea didn't discuss—with anyone. That bothered Sam. A lot, actually. Mostly because Drea knew everything about her. She had seen Sam at her absolute worst. If it hadn't been for Drea, Sam wasn't sure if she would have survived losing Anna.

It just didn't feel right not to be able to be that kind of friend for Drea. Sam didn't like asymmetries like that. Not with the people that mattered.

Sam convinced Ash to let her plan the second date. Maybe it was the competitive streak in her, wanting to top their amazing first date. Ash definitely set the bar high. But mostly, Sam wanted to make her feel special. She sensed Ash didn't think she deserved that kind of treatment, and Sam wasn't having any of that.

At just after five o'clock, Sam parked in front of the bright blue shotgun-style house with vibrant yellow shutters and started to get out of the car. When Ash emerged from the house wearing a tight, black V-neck wrap-around shirt with three-quarter sleeves, dark jeans, and her black ankle boots, Sam beamed. She wore her hair down, which Sam was learning was an infrequent occurrence. *God, she looks sexy.* Sam hopped out of the car and ran around the front to hold the door open for her. "You look beautiful," Sam said as they hugged. She breathed in Ash's perfume, a hint of lavender—it was intoxicating.

"You look pretty amazing yourself," she said, stepping back and looking Sam up and down.

Sam felt her ears heat up.

"So where are we headed?" Ash asked eagerly as Sam headed down Laurel Street. She didn't realize Ash lived so close to the zoo. They were practically neighbors.

"Uh-uh." Sam shook her head. "Tonight's your surprise."

As Sam took US-90 past the round, metallic Superdome that held the heart of New Orleans—as a refuge for people during Hurricane Katrina, and as the home stadium of their beloved Saints—Ash glanced at Sam. "Road trip?" she asked curiously.

Sam flashed a coy smile. "You'll see."

Ash became increasingly interested in the surroundings as they exited the highway. Sam snuck glances at her, noticing the mild confusion on her face. Sam had never asked if Ash liked surprises and hoped she hadn't made a big mistake in her choice of destination.

As they turned down Poland Ave., deep in the heart of Bywater, largely desolate with a sprinkling of houses, Ash snuck a cautious glance at Sam. As Sam drove toward the end of the road and parked along the curb—a rather glum area with a faceless defense complex behind a fence across the street and an abandoned train yard in the distance—she looked at Sam hesitantly. "So, did you bring me here to kill me?" Ash glanced in the back seat. "Beat me to death with a booster seat?"

Sam smiled. "Guess it depends on how the night goes. Come on."

They walked to the corner of the fairly empty street before Sam turned to Ash. "Here we are."

Ash arched a brow at her, clearly unsure. "Where?"

Sam grinned, nodding at the forest green double doors on the unassuming two-hundred-year-old building behind her. It was a two-story with patches of red brick peeking out underneath swaths of plaster—the remains of past layers. Sam held the door open for her. "After you," she said, with a flourish of her hand.

Ash looked skeptical as she stepped inside the dilapidated, dank, musty front room of the business, which had eye-level towers of wine bottles throughout the space. Ash turned to Sam with wide eyes.

"Pick a bottle. Anything you want."

She meandered amongst the towers and chose a Riesling.

They walked up to the chest-high counter against the wall, and glanced at the chalkboard hung behind it, listing different cheeses and specials. They chose an assortment of cheeses along with a mango chutney, and some nut and jelly accoutrement. After Sam paid, the friendly woman behind the counter took their bottle and told them their wine and cheese would be out shortly. Ash looked at Sam expectantly since there were clearly no places to sit in the room.

"Follow me," Sam said, grinning.

They walked through a mostly empty room and out into a noisy, lively fenced backyard, where a crowd of people sat laughing and talking at wrought iron and wooden tables.

"Wow," Ash said as she stood gaping.

"Welcome to Bacchanal." Sam grinned.

They found an empty round wooden table toward the back of the yard, and sat down in unpretentious plastic deck chairs. A man walked up with the wine, two glasses, and a small, white plastic bucket full of ice. Sam and Ash watched as he uncorked the bottle and poured them each a glass.

"Ladies," he said with a smile, before placing the bottle in the bucket, and walking away.

Ash met Sam's gaze, surprise still clear on her face.

Sam picked up her glass and raised it toward Ash. "To an amazing night."

Ash raised her glass. "I'll say," she muttered.

Sam sipped her wine—the crisp, cold sweetness mixed with a hint of apricot. They took in everything around them as the waiter returned with their cheese plate. As the sun set in the distance, casting a warm glow over the patrons, and strands of small white lights along the fence turned on, Sam looked at Ash, stunned by how beautiful she was. Ash caught her looking.

"What?" she asked.

Sam shook her head. "Nothing," she said quietly. "I'm just happy."

Ash took Sam's hand in hers. "I'm glad."

They sampled the different cheeses and drank more wine, enjoying each other's company and the jovial, laid-back atmosphere. As darkness enveloped them, three men walked to the lean-to against the fence that served as a minimalist stage and began unpacking instruments. A few small spotlights shone down from the wooden canopy of the stage, leaving them mostly backlit against the strands of white lights. It was pretty magical, even more so once the upbeat sounds of zydeco filled the yard. It felt unpretentious and inviting, as if they were at a close gathering of friends, lots of friends, in a backyard, with front-row seats to a band whose guitar, accordion, and washboard commingled to inspire everyone to breathe deeply, laugh loudly, and dance in their chairs.

"God, I've missed this," Ash said, grinning.

"Are you hungry?" Sam asked, after they listened to a few songs.

Ash looked at her with disappointment. "I am, but I hate to leave this place. It's so much fun."

"Oh, we're not going anywhere. Come with me." Sam led her to a portable kitchen in the corner of the yard. Pork loins sizzled on the large grill as hints of rosemary filled the air. Sam and Ash perused the three dinner options scrawled across the small whiteboard on the counter, before making their selections. When the waiter brought their food to them a short while later, Sam glanced at Ash, who had a surprised look on her face.

"Paper plates and plastic utensils? This is definitely a first."

Sam rolled her eyes playfully. "Don't knock it till you try it."

Sam watched as Ash took a bite of her grilled fish, closed her eyes, and moaned. "Oh, my god." Ash's eyes widened. "This is incredible."

Sam couldn't hide her huge grin. *Success.* "You act as if you didn't expect much from me or my plan for our date."

"No, it's not that," Ash replied quickly.

"I'm just kidding." Sam grinned. "You like to cook, so I wanted to take you to one of the best restaurants I know." She shrugged. "One of the best places I know, period. You can't beat the atmosphere, the food, and the wine. This place is magical, every time."

"Well, you're right about that. And I guess it's my turn to thank you now."

"For what?"

"For showing me something new and amazing about my hometown."

"Well, Bacchanal wasn't open last time you lived here. It's only been here about ten years. And it's gone through a few iterations during that time—between the hurricane and a police raid."

"Police raid?"

"Yeah, I guess the city takes its food license permits fairly seriously." Sam paused, sipping her wine. "I have a feeling that amazing oak tree has been here a little longer than ten years."

Ash laughed. "I'd say at least fifteen."

They spent the next couple of hours eating, drinking, talking, and listening to the music. As ten o'clock approached, Sam suppressed a yawn.

"Tired?" Ash asked.

Sam gave her an apologetic look. "Sorry. I guess I'm not used to late nights."

"Jake doesn't party into the early morning hours? That's surprising," Ash teased.

Sam laughed. "No. My usual night is a bedtime story with some plot variation of Optimus Prime saving the world."

Ash twirled her water glass between her fingers.

"I know. Pretty lame, huh?"

"No." Ash shook her head. "I think it sounds pretty amazing, actually."

The admission surprised Sam. "Did you ever want kids?"

She regretted asking the question the second she saw the hesitant expression on Ash's face. "I'm sorry, that's none of my business."

"No, it's fine. Really." Ash sipped her water, glancing off in the distance. She looked back at Sam and shrugged. "It was never anything I thought much about, honestly. I think because things were so rough when I was a kid. The worst thing I could imagine was being like my parents, and I would never want to put a child through that."

Sam nodded. She didn't know how to respond when Ash talked about her childhood. How could she understand what Ash had been through? She could tell how much it had affected Ash though. And how hard that must have been to work through as an adult.

Sam sensed Ash was watching her.

"Wanna head back?" Ash asked.

Sam nodded. They tossed their dishes in the large trashcan as they headed across the yard and back to the car.

The car ride to Uptown was pretty silent—both of them lost in their thoughts. When Sam pulled up to Ash's house and turned off the engine, Ash turned to her. "Would you like to come in for a little bit or are you too tired?"

Sam's heart started racing. She wasn't sure what the invitation meant. *Was that date code for having sex?* Or was Ash really just asking her to come inside? She didn't know what the rules were, but she did know she wasn't ready to go home.

Ash smiled at her as Sam overthought her answer to the simple question. Sam was pretty sure her thoughts had been written fairly clearly across her face.

"Sure. I think I just got a second wind."

Ash held the door as Sam entered the house first, greeted immediately by a blur of shaggy fur at her feet. She crouched down, petting the excited little terrier puppy. "Who's this little guy?" She peered under its low belly. "Or girl?"

Ash laughed. "Guy. Sorry about that. Meet Goose—my very untrained, but lovable, puppy."

Sam scratched behind the puppy's ears as he furiously wagged his tail. "You're a *Top Gun* fan?" She looked up at Ash.

Ash tilted her head with a half frown. "Not particularly, no."

"Okay . . ." Sam stood and followed Ash through the foyer.

Sam stopped when they entered the living room and nearly drooled. It looked like something out of *Architectural Digest*. The room was an intricate blend of rich blues, grays, and creams. Everything, from the furniture to the smallest accents on the bookcase, tied together in one unique vision. The play of textures and colors amazed her. "How long have you lived here?" she asked from her stupor.

"Um, about three months. It's just a rental."

"God, Ash, if I had known your place looked like this, I would've never let you in my house."

"Oh, stop it. I love your place. It's so comfy and homey."

Sam blinked at her. "I'm pretty sure that means unattractive."

Ash walked toward Sam and placed her palms on her shoulders. "Sam, believe me when I tell you, *nothing* about you is unattractive." Sam felt her neck heat up and wished her body wouldn't betray her so easily. "I'm gonna let Goose out real quick. I'll be right back."

Goose beelined it out of the room ahead of Ash. Apparently, he knew the drill. Sam examined the books on Ash's bookcase—lots of classics, and many on home design. Sam perked up as she recognized some familiar names. Audre Lorde, Betty Friedan, bell hooks, Angela Davis. She warmed, as if reminded of long-lost friends.

The room was beautiful, but something felt off. She gazed around, settling on a photo of Goose on a side table. Realization dawned. That was the only photo. In a room so well-thought out, right down to the accent pillows, it was a glaring omission that spoke volumes about Ash's life and what it didn't include.

"How about a drink?" Sam jumped at Ash's voice from the hallway. She wondered how long Ash had been watching her.

Sam followed her into the kitchen. "I'm not sure I should have any more alcohol . . . holy cow!" Sam's jaw dropped at the shiny gas range built into an island big enough to fit four people, with a wooden rack full of pots and pans suspended above it.

Ash grinned. "You like?"

Sam gave her an incredulous look. "You're not allowed to my house anymore."

She laughed. "The kitchen sold me too." She opened the back door as Goose sped in. "How about a fruit spritzer? Non-alcoholic."

"That sounds amazing, actually," Sam said, still taking in her surroundings.

"Great. Would you grab the seltzer water out of the fridge for me? Right side. On the bottom." She grabbed some fresh fruit off the counter and began rinsing it in the white farmhouse sink.

"Sure." Sam walked over to the fancy stainless steel fridge, opening it and bending down to look for the seltzer water, which took a second because the fridge was *packed*. Before she could grab the water, a swift pinch to her butt made her jerk.

"Feeling a little feisty?" she teased. She turned around, expecting Ash to sweep her into her arms, but Ash wasn't there. Sam's eyes dropped to the floor where the little puppy stared at her with twinkling brown eyes, his pink tongue hanging out of his mouth as he panted away. "Now I get it," she muttered.

Sam looked across the kitchen to see Ash shaking with laughter. "Well, I can't fault him for his taste."

Grinning, Sam rolled her eyes.

Ash and Sam sat on the sofa, sipping their drinks. They were quiet and smiled shyly at each other. The silence in the house was awkward and Ash felt like a teenager accidentally left alone to make out with her crush. Goose sat on the floor on the other side of the ottoman that doubled as a footrest and coffee table. He looked back and forth between them, his tongue lolling out the side of his mouth.

Sam broke their silence. "So . . . what made you end it with Ali?"

Ash nearly spit seltzer across the room. "Wow, you really jump right in, don't you?"

Sam shrugged. "I guess I'm not very good at small talk."

Ash nodded. She still felt bad about how things had happened with Ali. "There's not much to it, really. She was a cool girl, but we weren't right for each other. And that became hard to ignore."

"Were you together long?"

"Only about two months. The day you and Jake ran into us at the pizza place was our first date actually."

"Ah. That explains why you were so dressed up I guess."

Ash raised a brow at her. "You noticed what I was wearing?" A sly smile spread across her lips as she raised her glass for another sip.

Sam rolled her eyes and looked away. "Easy. I don't want your head to explode."

"Well, you do have that effect on me."

Sam scrunched her face. "Making your head explode?"

"In a good way . . . along with other parts of my body."

Sam swallowed audibly and sipped her drink, suddenly very interested in Goose.

Amused, Ash just watched. "What about you?"

"What about me?"

Ash paused, knowing this was a delicate topic and wanting to move carefully. "I understand if you're not ready to talk about it yet, but I was curious about your last relationship."

"Oh." Sam blew out a slow breath.

"You don't have to, Sam."

"No, it's okay. I just haven't talked about her much." Sam absently scratched at her neck, leaving a red mark behind. "What would you like to know?"

Ash shrugged. "Well, how did you two meet?"

Sam nodded, staring at her drink. "Through Drea, actually. Drea and Anna worked together at a publishing company. Anna was an editor and Drea was—still is, actually—the graphic designer. Drea hit on her of course because, well, it's Drea. Anna was probably the only woman who's ever said no to her."

Sam smiled. "As Drea and Anna became friends and got to know each other better, Drea got it in her head that Anna and I would be good together." She looked at Ash. "She was right." Sam paused, taking a sip. "We were together for three years before we had Jake. When same-sex marriage became legal in Louisiana, we started planning a small wedding for family and friends in October. That was . . ." Sam looked up at the ceiling, "2015, when Jake was two. The following spring, she was gone."

Ash couldn't hide her pained expression. "I'm so sorry, Sam. I can't imagine how hard that must have been for you and Jake."

Sam shrugged and gave her a half smile. "Thanks." They sat in silence for a few moments. "So, when did you know you were gay?"

Ash's stunned expression must have been obvious because Sam laughed.

"I don't remember that about you back in high school . . ." Sam winked at her.

Ash grinned. "Well, you know, college softball player . . ." She waggled her eyebrows. "I had a few opportunities there to figure it out."

"Are you trying to tell me you were a player? More than just softball?"

Ash laughed. "Player is a bit strong . . . I just . . . enjoyed my new-found freedom and the chance to explore a new side of myself. That's all." She flashed an overly innocent look at Sam.

Sam scoffed. "Player." Ash laughed. "You didn't know until college, though?"

Ash became a little more serious. She hadn't figured out how to tell Sam she was attracted to her in high school. Things seemed to be going well between them. She was afraid Sam would take it badly. And she didn't want to lose Sam. "I had an inkling or two in high school." She avoided Sam's eyes and sipped her drink. "What about you? When did you know?"

"My last year in college. I was a bit of a late bloomer, I guess. Drea figured it out in high school and came out to me. She slept with nearly every lesbian on campus our first year at Tulane—might as well have been a second major. Somehow I was still clueless until we went to a club our last year to see this girl she liked sing with her band. I still don't know what it was, but as I watched her sing and dance on stage, it was like my body awakened. I felt sensations in places I never had before. I thought it was a fluke at first, but then it kept happening."

Sam looked at Ash, and kept going. "When I finally told Drea just before graduation, she was ecstatic, and made it her job to introduce me to all the hotspots in town."

Sam laughed. "I met my first girlfriend at a dance club on ladies' night, and my first time with her confirmed everything I needed to know." She shrugged. "I didn't have quite the same tactics as Drea when I came out, but I never looked back."

Amused, Ash watched Sam.

"What?"

"Can I tell you something?"

"You can tell me anything."

"When I saw you at Charlie's with Drea, I thought I was going to faint."

"Why?"

"Partly because I thought you might be gay. And that? Well, *that* blew my mind." She shook her head.

"And the other part?" Sam asked quietly.

"I thought you and Drea were together. And that made me jealous as hell."

Sam stared at her. "Jealous?"

Ash nodded. "When I saw you at the pizza place, I wasn't able to get you out of my head for days."

Sam's mouth hung open. "But . . . you were there with Ali."

Ash grimaced. "I know. That was tough." Ash ran her thumb down the side of her glass, leaving a streak in the condensation. "I tried to ignore it. But the more time I spent around you, well, it was clear that no one came close to affecting me the way you did." She smiled at Sam. "Completely effortlessly, I might add."

Sam looked shocked. And as the moments ticked by, Ash felt an increasing sense of regret for being so open. It was too soon to tell Sam all of that. *What was she thinking?*

Ash placed her drink on the glass end table and faced Sam. "Sam,

I'm sorry. I shouldn't have said anything. I didn't mean to make you uncomfortable."

Sam waved off Ash's words. "No. You're fine. I'm just . . ." Sam shook her head, seeming at a loss for words. She placed her drink down on the floor and scratched the back of her head. "I guess it's just hard for me to believe that you're into me."

"Are you kidding?" Ash's voice was louder than she intended.

Sam shook her head no, a blush coloring her neck.

Ash rubbed her forehead and moved closer to Sam. They sat with their legs crossed on the sofa, facing each other. "Sam." Ash didn't want to belittle Sam's feelings, but she needed to set her straight. She placed her hand on Sam's knee. "I've never felt as connected to anyone as I do to you. There are no pretenses with you. You're just you, and you let me be me. You have a way of calming me down without even trying." Ash smiled and shook her head. "Not to mention, it takes every bit of restraint I have to keep my hands to myself when we're together."

"Really?"

"Really."

A smug smile formed on Sam's lips. "I have been having a hard time with that as well."

"Really?"

"Really." The flirtatious tone in Sam's voice sent a shot through Ash, making her throat dry.

She ran her finger slowly along Sam's knee. "Maybe we shouldn't try so hard." Ash watched Sam's breaths deepen, her eyes following Ash's finger as it traced along her leg.

Sam finally looked up, her eyes dark. A wave of butterflies fluttered in Ash's stomach. Ash couldn't wait any longer. She reached behind Sam's neck, pulling her into a kiss.

Sam's lips were soft and full. Her breath hot. Ash couldn't get enough and wrapped her arms around Sam, pulling her deeper into the kiss. Ash slid her tongue into Sam's mouth and heard her moan, amazed how good it felt to kiss her.

Sam balled Ash's shirt in her fist against the small of her back. Ash moved her hand to the front of Sam's white button-down shirt, but as she started to slide her hand underneath to Sam's stomach, Sam stopped her.

Sam broke the kiss, pressing her forehead to Ash's. Ash wasn't sure what had just happened. They sat in silence as their breaths slowly returned to normal.

"Sorry," Sam finally said.

"It's okay. Sorry if that was too much, too soon." Ash couldn't hide the concern in her voice.

"No. I'm sorry." Sam pulled away and sat against the arm of the sofa. She sighed. "This is just really new for me. I haven't been with anyone in a long time, Ash. I think I need to take things slower."

Ash nodded. "Of course."

Sam gave her a small smile. "Thanks." She turned and placed both feet on the floor. "I should probably get home."

Ash's head was still spinning from the sudden change of events. She felt bad for upsetting Sam. She could feel the distance increase between them. "Okay. I'll walk you out."

Sam turned to Ash at the door. "Thank you for tonight. I had a great time." She smiled and kissed Ash on the cheek. And then she was gone.

Chapter 12

"Good job, bud. That looks really good." Sam rubbed Jake's arm as he finished writing "book" on loose-leaf paper.

The timer on the microwave beeped and she got up from the kitchen table to drain the pasta. Even she could handle buttered noodles. She had chosen something easy tonight because she was stressed. Despite her minor freak-out with Ash last night, she had decided to tell Drea about Ash. And she was pretty sure it wasn't going to go over well.

She drained the pasta and added a couple thick pats of butter to the pot. It was soothing to watch the butter melt as she stirred. She spooned the noodles onto two plates and carried them to the table.

"El—el—ela," Jake sounded out one of his more challenging homework words.

"Good job. Way to sound it out. Think, what's Babar?"

"An elephant!" Jake exclaimed. He ran his finger over the word as he spelled it out. "E-l-e-p-h-a-n-t."

"Right. That's how you spell elephant." Sam placed the plates on the table and pointed to each syllable as she and Jake sounded out the word together.

"Okay, can you put that somewhere so we don't get noodles on it?" Jake nodded and walked the paper to the kitchen counter.

"Thanks, bud."

After dinner, Drea came over and they all watched a movie. Once Sam put Jake to bed, she joined Drea in the kitchen for adult talk.

Drea sat at the table as Sam poured them each a glass of Malbec. "This better be good."

Sam handed Drea a glass and sat. She stared at her glass for a moment, steeling herself. "There is . . . *something* I need to tell you."

"I knew it! This is going to be good." Drea got more comfortable in her chair and took a sip of wine, gazing at Sam expectantly, a twinkle in her eyes.

Before Sam could open her mouth, Drea continued. "Is it work? You finally told Pete to go fuck himself?" Drea's enjoyment of this guessing game made Sam smile.

"No. But, he has been a colossal—" Sam leaned in and lowered her voice to an almost whisper—"asshat." Sam's conscience took over with curse words when Jake was nearby.

Drea raised a palm. "Whoa. Sam. Language, please."

Sam rolled her eyes.

Drea's mockery switched to glee. She was like a kid in a candy store. "Is it a girl?"

Something in Sam's expression must've tipped her off, because Drea's face lit up. "It is! You met some hot twenty-year-old and are getting it on." Drea did a lewd dance in her chair.

"That's really more your MO, isn't it?"

"Okay. A forty-year-old in mom jeans?"

Sam narrowed her eyes at Drea. "You do know those aren't the only options, right?"

Drea stared at her, unimpressed. "Fine. Tell me."

Sam took a long sip of wine. She had been playing this conversation over in her mind since their phone call Wednesday night. Drea, more than anyone, had been by her side through everything with Ash in high school. She rubbed Sam's back when she cried, and belted out songs in overly dramatic voices to make Sam laugh. She had stuck by Sam through all those terrible years, trying to convince her that everything the bullies made her believe about herself wasn't true.

Sam chose to forgive Ash and give her another chance—a chance that allowed her to get to know one of the most amazing women she had ever met—but she wasn't so sure Drea would be so forgiving.

And how could she blame her? Drea was as loyal as they came. Sam wondered how much of a fight it would be to get Drea to give Ash another chance. To see what Sam saw, and not the nasty bully from high school.

Of course, Sam wasn't even sure Ash would speak to her again after how she had left things the night before. She grimaced at the thought of how badly she handled it. But, she knew how she was feeling about Ash and she couldn't stand hiding it from her best friend any longer.

"You know how I told you that Ash and I had that conversation in the elevator and we decided to give each other a fresh start?"

Drea's eyes narrowed. "Yeeaahh."

Sam sipped her wine. "Well, we did—give each other a fresh start, second chance, whatever—and when I got the concussion, she took care of me. She stayed on the sofa all night, actually, to make sure I was okay. And she made food for Jake and me the next day." Sam glanced at Drea, nervously spinning her glass in her hand. Drea watched Sam intently with narrowed eyes.

"You told me a teammate took you home. You somehow left out the rest of those details," Drea said, raising a brow.

"I know," Sam said apologetically. "I didn't know how to tell you. I didn't ask her to stay. I didn't ask for any of it."

Drea sat back in her chair and crossed her arms. "So?"

"So, what?"

"So, what should I think?"

Sam looked at her, pitifully.

Drea sat up straight, her eyes wide. "Oh, god!"

Sam closed her eyes.

"Oh, my god. Sam! What did you do?"

"Nothing, really, yet." Sam looked down at her lap, her face hot from embarrassment. "We went out on a couple dates," she said quietly.

"You what? You're fucking her?" Drea leapt out of her seat and started pacing erratically. Sam grimaced in anticipation of Drea's Italian temper. Drea stopped suddenly and stared at Sam. "Are you insane?"

Sam avoided Drea's stare.

"Sam, this is Ashley-fucking-Valence. Your nemesis. Ring a bell?"

"She's not like that anymore," Sam whispered.

"Excuse me?" Drea put her hand to her ear. "I couldn't hear you over the sound of hell freezing over."

"I don't think that would really make a sound." Sam raised her head.

"Shut up! Just . . . shut up." Drea resumed pacing.

Sam had never seen Drea flustered before. Not like this. She held out a palm toward her. "I'm sorry. I know I should've told you. I just . . . I wasn't sure what was happening and I wanted to be sure before I said anything."

"Sure?" Drea stopped pacing. "Sure of what?" Her voice was cautious.

Sam met her gaze and sighed. "I care about her, Drea."

Drea dropped into her chair like the air had left her body. She stared at the table, slowly shaking her head.

"Drea, I know this sounds crazy to you. I know you want to protect me. You always have." Sam reached out and took her hand. She looked up at Sam, her jaw hanging open in disbelief. "And I love you for that." Drea stared back at the table. "But honestly, she's not the same person anymore. She's actually, well, pretty amazing."

Drea met Sam's eyes with a guarded expression.

"I need you to trust me on this one. I'd like you to make up your mind for yourself by spending time with us at some point. It would be important to me. But for now, can you at least give her the benefit of the doubt?"

Drea took a long sip of wine. She regarded Sam for a bit before she spoke. "I hope to god you're not wrong about this, Sam."

The final game of the regular season was Tuesday night. The Lady Lobbers were rocking an undefeated season and the opposing team tonight wasn't a big threat to that record. Assuming they won, they'd be the top seed in the championships slated for the weekend. Two games Saturday, followed by semi-finals and finals on Sunday.

It was a fairly uneventful game. Sam's mind was mostly focused on her budding relationship with Ash. After Drea left Saturday, her words had stayed with Sam the rest of the night. Sam worried she was being blind and Drea was right. But as she considered the evidence—everything that had happened since Ash moved back—she knew she wasn't wrong about Ash. She felt it in her gut. If anyone was acting poorly, it was Sam. And she needed to fix that. ASAP. She had texted Ash later

Friday night to say she was sorry for leaving so abruptly, and to see if they could talk after the game tonight. Ash agreed but the text felt a bit impersonal. Sam couldn't help but worry she had messed everything up. Or worse, that she had hurt Ash.

As Sam watched Ash pitch, she couldn't fathom how much things had changed between them since the beginning of the season. It still made her a little nervous how quickly things were progressing, but it also made her happy. She just hoped Ash gave her the chance to explain that.

After the win, Lace jogged over to Sam, who was packing up at the bench. "Good game, Sam."

Sam tossed her glove into her bag. "Thanks! You too. Championships, baby!" They cheered and the rest of the team chimed in.

"Walk you to your car?" Lace asked.

Sam tried to be nonchalant as she looked past her to find Ash, who was busy being talked to by Marci, nodding occasionally in response to Marci's wildly gesticulating hands. She caught Sam's eye and winked. Marci didn't even notice. Sam smiled, returning her gaze to Lace, who eyed her intently. Sam's ears grew hot. She turned and grabbed her bag. "Sure."

They crossed the parking lot, dodging cars rushing to get on the road. "So, are you two an item now?"

Sam stumbled, gawking at Lace. "What?" Sam was thankful for the sparse lighting, hoping Lace couldn't see her blushing.

"You and Ash," she said matter-of-factly. "Are y'all together now?"

"I, I don't . . . what gave you that idea?" They reached Sam's car and faced each other.

"Oh, I don't know. The way you nearly sucked each other's faces off a couple weeks ago."

Sam closed her eyes. "You saw that?"

"Me . . . and half the team. You two weren't exactly subtle."

"Oh, no. Marci too?" Sam asked sheepishly.

"I don't think so. She was too busy envisioning future trophies. So?"

Sam swallowed, staring at a very interesting spot of gravel nearby. She wasn't good at lying and couldn't think of anything believable to satisfy Lace. She nodded slowly. "We're . . . seeing each other, yes." She really wanted that to be true and hoped she hadn't just stuck her foot in her mouth.

Lace pushed Sam's shoulder lightly. "That's great! It's about time you got some." Lace giggled as Sam's mouth dropped open. "Oh, come on. You know it's true."

She glanced behind Sam. "Well, there's my cue." She looked over her shoulder as she walked away. "See you Saturday," she said in an overly flirtatious voice. Sam just shook her head.

"Hi."

Sam turned at Ash's voice. "Hey," she said with a warm smile.

"What was that about? Everything okay?"

"Well, apparently half the team saw us kiss the other night. I guess we weren't that discreet."

"I see." Ash nodded, but Sam couldn't read her expression. "So, you wanted to talk?"

Sam tried to swallow, but her throat had gone dry. She was nervous. She hadn't expected to feel so nervous.

Sam blew out a small breath. "Ash, I'm really sorry about Friday." She shook her head. "I had an amazing time. I always have an amazing time with you." She gave Ash a meek smile. Ash just listened, her expression unreadable. "I told you that I haven't been with anyone in a while. And that's true . . . but, that's only part of the truth. I haven't been with anyone since Anna."

Ash's eyes softened as Sam continued. "I thought I was ready. To try being with someone new. But it hit me all of a sudden on Friday. I wasn't prepared for it."

Sam took Ash's hand in hers. "I like you, Ash. But I need you to be patient with me. I want to move forward with you, but it's probably more complicated than I even realized." Sam looked at the ground. "If that's too much for you, I will understand."

"Sam." Ash ran her thumb over Sam's hand. "I like you, too. That's not going to change."

Sam's entire body relaxed at her words. *How did Ash know exactly what she needed to hear?*

Ash smiled and pulled her into a hug.

"So, you still want to date me?" Sam asked into Ash's neck.

Ash chuckled. "Um, *yeah.*"

Sam laughed, stepping back. "Okay good, because I may have just told Lace that we're seeing each other . . . so the whole team should be briefed on this by Saturday."

Ash looked a little stunned.

"Sorry. She kind of cornered me. I didn't want to lie, but I realize maybe . . ." Ash pulled her into a kiss that left her dizzy. Sam looked at her in surprise. "So . . . you're not angry?"

"Definitely not. Besides . . ." She put her hands on Sam's waist and tugged her forward. Sam felt woozy at Ash's closeness and the hot breath on her face. "That means I don't have to be subtle about kissing you in front of them." She pulled Sam into a long, exploratory kiss. Just as Sam relaxed, wanting more, Ash pulled away. "I've been wanting to do that all night," she whispered.

"Uh huh." Sam nodded dumbly, still trying to regain her senses.

Ash leaned forward and placed a quick kiss on Sam's lips, before gazing into her eyes. "Good night, beautiful."

"Good night," Sam murmured belatedly. She watched Ash walk away, mesmerized by the confident sway of her hips as she strode toward her car.

I'm in so much trouble.

Because of the chaotic schedule with championship games all weekend, Drea gave Sam a pass on Friday night to have her third date with Ash. Sam would see her on Sunday anyway when Drea watched Jake for her. Sam didn't think Drea had fully accepted her relationship with Ash yet, but she was giving Sam space to pursue it and figure things out. Sam appreciated that.

Sam pulled up to Ash's house and took a deep breath. She had stopped herself from going too far with Ash last week, but she wasn't sure she had the strength to resist her again. She wasn't sure she wanted to anyway.

Ash opened the door before Sam's second knock. *Holy shit.* She wore a white UCLA softball T-shirt and faded jeans which clung to her sculpted legs. Her hair was up in a ponytail, sporty, yet sexy as hell.

"Hi," Sam muttered.

140

Ash smiled warmly, looking her up and down. "You look beautiful."

Sam suddenly felt overdressed in her cream V-neck sweater, dark jeans, and gray suede boots. Sam smiled shyly. "So do you."

Ash gestured her inside. "Hi, Goose," Sam said as the dog sat down beside Ash's bare feet. He stayed seated but wriggled his whole body in excitement. He had a perpetual smile on his face, which Sam found adorable.

"Come here." Ash took Sam in her arms and Sam inhaled her lavender scent, feeling woozy. She let Ash's warm strength envelop her. *Man, she gives good hugs.* Sam stepped back and met her eyes.

Sam's boots gave her a couple inches, which matched Ash's bare feet nicely, making them nearly eye to eye for once. Sam liked being able to look straight into her deep green eyes. The more evenly matched footing ratcheted up the heat as they stood gazing at each other. Sam swallowed hard.

Ash smiled and took her hand, leading her into the kitchen. Only then did she notice the mouth-watering aromas. There was a large stainless-steel pot sitting atop the island's range alongside a pot of white rice, but nothing else to take responsibility for the tantalizing play of smells.

Ash handed Sam a glass of Riesling before picking up her own half-filled glass and taking a sip. "Why don't you take a seat while I finish dinner?" She gestured toward one of the brushed nickel stools around the island. "I hope you like gumbo," she said with a wink.

"You'd have to kick me out of town if I didn't."

Sam watched as Ash stirred the pot with a wooden spoon, and took a taste. She hummed to herself as she sipped her wine, swaying her hips—a side of her that was pretty adorable and alluring at the same time. She put her glass down and dipped the spoon back into the large pot before walking toward Sam, her hand underneath the spoon to catch any drips. "Tell me what you think," she said, holding the spoon to Sam's mouth. Sam closed her eyes at the enchanting concoction playing on her tongue, and let out a moan. Her mind flipped through each taste, the Cajun seasonings, garlic, tomato. It tasted like home.

"Oh, my god, Ash. This is amazing." She opened her eyes to see Ash looking at her with undisguised passion. Ash blinked a couple of times and walked back to the range.

Sam watched Ash add some finishing touches to the gumbo. "I like watching you cook."

Ash looked up. "Oh yeah?"

"Yeah. You get this little grin. It's cute." Ash's cheeks turned pink. "And you have a twinkle in your eye. You seem happy."

"I'm happy when I'm pitching. Do I have a twinkle in my eye then?" Ash asked as she approached Sam.

"Oh no. You get a completely different look in your eyes when you pitch. Probably has something to do with you being so competitive." Sam smiled sweetly at her.

Ash pointed to her chest. "I'm competitive? That's pretty funny coming from you."

Sam pulled Ash's shirt, tugging her forward into a kiss.

Ash leaned back, breaking the kiss. "Don't think just because you're kissing me, this is over."

Sam smiled, placing a finger against Ash's lips. "Shhh."

Ash grinned and leaned in for more.

Over dinner, they talked about the upcoming championship games, their chances of winning, and Ash's time playing college softball.

"So, what made you choose to major in interior design?"

Ash shrugged. "Well, as much as I loved softball, I knew, obviously, it wasn't an option as a career. And I always liked putting my touch on the few places I had decorated . . . mostly my college dorm room and then the apartment I shared with some friends during my last few years there. It was creative and fun. Very different from the strict regime of training for softball that had structured most of my high school years."

Sam nodded. "I totally get that. With marketing, it's a really interesting mix of graphic design and word play, but also finding the right combination to appeal to the demographic you're targeting. So, it satisfies my analytical side and love of words, as well as my creative side."

"It sounds like you really like what you do."

Sam frowned. "For the most part, but there are some colleague issues that have made it a bit less enjoyable lately." Sam regarded Ash.

"I'm impressed by your courage, starting your own company. That must be amazing."

"Maybe you should think about it for yourself," Ash suggested gently.

Sam shook her head. "I wouldn't even know where to start. As cool as it would be to have my own company, the idea terrifies me. I don't know if I could handle that kind of pressure. And with Jake . . . well, failure is not an option."

Ash nodded and twirled her glass on the table. "Well, I think you'd be a great business owner." She glanced at Sam. "Don't discount it or yourself just yet, okay? It can be tough, but in my experience, it's worth it."

Sam picked up the last bit of her baguette and mopped up the remains of the gumbo. "I choose you as the official chef."

Ash raised a brow. "Oh, yeah? The official chef of what?"

"Our relationship."

Ash's cheeks flashed pink and she smiled down at her bowl. "I'd like that."

"Which part?" Sam watched her intently. At her look of confusion, Sam clarified. "The chef part or the relationship part?"

Ash grinned and placed her hand on Sam's thigh. "Both."

Sam couldn't hide her smile. "Good."

"You want to take this outside?"

Sam's eyes widened.

"To the porch . . . to sit on the porch." Ash laughed and bent down to hand Goose a piece of sausage.

"Wow. How did I not notice this before?" Sam said as she swung on Ash's white porch swing, watching the sun set in the distance.

"I hope because you were busy noticing other things."

"Maybe . . ."

Ash smiled. "It's the other thing that sold me about this place, besides the kitchen. I used to love sitting on the porch swing at my house growing up. Hearing the hum of cicadas fill the night and watching the neighborhood settle down for the evening." Ash glanced at the grass in her front yard, remembering those few times she had felt comfort as a kid.

"I know what you mean. The sounds of this place, of the South in general. Growing up hearing them, and watching the lightning bugs at night. That's what I wanted for Jake. For him to have a home filled with heart and soul. I couldn't imagine a place with more of that than New Orleans."

Ash felt like Sam had read her mind.

"What?"

Ash shook her head. "I'm just surprised. That's exactly why I moved back here. I've never known a place with such a heartbeat of its own. So much of who I am as a person is because of growing up in a place filled with culture and life. I dreaded coming back here for so long, but in the end, I chose to make a home for myself here because those things outweighed the bad memories."

"Well, I for one, am glad you're back." Sam smiled at her.

"Me too." Ash leaned back against the swing and put her arm around Sam, as Sam rested her head against Ash's shoulder.

They sat in silence for a little while as dusk descended into night. Listening to the calming chirps of crickets, and watching as Goose methodically sniffed each shrub in the front yard.

As Ash stroked her fingers up and down Sam's upper arm, Sam leaned into her, nuzzling under her chin. Ash began using her whole hand to rub up and down Sam's arm with more pressure. Sam turned into her and Ash stilled as she felt Sam's lips against her neck. She gripped Sam's arm as heat spread through her body and she leaned her head back. Sam kissed and nipped at her neck, pulling a low growl from Ash. Ash's breath hitched as Sam slid her hand underneath her shirt and bra, cupping her breast and caressing it before rolling Ash's nipple between her fingers. Ash whimpered at the sensation.

"Ash," Sam whispered before taking Ash's mouth in hers. Ash placed her hand behind Sam's neck, pulling her closer, as she slid her tongue past Sam's parted lips. Sam let out a sexy moan. Ash wrapped her arms around Sam, pulling Sam tight against her chest. She needed her closer.

Sam slowly broke the kiss and met Ash's eyes. They stared at each other for a long moment, Ash feeling Sam's breath on her lips as they breathed each other's air.

"You're killing me," Ash whispered.

Sam stroked Ash's hair. "Why?"

"I want you so bad, I can hardly stand it." Her voice was strangled with the desire she could barely contain.

"I want you, too," Sam whispered.

"I thought you wanted to wait."

Sam smiled warmly. "I did. But now . . ." She shrugged and her smile turned mischievous. "I'm ready . . . if you are."

Ash nearly leapt from the swing, taking Sam by the hand, hurrying her to the front door. She held the door open as Goose rushed past them into the house. She barely locked the door before Sam's lips were on her again.

They stumbled toward the bedroom, knocking into walls as they kissed and pawed at each other like teenagers. Ash paused once they reached the bedroom and met Sam's heated gaze. "Are you sure?" she whispered into Sam's ear. "Because once I touch you, I don't think I'm going to be able to stop."

Sam leaned forward and kissed her softly on the lips. "I'm positive." The kiss was sweet, but the tone of her voice sent a surge of passion through Ash.

Ash laid Sam gently on the bed and lowered herself on top of her. The pressure of Sam's hips against her own ratcheted Ash's desire even higher. She leaned down and kissed Sam's soft, full lips. Sam's tongue teased her own and Ash felt like she was going to melt into her. As their tongues mingled together, Ash thrust her hips into Sam.

"Fuck." Sam groaned.

Ash broke the kiss and held Sam up off the bed, pulling Sam's sweater up and over her head before effortlessly unclasping her black lace bra. She slid the straps gently down each arm and tossed it to the ground. She swallowed hard, staring at Sam, the passion in Sam's eyes gripping her. Ash couldn't help but admire the expanse of creamy skin and swell of Sam's full breasts. "Sam, you're so beautiful."

Sam flashed a small smile and pulled Ash down into another long kiss, before Ash began slowly trailing kisses down her neck and chest to her breasts. She licked around Sam's nipple and took her breast fully in her mouth as they both let out a ragged moan. Sam ran her hand through Ash's hair as Ash placed gentle kisses across her chest on the short journey to her other breast.

As Ash kissed down to Sam's stomach, she felt Sam still beneath her. She glanced up and saw that Sam was looking away.

"Hey," she whispered.

Sam looked down at her.

"You're beautiful." She grasped Sam's hand and squeezed as they smiled at each other. When Ash kissed down to the waistband of Sam's jeans, she glanced up, a question in her eyes. Sam stroked her hands through Ash's hair and gave a small nod. Ash slowly undid the button and painstakingly pulled the zipper down. She paused and rested her cheek against the warm skin of Sam's lower abdomen. Sam clutched Ash's head against her, stroking her hair gently. Ash's heart raced in her chest, knowing they were about to cross a threshold that she had never wanted more in her life. She sat up and slid Sam's jeans and hot pink underwear off.

Ash stood, holding Sam's gaze, and quickly removed her own shirt and jeans. She pulled her hair tie off, letting her hair fall down onto her shoulders, before unclasping her red satin bra and letting it fall to the floor. As she slid her red lace underwear down her legs, she was surprised at how vulnerable she felt, so exposed, so seen. When she raised her gaze, the look in Sam's eyes shot straight through her. It felt like it was her first time again. She crawled up Sam's body, holding her gaze, and lowered her body onto Sam's, closing her eyes for a moment at how perfect Sam's body felt against her own.

"Ash . . ." Sam whispered. "You feel so good."

Ash opened her eyes and smiled. "So do you."

Sam claimed her mouth in a passionate kiss as Ash reveled in all of the sensations. Sam's lips, hands, body. They were everywhere and everything.

Everything blurred together as they moved seamlessly together. Every kiss. Every touch. The way Sam's body moved in response. The sounds she made. Ash wanted to remember all of it because something deep inside told her this one mattered.

When Sam's back started to arch off the bed, Ash held her there, wanting to delight in the moment and take her over the edge. She watched as Sam's body stilled and she screamed out before collapsing onto the bed.

Ash laid her cheek against Sam's thigh and reached up, taking Sam's hand in hers. They locked eyes and Ash was overwhelmed by how connected she felt to Sam. They stayed like that for several long moments, as Sam ran her fingertips gently along Ash's upper back.

Ash felt Sam reach for her arm. "Come here."

Sam watched lazily as Ash crawled up her body, placing kisses along the way. She shook her head at Ash in disbelief. "That was incredible. *You* are incredible."

Ash smiled at her. "I dreamed about what it would be like between us, but the reality is better than anything I ever imagined."

Sam kissed her lips. "I know." She wrapped her arms around Ash's neck, and held her close.

Ash felt Sam shudder. "Are you cold?" she asked, propping her head on her fist to look at Sam.

Sam shook her head. "No, just feeling the effects of you." Sam leaned forward and kissed her softly. "Now . . . get ready to feel my effects." She waggled her eyebrows at Ash.

"With a line like that."

Sam placed a finger against her lips. "Shhh."

Ash smiled and kissed her finger, letting out a small yelp as Sam flipped her on her back and kissed her deeply.

It was early morning before they finally drifted off to sleep, wrapped in each other's arms, and completely exhausted.

Sam woke to the insistent beep of an alarm clock, not recognizing its tone. She felt a weight against her back, which moved, as the beeping stopped. Before she could turn around to look, the weight, which she now realized was Ash's body, returned behind her. Ash laid a hand across her stomach. Sam smiled to herself as memories of last night— and this morning— came back to her. She took Ash's hand and raised it to her lips.

Sam felt Ash's lips turn up into a smile against her shoulder, and she rolled over to face her. Sam's stomach flipped when she met Ash's eyes. It was ridiculous how easily Ash affected her. They smiled at each other, lips inches apart.

"Good morning," Ash said quietly.

"Good morning." Sam's face lit up into a smile—she couldn't help it. "Do you always look this good when you wake up? Because it's seriously unfair to the rest of us."

The early morning light spreading through the room illuminated Ash's green eyes and cast a soft glow on her immaculate hair.

"I put my pants on one leg at a time, just like you, sweetheart." Sam rolled her eyes and Ash chuckled. "That wasn't exactly the right metaphor. I apologize. Someone kept me up all night."

Sam closed the distance between them, kissing her gently. "It was worth it."

"I'll say." She rolled Sam onto her back as she lay on top of her. Sam groaned at the surge of pleasure that went through her body. "Last night was amazing," Ash said, gazing down at Sam. "But waking up to you, naked in my bed, wrapped in my arms, well, that may be the winner."

"Sweet talker."

She leaned down and kissed Sam long and slow. When Ash broke the kiss, Sam's body was aching for her.

Ash frowned. "As much as I want to continue this, we should get going if we want to get to the game on time."

Normally, Sam loved the excitement and competitiveness of the championships, but she was seriously considering blowing the whole thing off to stay right here with Ash.

"Wanna join me in the shower?" Ash flashed a naughty grin.

Sam groaned. "If I do, we'll never make it to the game."

Ash pressed her hips into Sam. Sam's eyes widened and she moaned at the sensation. "That's just cruel."

"I just wanted to give you something to remember me by . . . it's going to be a long day," Ash whispered into Sam's ear, causing shivers to run through her body.

"Honestly, I'll be surprised if I can think of anything other than you today . . . which is not ideal as we face a weekend full of games. All of which we need to win."

Ash nodded and grew more serious. "I guess you need to go home and get your gear, huh?"

Sam's shifty gaze gave her away.

Ash's eyes narrowed. "What?"

"I may have my gear in my car." Sam continued to avoid eye contact.

"Well, Samantha Parker, you were planning on seducing me last night, weren't you?" She gave a mock gasp.

Sam met her eyes, determined to restore her honor. "I most certainly was not. I just . . . wanted to be prepared in case you wanted me as much as I wanted you."

Ash looked at her like she was a child who had just blamed something on the dog. "Sam . . ." Sam's heart skipped a beat at the affection in her voice. Ash kissed her, soft at first, before deepening it. Sam's head was spinning when Ash pulled back and gazed at her. "Do you honestly have any doubt about that?"

Sam tilted her head. "Maybe just a little still," she teased.

Ash slammed her mouth against Sam's, stunning her with the level of passion she found there. After a brief moment of surprise, Sam gave as good as she got, and they rolled on top of each other, fighting for top position, in a flurry of passion.

Ash ended up on top, and pinned Sam's arms up by her face, just as she had done that night on the softball field. Their eyes met, chests heaving, as she straddled Sam. She leaned down slowly, the mix of desire and adoration in her eyes stilling Sam's breath. Ash kissed Sam in a way that somehow felt even more intimate than all of last night. When she pulled away, she whispered. "*That's* what I wanted to do to you on the softball field that night . . . just in case you were wondering."

Sam stared at her—the compassion and vulnerability in her eyes, mixed with raw desire. She felt so much for Ash already. It was almost ridiculous.

Ash glanced at the alarm clock on the bedside table and sighed. "We have to get going. There's a shower and towels in the bathroom down the hall, since you won't join me." She kissed Sam once more and got off the bed. Sam watched her naked form walk toward the bathroom, hips swaying. Ash glanced over her shoulder and winked. "I'll be thinking about you."

Chapter 13

Sam's parents brought Jake to the second game on Saturday. Sam's team won the first game by six runs, and was beginning to believe they could actually win the whole thing. The day had been quite the struggle already, and not just with their opponents. Having Ash in front of her for an entire game, as she watched those strong arms throw ball after ball was a major distraction. It was a marathon of willpower not to take Ash on the softball field, in front of everyone.

During the second inning, Sam jogged over to the bleachers to say hello to her parents and give Jake a hug. "Enjoying the game, bud?"

Jake nodded vigorously. "Are you winning, Mom?"

Sam smiled at him. "We are, bud. It's still early though. This is a pretty tough team. Cross your fingers for us, okay?"

"Okay." He nodded, trying to cross his fingers on both hands. He glanced over at the bench. "Hey! There's Ash!"

Sam glanced over her shoulder at Ash, who smiled and started to walk toward them.

Sam turned back to Jake and noticed her mom sit up straight, a stern expression transforming her face. Sam shuddered and glanced back at Ash, who stopped walking toward them. She turned quickly and walked back to the bench.

Jake sagged with disappointment. "Don't worry, bud. You can say hello after the game."

"Okay," he mumbled.

Sam glanced at her mom who no longer seemed so stern. *Note to self, don't bring Ash home for a while.* When she looked at her mom a few moments later, she was leering at Ash. Thankfully, Ash wasn't looking. *Okay, don't bring her home, maybe ever.*

It was a close game with their lead dwindling toward the end, but they held out and won by two runs. After Sam collected Jake from her parents and said goodbye to them, she walked over to Ash, waiting a safe distance away.

Jake ran ahead, hugging Ash around her waist. She smiled and tousled his hair.

"Jake, how about pizza for dinner?" Sam asked. "We can pick it up on the way home."

Jake jumped up and down. "Yay!" He looked up at Ash. "Can Ash come?"

Sam looked at her innocently as if she didn't already know the answer. "Ash, if you don't have any plans tonight, would you like to join us?"

Ash leveled Sam with a seductive gaze, the effect of which shot straight to Sam's groin. Her expression must have indicated as much because Ash started laughing. "I'd love to."

Later, Jake sat nestled between Ash and Sam on the sofa, the remains of a pineapple pizza—Jake's favorite—and pepperoni pizza in open boxes on the coffee table. They were forty-five minutes into *WALL-E*—that damned robot got Sam every time—when her intense concentration was broken by Ash grazing her fingernails along the most sensitive part of her neck below her ear.

Sam clenched her jaw to fight the sensations running through her body, trying to focus on the movie.

The nails stroked her neck again. Sam slowly turned toward Ash, the heat in her eyes making Sam instantly wet. They held each other's gaze as butterflies danced in Sam's stomach.

Sam glanced down at Jake who was engrossed in the movie. "Hey bud, do you want some popcorn?" Jake didn't blink or respond at all. She bumped his shoulder. "Jake, do you want some popcorn?"

"Yeah," he responded slowly as if drugged.

Sam looked at Ash and laughed. "Movie coma. You wanna help me clean up and make some popcorn?"

The heat in Ash's eyes hadn't dissipated and Sam shot her a mock stern look. Ash cleared her throat and shrugged innocently. "Sure."

As Sam headed to the pantry, she heard the thud of pizza boxes on the table, just before Ash grabbed her hips, spinning her around. Ash backed her against the wall, grasping Sam's face in her hands, and kissed her deeply. When she pulled away moments later, Sam's head was spinning.

"Sorry. I needed to kiss you." Ash gave her a seductive smile.

Sam stared in shock, finally remembering to blink. "Um, you can do that anytime."

Ash grinned. "Good to know." She kissed Sam's cheek and sauntered into the living room. Sam stared after her in disbelief before mentally shaking herself and grabbing the popcorn.

Jake fell asleep before the movie ended. When Sam picked him up off the sofa, he sleepily wrapped his arms around her neck and laid his head on her shoulder. In these little moments, Sam felt overcome with such boundless love that she almost couldn't stand.

Though it only took a few minutes to put Jake to bed, when Sam returned, she found Ash on the sofa, head flopped back on the cushion, sound asleep. Sam bent in front of her, placing her palm against her cheek. "Ash? Sweetie," she whispered. Ash's eyes fluttered open. "Come to bed." Sam held out her hand and helped her up.

Sam hadn't expected Ash to stay the night, but seeing how tired she was, Sam knew she couldn't ask her to drive all the way home. Though Sam had an uneasy feeling in the pit of her stomach, she was too tired to worry about it right now. One thing she did know, she'd ask Ash to leave before Jake woke up in the morning.

They crept past Jake's room and closed Sam's bedroom door behind them. Ash was still half-asleep as Sam helped her out of her shirt and shorts. She gave Sam a tired frown. "I'm sorry, Sam. I so wanted to continue what we started earlier."

Sam kissed her gently. "It's okay. We're both exhausted. Let's get some sleep so we can kick some ass tomorrow."

Ash grinned and slid under the covers. "Have I told you how awesome you are?"

Sam undressed—too tired to put on pajamas—and joined Ash in bed. They fell asleep instantly.

When the familiar sound of Sam's alarm clock woke her, she recognized the body pressed against her back immediately, and smiled. As she leaned over to turn off the alarm, her gaze landed on the photograph of Anna. Sam's body stiffened, a sense of guilt gripping her.

"Sam, you okay?" Ash must have felt her reaction.

"Yeah, just a back spasm." *Great, starting a relationship with lies. Perfect.*

Ash massaged Sam's back for a couple minutes. "Did that help?"

Sam nodded, trying to ignore the wave of guilt spreading through her. She rolled over to face Ash and kissed her gently. "Good morning," she said, smiling at her.

"Good morning. Game day. It's today or nothing."

"I have confidence you'll drag us to a victory. I'll enjoy the view as you do." Sam winked.

Ash laughed.

"Ash?"

"Yeah?"

"I don't mean to be a jerk, but I haven't told Jake about us yet. I don't think it would be a good idea for him to know you slept over just yet."

Ash nodded, but Sam could tell her comment had stung a little from the look in her eyes. "Say no more." She leaned forward and kissed Sam before sliding to the edge of the bed. She stopped, noticing her lack of clothes, and glanced back at Sam.

Sam raised her hands. "I was a perfect lady, I swear. No funny business."

Ash gave Sam a smile as she stood. Sam propped up on her elbow, watching Ash get dressed. She walked over to Sam's side of the bed, and leaned down to kiss her once more. "See you at the game."

As Ash walked out of the room and tiptoed past Jake's door, Sam felt a small sense of dread that she had just messed up. She hated that she had just treated Ash like a college student doing the walk of shame after a meaningless hook-up. Ash mattered to Sam and she promised herself she would make sure Ash knew that when she saw her later. Sam just hoped she'd give her the chance.

The first game was much less of a challenge than Sam had expected. Their team kept a four-run lead nearly the entire game. Drea and Jake arrived toward the end of the game.

As the team jogged off the field after the final out, Sam headed in their direction. Jake sat atop Drea's shoulders in his neon green Teenage Mutant Ninja Turtles shirt and navy shorts, as Drea flirted with a woman from another team by the bleachers. Drea quickly ended the conversation when she saw Sam.

"You looked good out there," Drea said with a grin.

"Hi, Mom."

"Hi, honey." Sam reached up and rubbed Jake's arm.

She glanced at Drea. "Oh, really? I'm surprised you saw anything. Seemed like most of the action was out here."

Drea stifled a grin.

"Honk, honk! And the ride is over." Drea lifted Jake off her shoulders and swung him around in a circle, causing him to squeal with glee.

"So, what have you two been up to all morning?"

"I'm helping Aunt D make sleepovers," Jake said with pride.

Sam glared at Drea. "Would you quit using my son as your wingman?"

She shrugged. "But he's so good at it."

"You're shameless, you know that?"

"I do." Drea gave Jake a high-five, then eyed Sam for a moment. "What?"

"Well, with Jake's superpowers, it kind of baffles me that you're still single. Although I guess one person has gotten through that force field surrounding you, keeping women away."

"Yeah, me!" Jake yelled, and hugged Sam around the waist.

Sam patted him on the head, smiling down at him. "This is why you're my favorite child."

He giggled. "Mo-om, I'm your *only* child."

Sam looked at Drea, pointedly. "Sometimes I forget."

With only an hour between games, Drea, Jake, and Sam decided to have a quick lunch at the ballpark. Sam invited Ash to join them, but she had to go home to let Goose out. They sat under the shade of an oak tree and chowed down on hot dogs. Sam gave them a pass on nutrition today. She felt nervous about the championship game coming up and wasn't very hungry, but knew she needed to eat while she could.

After lunch, Drea and Jake stayed to watch the final game, but when Sam jogged over to them after the third inning, Jake was fading fast. "Hey bud, you tired?"

He nodded.

"You wanna go home with Aunt D and play with Pickles?"

He brightened. "Yeah!"

Sam laughed. "Okay. Have fun." She kissed the top of his head. "I'll pick you up later."

Sam turned to Drea. "No R-rated movies this time. He had nightmares for weeks."

Drea saluted her. "Aye aye, boss."

"I mean it."

Drea smiled sweetly and batted her eyes. "I know you do."

The game was a nail-biter. Their opponents, the Bywater Babes, had won first place the last three years. No one expected Sam's team to win, but by the fifth inning, not only were they holding their own, they were ahead by one run.

The frustration was clear on their opponents' faces. There was an incredibly hot, all-star pitcher who kept getting them out without breaking a sweat.

Ash turned as Jenny tossed her the ball from first base after smothering a grounder up the line. She flashed a lascivious smile at Sam, looking her up and down.

Sam's jaw dropped open as her body started tingling all over, her mind on anything but the game. Ash winked and turned to face the next batter.

Seriously? Oh, we're going to have a talk about that. Could she really pitch this well without being completely focused on the game? If she could, then Sam had drastically underestimated her abilities.

By the top of the seventh, they were still up by one run. Sam reminded herself to breathe, knowing how close they were to victory. Marci, on the sidelines, looked like she was about to pass out with anticipation. Unfortunately, the next three batters were the best hitters on the other team. The first woman up to bat—a leggy brunette, who had been slinging some fairly uncreative zingers at Sam's team all game—swung once, too high. Swung again, too low. Ash walked a small circle around the mound, catching Sam's eye under the rim of her cap with a seductive and equally devilish grin.

Sam stared at her. *Really?*

Ash set up for her next pitch. She wound up and let it fly—straight at the catcher with just enough rise at the end for the brunette to swing with all her might, nearly falling over when air was the only resistance her bat met. Ash turned and winked at Sam, who grinned back in disbelief, feeling like her hero had just slain the dragon.

The next batter was a stout dirty blonde powerhouse. She was the main one Sam worried about. She swung and missed the first pitch as it curved outside. With a determined look, she waited for Ash's next pitch.

Ash focused completely on the batter this time, rather than flirting with Sam. As the ball flew toward the plate, the batter swung and made contact. Sam held her breath, watching the ball arc high in the air, flying deep toward left field. Lace ran underneath it, flinging her cap to the ground so she could see better. She held out her glove, the thud of the ball meeting leather resonating across the field. Sam and her teammates cheered.

They only needed one more out, and the second-best hitter was up. As tall and blonde as Ash, and about double the size, she was a force. She stared Ash down with a look of pure hatred. Sam stepped back involuntarily in response. She couldn't tell if Ash felt nervous—everything about her stance and windup seemed typical.

She released the ball and it flew straight at the plate. The batter swung, sending the ball hurling toward Ash's head and she ducked just in time for it to miss knocking her out. Thankfully, this time, Sam paid full attention and lifted her glove just in time to catch the ball as it sped toward her face. Pausing at the sting of the ball through the leather, it took a second before she realized they had just won the game. Her teammates yelled, tossing their gloves in the air as they all ran to her. Sam ran toward Ash and jumped up. Ash caught her around the waist and twirled her around. She slowly lowered Sam and kissed her cheek as she leaned into her ear. "Nice catch, Ace."

They joined Marci, who was nearly hoarse from screaming on the sideline. Lace and Jenny snuck up behind her, shaking champagne bottles and letting them spray bubbles all over her.

Then, the team relaxed on the grass under some nearby trees, while Marci handed out championship T-shirts, followed by their first-ever championship trophy. The players all hung out for a bit, laughing and talking before they headed to the local pizza place to celebrate the end of their season.

Marci congratulated everyone, encouraging those playing on the summer team to keep in shape, and she had even more words of warning for those taking a break until fall. As their teammates trickled toward the parking lot, Sam waited for Ash, who was talking to Marci.

Ash walked up to Sam, circling her hand around the back of Sam's waist as they headed toward the parking lot. She felt the damp sweat through Sam's T-shirt, heat radiating off her body. It was hot, even for early May. Ash had sweated just walking to the field from her car this morning. It was stifling, but her mind had been so focused on the games—well, mostly—she had forgotten how hot it was.

"You were pretty hot stuff out there today."

Ash grinned. "So were you."

They walked the rest of the way to Ash's car in silence. Ash felt a weight to their unspoken words, but wasn't sure what Sam was thinking.

They paused at Ash's car door, facing each other. "Could we talk for a minute?" Sam asked hesitantly.

Ash nodded. "Go ahead and hop in. I'll turn on the A/C." She tossed her stuff in the back and started the engine before turning to Sam.

"Can I have a hug first?"

Ash nodded and held her tight for a few moments. Sam rubbed her back gently and held her close. The intimacy of it almost made Ash cry.

Sam spoke next to her ear as they held each other. "Ash, I'm so sorry about this morning. I was stupid and I'm so sorry if I hurt you."

Ash was quiet as she leaned her head down, resting her forehead against Sam's shoulder. Maybe it was the exhaustion of the day or the intimacy of the moment. Ash wasn't sure. But the strength of her emotions overwhelmed her. She had tried to play it off this morning, just how much Sam's comment hurt her. She knew it shouldn't have, but it felt like a rejection. She had spent the morning wondering if the moment would ever come when Sam was ready to commit to her. It was early for them, sure, but Ash had a lingering feeling, something deep in her gut, that kept telling her this was never going to work out.

She had tried to just focus on the game. To act normal and flirt with Sam—well, that was pretty fun, actually—but it was still there, the hurt, like a memory you couldn't fully recall. It left her a little unsteady.

"You mean a lot to me, Ash. And the last thing I want to do is make you feel insignificant."

How could Ash doubt Sam with words like that? They were everything she needed to hear. She swallowed the lump in her throat, willing the doubt away.

Ash raised her head off Sam's shoulder, placing a gentle kiss on her cheek. "Thank you," she whispered.

When she pulled back and met Sam's eyes, she saw sadness there.

Sam took Ash's head in her hands, wiping away the tears Ash hadn't realized she was crying. "Can you forgive me?"

Ash let out a trembling breath and nodded, before Sam took her mouth in hers. They kissed for several moments. It wasn't passionate or heated, but the emotions behind the kiss made it the most intimate one they had shared. There was a gentleness and compassion to it, and when they broke the kiss and rested their foreheads together, Ash knew she was falling in love with Sam.

They sat together for a while, Sam's head resting on Ash's shoulder, their arms wrapped around each other.

"So, what do we do now?" Ash asked.

Sam lifted her head. "Well, I'd like to keep seeing you. I'm . . . hoping you feel the same," she said hesitantly.

Ash rolled her eyes. "Of course, silly. I meant about Jake—are you going to tell him or should we just say we're friends for now?"

Sam let out a relieved breath. "Oh! Well, I don't know. This is all new territory for me. I've never had to tell my son I was seeing someone, even someone as great as you. I guess I'm just a little afraid to move too fast with him. He's been through so much already. I couldn't handle him getting his hopes up and then it not working out."

Ash nodded. "I understand. But, just so we're clear. I'm planning on this working out."

Sam smiled. "Me too."

Ash gave Sam an encouraging smile. "Look, we don't have to figure out everything right away. I can be patient, as long as I know you're in this with me."

Sam placed her palm against Ash's cheek. "I am."

Ash kissed Sam's forehead. "Just know that I care about you and Jake, and . . . when you're ready, I'd like to be a part of both of your lives."

A huge grin spread across Sam's face. "I want that too." She leaned in and took Ash's lips in hers. Ash could feel the promise in her kiss.

Later that night, Sam leaned her back against the wooden headboard of Jake's bed, perched atop the comforter, as he lay nestled under the covers beside her. He peered at the book in her lap with intense interest as she read to him about Optimus Prime's attempts to save the country from the Decepticons.

When she reached a good stopping place, Sam closed the book and yawned. "All right, bud, time to go to sleep."

He groaned, but didn't argue, thankfully.

Sam got up, walked around the end of the bed to Jake's side, and pulled the comforter up under his chin.

He frowned, which wasn't like him.

"What's wrong?"

He bit his bottom lip—the tell-tale sign that he was thinking about something. Sam was thankful that at least some of his behaviors were easy to decipher.

"What is it, honey? You can tell me."

He looked up at her. "I like Ash."

Sam nodded, exhaling internally at the topic. "Good, because I like her too." She smiled down at him.

His eyes were sincere. "Do you *really* like her?"

The question surprised Sam. She thought she had been casual with Ash in front of him. She wanted to be sure of her own feelings before she made any sort of announcement. That was the plan—at least, until this bright little guy saw right through her.

How was she supposed to answer this? She didn't want to lie to him. Of course, she liked Ash. She was crazy about her—something Jake had apparently picked up on. But there was a big difference between having feelings for Ash and endless thoughts about her, and telling her son that she had feelings for another woman. He had already been through so much in his short five years. She wanted to protect him from any more hurt. If she was being honest, she wanted to protect herself too. But as she thought about Ash, a smile formed on her lips and a warmth spread through her. Yes, it was still early, but Ash did mean a lot to Sam, and she didn't plan on that changing any time soon.

Sam nodded at Jake. "I do." She bit the inside of her cheek. "Is that okay with you?"

He looked down at the bed. "I *think* so."

"But . . . you're not sure?" she asked gently.

He looked up. "I like Ash a lot. She teaches me to cook and is nice and funny." He frowned again.

"What is it?"

"I'm afraid you'll be mad," he said quietly, staring at the bed again.

"Honey." Sam lifted his chin with her finger until he met her eyes. "You are the most important person to me in this entire world. I could never be mad at you." Jake's eyes filled with tears as his bottom lip quivered. "Come here." Sam pulled him into a tight hug. He wrapped his little arms around her neck and squeezed back. It pulled at Sam's heart.

She held him for a while, knowing they both needed it. When he pulled away, she wiped away his tears with her thumb.

"I don't remember Momma anymore," he muttered, tears starting.

"Oh, honey." Sam placed her palm against his cheek. "Is that what you're upset about?" He nodded. "You were so little when Momma passed away. No one can remember things from that long ago. Not even someone as smart as you."

She smiled at him and he returned a halfhearted smile. Sam's heart was being crushed inside her body, but she knew how she handled this moment would be significant. "I know you love Momma. She knows it too. I promise you that. And whenever you want—if you ever want to talk about her or ask questions about her—you can always ask me anything. Okay?" He nodded.

Sam put her finger under his chin again to make sure he heard what she was saying. "No one will ever replace Momma. No one ever could." Jake nodded, but the look in his eyes was doubtful. "I'll tell you what . . . I promise to remember her enough for the both of us. Deal?"

He nodded. "Deal," followed by a hint of a smile.

Sam leaned forward, kissing his forehead, as Jake wrapped his arms around her neck again. She blinked back tears as she hugged him.

Chapter 14

Early Tuesday morning, as Sam lay in bed, still half asleep, light just beginning to stream through her windows, she blinked her eyes open and saw a figure staring at her. A hooded figure. She screamed as loud as she could until the sound of giggling filled the room. "Mom, it's me!" Jake hollered, pulling off his mask, then grinning.

Sam stared, taking in the red and blue Nacho Libre mask in his hand, and forced a nervous laugh.

"Drea got me this. Isn't it cool?" He spun the mask on his hand. "She said I should wear it and wake you up one morning. She thought you'd like it."

Sam blew out a shaky breath, still unnerved. "Jake, please don't ever do that to me again." At his frown, she added. "But yes, it's a really cool mask."

Jake grinned as Sam held her forehead in her hand. She glanced at the clock, realizing it was almost time to get ready for school anyway, and sighed. "You ready for breakfast?"

After Sam fed Jake and got him onto the bus, she headed to work. She was still exhausted from the weekend, the heat, the softball games, everything with Ash. It was all good, but still tiring as hell. It had taken three cups of coffee to give her the energy to shower yesterday. Today was a little better. It only took two. Thankfully the morning at work was filled with mostly mindless tasks she could do in her sleep.

At the sound of a man clearing his throat nearby, Sam glanced up from her computer. "Hi, Pete." She tried to hide her dismay at seeing him, feigning collegial professionalism. Pete normally ignored her except for the few times he needed something from her.

"Sam, hi." He always seemed to struggle trying to be friendly.

When he didn't continue, Sam tried moving the conversation along. "What can I do for you?"

He stood a little taller. "Do you have the monthly reports on our current campaigns?"

"I do."

"Great. Could you send those to me before the end of the day?"

Sam's brow furrowed. As the two project leaders for their team, Pete normally handled the design concepts and Sam handled, well, everything else, so she was confused by his sudden interest in what Sam and the rest of the team did to keep them afloat. "Um, do you mean where we stand with the designs or—"

"No, the whole report for each client."

Sam frowned. "Sorry, why are you wanting this? Normally you don't handle this side of things."

"Oh, you haven't heard?" The corners of his lips turned up into a slimy grin.

Sam had a sinking feeling. She was pretty positive she didn't want to know the answer, but also knew it was only a matter of time before she found out from someone what was going on. "Heard . . . what, exactly?"

"I'm the new Audrey," he said excitedly. "I'll still be heading up the designs on our team's campaigns, but will source a bit more out to the rest of the team, since I'll have a few more . . ." He stood up even taller and straightened his tie—the light green and yellow paisley would have looked fine on anyone else, but on Pete, it just accentuated his air of sliminess. "Responsibilities."

Sam managed to swallow the bile rising in her throat and do her best impression of someone happy about the news. She forced a smile. "Congratulations, Pete."

"Thanks. I mean . . ." He leaned toward Sam and placed his hand by his mouth as if whispering a secret, but didn't lower his voice at all. "No big surprise, but it's still a step up." He smiled at Sam genuinely. Sam couldn't figure out if he was completely unaware of his bravado, or just a total asshole. Her money was on the latter.

She smiled past gritted teeth. "That's great." She turned back to her computer for a moment, but could still feel him standing there. She glanced back at him. "All right, well, I'll have the reports to you later today. Did you need anything else?"

"Nope, that's all for now." He left, smiling.

Sam stared at her computer for a few minutes trying to rectify in her mind what had just happened. Every part of her wanted to grab her things and go home. Maybe swallow about three margaritas and drift off to a peaceful sleep, where people like Bill and Pete didn't exist. Had it been six years ago, maybe she would have. But getting drunk midday wasn't exactly parent-of-the-year material.

Instead, Sam emailed Audrey to see if she had any time to meet this afternoon. She'd try to find out what the hell had led to this catastrophe. With Pete at the helm of their team, they might all be out of a job in record time.

Then she called Ash to see if she could meet for lunch. Sam was going to take a real, full-hour lunch break today, damn it.

Ash found an open parking spot behind Mother's Restaurant and let out a sigh of relief since she was already running late from a client meeting. Mother's was a city stronghold. Even its three-story red brick façade seemed to laugh in the face of the glass and concrete modern high-rises surrounding it. Downtown New Orleans was a mix of forward progress and tradition.

Mother's was unassuming—cafeteria-style with basic tables and chairs that made Subway seem gourmet. But the framed photographs that hung on the brick walls spanned decades and the steady crowds hinted at something much larger than its humble appearance. And the food, well, it spoke for itself.

Ash searched the room for Sam. She stood in line, reading the specials from the chalkboard menu on the wall. She wore a short-sleeve, thin black sweater offset by a high-waisted, long cream pencil skirt hugging her hips. Ash stared at the expanse of leg left uncovered. She swallowed hard and continued toward her.

Sam turned as Ash reached her side. "Hi," she said warmly.

"Is this what you wear to work?"

A look of uncertainty filled Sam's eyes. "Um, yes."

Ash shook her head slowly. "Sam, you look incredible. My god."

Sam smiled for a moment before her brow furrowed. "Does that mean I don't look incredible the rest of the time?"

"That's not what I meant. You always look beautiful to me, but you have to admit, this outfit is a little more upscale than the sweat-drenched, holey T-shirts we're used to seeing each other in."

"Nice save." The air seemed to thicken between them as Ash watched Sam's eyes wander down her body. "You look pretty incredible yourself."

Ash glanced down at her light green sleeveless blouse, black dress pants and black heels, and shrugged. "I might have to step it up if I'm going to keep up with you."

Once they had their po' boys—fried shrimp for Sam, grilled shrimp for Ash—and grabbed a table, Ash could tell something was wrong. Sam's energy was dulled and every smile seemed to take effort.

Sam bit into her sandwich as crumbs from the crispy French bread fell to her plate, and closed her eyes. "Mmm. I needed this."

"What's going on? You sounded upset."

Sam nodded, staring at the table as she finished chewing. "I don't know if I can do it anymore."

A jolt of fear shot through Ash. She reached across the table and took Sam's hand. "Do what?" she asked gently.

"Pete, the guy at work who makes my life a living hell with his ineptitude, is now my immediate boss. I found out today. When he stopped by my desk and told me. No heads up, no warning."

A sense of relief washed over Ash. *Why had she assumed the bad news was about them?* "Sweetie. I'm so sorry."

Sam tried to smile as she met Ash's eyes. "Thanks."

"What do you think you're going to do?"

Sam shrugged. "I'm meeting with Audrey—my main boss—this afternoon to find out what happened. The CEO retired a few weeks ago and appointed Audrey to run the company. Pete got her previous position." She shook her head. "I just feel like nothing I do matters."

"Did you want the position?"

Sam looked at her in surprise. "No!" The look of shock dimmed into a frown. "Maybe. I'm just tired of working so hard and it not mattering. Especially when an idiot like Pete barely does anything and keeps reaping the rewards. I've had to do damage control so many times with clients after he's annoyed or insulted them." She shook her head. "It would be funny if it weren't so sad."

Ash gripped her hand encouragingly. "Well, there is a solution."

Sam gave her a faint smile. "I don't think that's really an option right now."

Ash held her gaze for a moment, trying to decide if it was worth convincing Sam she should start her own company, if she would even listen.

"What?"

Ash shook her head. "Nothing."

"Ash, I want to know what you're thinking. If we can't talk about things, then, what's the point of all this?"

Ash stared at her for a moment. "I just wish you'd believe in your-self more. I believe in you. Why don't you? You said yourself that you keep your team running and keep the clients happy. Are you good at design?"

"Yes," Sam said quietly. "With the right graphic design team, I'm pretty awesome actually."

"There you go." Ash grinned. "Imagine if you had an awesome team like you do now, great clients, and didn't have to deal with Pete dragging you down."

Sam shook her head in wonder. "That would be amazing."

"It would." Ash rubbed her thumb over the back of Sam's hand. "Just think about it."

Sam knocked on the heavy wood door of Audrey's, formerly Bill's, office at four o'clock. Unlike Bill's permanently closed door, it was open. Audrey looked up with a smile and gestured Sam in.

"Hi, Sam. How are you doing?" Sam had always liked Audrey. She had a certain tenacity that had helped her stay in the marketing game for twenty-five years, but she also kept up with trends and technology, and, unlike Bill, understood that people mattered. Not just clients, but colleagues and employees as well. It was odd seeing her at Bill's massive desk. It didn't suit her.

"Hi, Audrey. Thanks for fitting me in today." Sam sat down in front of her desk and smiled. Audrey had always been a mentor to Sam and Sam felt a kinship with her she sometimes had to check. Especially now that Audrey was the head boss.

"Of course, of course. I think I know what you would like to discuss, but why don't you tell me anyway?" Audrey tucked a strand of salt-and-pepper hair behind her ear, the frame of her stylish black glasses holding it in place.

"I'm sure it's what you think. Pete stopped by to ask me for monthly reports today and shared his good news."

Audrey gave Sam a sympathetic smile. "I apologize for that, Sam. I planned to talk to you myself first, but got called into an investor's meeting first thing this morning. I'm sure it was a shock and not what you were expecting." She sighed. "I tried to fight for someone else for that position. You, actually. But it was Bill's final say and he was adamant. You know how he is about Pete. Lord knows why." She shook her head.

Sam didn't know what to say. While it was comforting to find out that Audrey had gone up to bat for her, in the end, it didn't matter.

"Sam, your job is still the same. Keep doing the excellent work you do with your team. Try not to focus on this change, if you can."

"Except, now Pete is technically my boss." Sam couldn't keep the indignation out of her voice.

Audrey frowned. "Technically . . . yes. I'm truly sorry, Sam, but my hands are tied on this issue."

"Thank you, Audrey, but you know as well as I do that he's a liability. He could cause us to go up in flames." Sam had to plead with her. This was too big a mistake to stay silent.

Audrey gave her a pointed look. "I'm counting on you, Sam, to make sure that doesn't happen."

Just before seven o'clock, Sam knocked on Ash's door. Jake was almost vibrating with excitement as she held his hand. It was the first Tuesday night in months with no softball game, so Ash had invited Sam and Jake over for dinner. When Ash opened the door, Jake launched himself at her, hugging her waist.

"Well, hello." Ash hugged him back. The shaggy brown dog spinning in circles a couple feet away finally caught Jake's attention.

"Puppy!" He squealed and ran over to pet Goose, both of them bursting with joy.

Ash hugged Sam briefly and shut the door. She gently rubbed Sam's back as they watched the lovefest unfold before them. Goose spun and whimpered as Jake petted and hugged him.

"Jake, this is Goose," Ash said.

"Hi, Goose! Goose, goose, goose."

"Jake, why don't you take Goose in the backyard to play? He has a ball out there. We can make dinner when you tire him out," Ash suggested.

"Okay!" Jake followed Goose as he ran through the kitchen to the back door.

Sam shook her head, still staring after them. "Well, it was a good run. Should I bring the adoption papers by tomorrow?"

Ash laughed. "How are you doing?"

Sam pulled her into a tight hug. "Better now."

Sam and Ash watched Jake and Goose play fetch for what felt like an endless period of time. Ash finally called an end to it when Goose's panting hit a new intensity, and they went inside to make dinner together.

Ash handed Jake a hunk of dough as he stood on a chair at the island. "Okay, I want you to roll this as flat as you can for me." Jake grinned at the challenge.

Sam stood next to Ash, sipping Malbec as she watched the cooking lesson. She had never seen anyone make their own pasta before. Goose lay nearby, his tongue resting on the kitchen floor as his panting calmed. As Jake worked the rolling pin over the dough, Ash sprinkled flour onto it.

"Why do you do that?" he asked curiously.

"So the rolling pin doesn't stick to the dough, and I put flour on the other side so the dough doesn't stick to the table."

Jake pondered her answer. "Oh." He kept rolling, but was getting visibly tired.

"That looks really good, Jake. How about you sprinkle flour while

I take a turn?"

With great skill Sam could only imagine came from doing this many times before, Ash quickly rolled the dough from its fairly thick state into a much thinner layer. Ash showed Jake how to put the dough through the pasta roller and helped him crank the handle until it came out so thin you could see light through it.

"Where did you learn to cook, Ash?" Sam asked. Ash had never mentioned going to culinary school, but from the little bit of her food Sam had already tasted, Sam assumed she had taken classes at some point.

Ash glanced up. "It's just something I liked doing, so I've perfected a few recipes over the years. I like trying new ones and putting my spin on them."

"When did you start cooking?" Jake asked.

She nudged his shoulder playfully. "I was a lot older than you. I started when I was in high school. My father didn't cook so it was either learn to cook or starve."

"What about your mom?" he asked.

"She used to cook, but she left when I was young."

Jake looked up at her. "So did my momma."

Ash rubbed his shoulder. "But at least your mom . . ." She glanced at Sam and grimaced. "Well . . . it's a good skill to learn."

"Hey!" Sam threw a dish towel at Ash, making Jake and her laugh.

Chapter 15

"There's just no theme. Nothing pulling the room together." Mrs. Devereaux gestured to her expansive living room, her large silver bracelets clinking against each other. "I tried displaying things from my travels and important photographs—things that mean something to me—but it just looks thrown together."

Ash nodded, taking in the eclectic mix of souvenirs and other mementos scattered throughout the room. Mrs. Devereaux had definitely traveled a lot. Ash was impressed by her collection, but she was right, there wasn't any real vision or purpose tying it all together. "Well, it's an impressive space. Intricate archways and built-ins. We can definitely highlight those. And there's tons of space here. What are your goals for the room?"

Mrs. Devereaux opened her mouth, then closed it, and looked around.

"If you imagined your ideal room, what would that look like to you?" Ash tried to clarify.

The woman's face lit up as she launched into a description of what she was looking for.

A while later, after Ash had taken room measurements and discussed different design options with her client, she headed to her car. Her phone buzzed in her leather tote bag and she dug around to find it, smiling when she saw the name on the screen. "Hi."

"Hi," Sam replied. "How are you?"

Ash propped the phone against her ear with her shoulder as she opened her car door. "Good. Just leaving a client's place. What about you?"

"Well, that's why I was calling. Um, I was wondering if I could ask a big favor of you." Sam sounded a little stressed.

"Of course. What's up?"

"I have to work late. There was a problem with the copy on an ad we were supposed to launch today and I need to fix it before I can leave. Lauren can't stay late, so I was wondering if there's any way you could pick Jake up from school and watch him until I can leave."

Ash paused for a moment, absorbing the information. A small wave of panic washed through her. "Sure. I can do that. What time does he get out of school?"

Sam let out a relieved sigh. "Thank you so much, Ash. You're a lifesaver. He gets out at three-thirty."

"Okay, no problem." Ash tried to sound confident, but she had never been completely alone with a kid before. Completely responsible. It made her nervous. At least she had Goose to help.

"Okay, great. I've got to go, but I'll call the school and put you on the pickup list, and I'll text you the school's address."

Ash nodded, then remembered she was on the phone. "Sounds good."

"Hey Ash." Sam's voice was warmer, more intimate.

"Yeah?"

"Thank you."

When Ash pulled into the school's pickup area, her eyes widened. The line of cars seemed endless as children screamed and ran around. A crossing guard in a neon yellow vest helped a few children walk in front of the line of cars. Thankfully, the line moved forward steadily and when Ash reached the loading zone, she spotted Jake standing by the school doors with an adult Ash assumed to be a teacher.

Ash got out of her car and walked to the sidewalk to wave at Jake. He smiled and ran to her, hugging her waist once he reached her. It was almost too cute to take. Jake wore a blue and white-striped polo shirt with khaki pants and tennis shoes, but the large Transformers backpack seemed about two sizes too big for his tiny frame.

Ash noticed a dark-haired little boy scowling at them about ten feet away. She wondered what that was about.

"Your mom asked me to hang out with you until she gets off work. Is that cool with you?"

"Yeah!"

Ash securely buckled Jake into the back seat—she didn't have a booster seat like in Sam's car—and opened the front passenger door to slide the seat as far back as it would go, just in case the seatbelt wasn't enough. She would have taped pillows all around his body if she'd had any. But this would have to do.

"Can we go play with Goose?" Jake asked as Ash pulled away.

"Definitely. But, I thought we could do something fun first. You want to?"

"Yeah!"

As Ash drove through the city to the French Quarter, she watched Jake grinning out the window. Maybe this wouldn't be that hard.

After parking the car, Ash and Jake sat down at one of the round marble tables under the famous green and white-striped awning of Café Du Monde. The outdoor patio space was crowded, as always. Ash placed her coffee mug and bowl of beignets on the table.

Jake's huge eyes looked possessed as he stared at the bowl filled with fried dough covered in powdered sugar.

Ash stifled a laugh. She felt the same way.

"Here you go." She handed him a beignet and grabbed another for herself. He took it eagerly.

"Whatever you do, don't laugh," Ash said, then made a face at Jake as he went to take a bite. He laughed, sending a cloud of powdered sugar up in the air. Now they both laughed.

"Did you have a good day at school?" Ash asked as they munched. Jake nodded.

"What's your favorite subject?"

Jake pondered the question and paused eating long enough to bite his bottom lip. "Science."

"Wow, you must be pretty smart then."

"I am."

Ash laughed and sipped her coffee. It was probably going to keep her up tonight, but she was exhausted and needed a pick-me-up. Her mind drifted back to the little boy in front of the school.

"Jake, who was that little boy in front of the school this afternoon?"

"What little boy?"

"He had dark hair. About your height. Is he a friend of yours?"

Jake frowned. "That's Max."

"Oh yeah? Are y'all friends?"

Jake's mood dimmed. "We were."

"Did something happen?"

Jake shrugged.

Ash decided not to push. It wasn't her business anyway. She pointed to the remaining beignet. "You can have the last one."

Jake smiled shyly at her. "Thanks."

They watched the people walking along Decatur Street. Ash entertained herself trying to determine which people were tourists versus locals. It was nice being here with Jake. Sitting at a café in the middle of the afternoon felt like a luxury. It felt like time had been suspended, replaced by an easy calm.

"He made fun of me for having two moms." Ash looked at Jake, stunned. He had put the beignet down on his napkin and was staring at it. "Then he made fun of me because Momma died." He looked up at Ash with tears in his eyes.

Her heart sank. She moved her chair next to his and wrapped her arm around his shoulders. "I'm so sorry, Jake." She tried to force a smile to make him feel better. "I know that must have hurt."

Jake shrugged. "Why did he say that?"

Ash tried to figure out how to respond. She thought back to her own motives in high school, none of it fun. "You know, it might be hard to understand this, but usually bullies are mean because they don't like themselves. So they take it out on other people."

Jake looked confused. "Why?"

Ash sighed. "Well, it might make them feel better to see somebody else feel bad. There are different reasons." Jake frowned at the table. "What's important to remember, is that it has nothing to do with you."

Jake faced her, absorbing her words.

"I know it can be hard when Max is mean to you and says hurtful things. But trust me when I say, he's the one with issues, not you." She rubbed his arm and smiled. "You're awesome."

A shy grin spread across Jake's face. She hoped she had helped and not made the situation worse.

"Hey Ash?"

"Yeah?"

"Can you not tell my mom?" he asked hesitantly. "About Max."

"Why don't you want your mom to know?"

Jake shrugged. "I don't want her to be sad."

"Don't you think she'd want to know what's going on if you're sad?"

"She's happy now. I don't want to make her sad again."

Ash was quiet. It was a lot to take in. How could she keep secrets from Sam, especially about her own son? And she certainly didn't want to lose Jake's trust. It was a lose-lose situation. Ash looked at the sad expression on Jake's face. "Okay," she smiled. "I won't tell her. Ready to go play with Goose?"

Jake nearly leapt out of his seat. "Yay!"

When Sam arrived at Ash's house around eight o'clock, she looked exhausted. "I'm sorry I'm so late. We had to go several rounds back and forth with the client."

"It's okay. We had a good time." Ash hugged her and led her over to Jake, who was passed out with Goose on the sofa.

Sam smiled and shook her head. "I can't thank you enough."

Ash took her hand. "Sam, you don't need to thank me. We're in a relationship."

Sam nodded and laughed softly. "I'm not good at asking for help."

"You're a great mom. And it's okay to ask for help. No one does it all on their own."

Sam didn't reply, but she smiled. "What did you do today?"

"Well, these two have been wearing each other out, as you can see." Ash smiled at Jake and Goose. "And I took Jake for beignets after school."

Sam's body straightened.

"You okay?" Ash asked.

"Um…yeah, I should get Jake home. It's past his bedtime." She kissed Ash briefly on the lips. "Thanks again."

After Sam left, Ash had an uneasy feeling. *What the hell just happened?*

On Friday night, Drea and Sam sat at their usual table. Drea talked about a new intern at her work, describing her plan for pranking the girl.

"What I don't understand is why you have to prank her at all. Why can't you just mentor her and let her enjoy her life?"

Drea stared at Sam like she was speaking in tongues. "*Because,* Sam. My job is boring." She dragged out the last word for added effect. "Plotting hijinks keeps my creative brain working . . . and it gives me a laugh."

"I thought you liked your job."

"I did . . . do . . . whatever. It's just becoming routine and I don't feel challenged anymore, which sucks because that *was* my favorite thing about what I do." She tipped her glass at Sam. "So, lay off me about the pranks. It's all I've got."

Sam held her hands up in surrender. "Sorry."

Over a second margarita, Sam filled Drea in on recent events at her office and how upset she had been.

"What did Ash have to say about all of that?"

Sam blinked in surprise. Ash was a topic they carefully avoided discussing lately. "That...I should think about starting my own company and . . ." Sam looked away.

"And what?"

Sam met Drea's eyes with a sigh. "She thinks I should believe in myself more."

Drea raised a brow. "Well, we agree on *one* thing."

"What? You're going to get on my case now too?"

Drea stared at her. Sam knew this was going to be bad and took a large gulp of her margarita to prepare herself.

"Sam, I know for a fact that you're awesome at what you do. I hate seeing idiots like Pete and Bill keep you from realizing it. Your whole career revolves around selling things to people, and yet you're the worst at selling yourself."

Sam blinked, surprised by her candor. She had never known Drea felt this way.

"Now, I'm going to tell you something that may be hard to hear," Drea continued.

"There's more?"

Drea shot her a stern look.

"Sorry, go ahead."

"All of your life, you've been surrounded by people who believed in you—your family, me, Anna—but, despite that, the bullying by stupid Jackie and her posse tormented you enough to make you doubt yourself. I blame those assholes for that. But if, nearly twenty years later, you're still doubting yourself, then that's on you."

Drea's words hit Sam hard. Before she could even react, Drea changed the subject and they moved on to other things, but Sam's side of the conversation had only half her attention. Drea's comment stayed with her. When the waitress dropped off the check, Sam reached for it, but Drea's hand stopped her.

"Oh, no you don't," Drea warned.

"I was going to treat you for watching Jake all day Sunday. It's the least I can do."

"Sam, Jake is my family. You don't need to pay me to spend time with him. I love the little guy."

Sam smiled, warmed by her words. "I know you do."

"Besides, who else is going to help me plan my pranks?"

Sam laughed at the thought of Jake and Drea plotting together. Her mind jumped to Ash taking Jake for beignets. Just another thing she had missed out on in her son's life.

"What is it?" Drea asked.

Sam realized she was scowling at her empty glass. She looked up and blew out a breath. "Ash watched Jake for me the other night when I had to work late."

"O-kaaaaay." Drea drew out the word.

Sam shook her head, feeling stupid. "She took him for beignets."

At Sam's silence, Drea prompted her. "And?"

"It was his first beignet. It's a big deal." Sam pointed to herself. "I wanted to be the one to take him."

Drea grimaced.

"What?"

"It wasn't exactly his *first* beignet."

"What do you mean?"

"I may have taken him a few months ago." Drea grimaced again.

"For fuck's sake, Drea!"

"I'm sorry. I didn't realize it was a thing."

Sam felt deflated. She hadn't really realized it was a thing either, but it was.

"What's really the problem?"

Sam felt tears forming. "I just feel like I'm missing so much. I'm trying so hard to do it all, but I know I'm not enough. I feel like a failure every day." She wiped at a tear rolling down her cheek. "I'm jealous that you and Ash had these moments with Jake that I didn't get."

Drea took Sam's hand. "First of all, you're not a failure. You love Jake more than anything." Sam looked down at the table. "And Sam—" Drea waited until Sam looked at her. "Jake knows that."

Sam wiped the tears that were flowing more steadily now.

"And second, would you rather control everything in his life or be happy he has people who care about him enough to do these things with him?"

Sam knew Drea was right. It didn't make her feel like less of a failure, but it did bring her comfort that Jake had so many people in his life who cared about him. She tried to pull herself together and smile a little.

"When did you become so wise?"

"Well, when you interact with as many people as I do, you can't help but gain some insight." Drea winked at her.

Sam rolled her eyes and laughed. "Let's get out of here."

They paid their bill and left Charlie's. By the time Sam drove to Ash's place, it was almost eleven. Ash opened the door before Sam could knock. "Is this a booty call?"

"It would be if we hadn't planned that I'd come over after drinks with Drea . . . you know, so I didn't become that girl who completely abandons her best friend when she gets a girlfriend."

Ash shrugged. "Just checking." She leaned in and kissed Sam gently on the lips.

Sam pulled a pink carnation from behind her back. "This is for you. There was a woman selling them on the sidewalk near Charlie's."

"You may come in, then." Ash took the flower and stepped aside so Sam could enter. She sniffed the carnation, smiling and playful.

"Good day at work? You seem happy."

"Yes, but can't I just be happy to see you?"

Sam felt her neck heat up and smiled at Ash.

Ash took her hand and started to walk backward down the hall, pulling Sam with her as she held the carnation under her nose, smiling.

"Should we put that in some water?" Sam glanced toward the kitchen.

Ash flashed a mischievous grin. "I've got some other plans for it . . ."

After Ash demonstrated her inventiveness with the carnation, they finally got some sleep.

The smell of pancakes and coffee roused Sam awake, and she paused for a moment, remembering when the same thing happened a few weeks prior. So much had happened between the two of them since then. She was still amazed by it all, but trying her best to follow her heart. As unlikely a pairing as it was, Ash made Sam happy. And every time Sam got nervous that things were moving too fast or they wouldn't work out, she focused on how right and easy it felt with Ash. Yes, issues could still come up, but she was trying hard not to waste energy on what-ifs as long as this beautiful, smart, funny, and sexy-as-hell woman made her smile and laugh more than she had in years.

There was one thing that wasn't getting easier though. No matter how much Sam believed in their burgeoning relationship, she couldn't escape the guilt she felt at having Ash in the same bed she had shared with Anna. That they spent most Friday nights at Ash's lately made things easier, though Sam wasn't sure how much longer she could avoid the issue.

Sam walked up behind Ash, who was standing by the range, a coffee cup in one hand and a spatula in the other as she waited for the pancakes to cook. Sam slid her hands under Ash's T-shirt and wrapped her arms around her waist. Ash leaned back against her and sighed.

"Good morning, sexy."

"Sexy, huh? Still thinking about last night?" Ash teased.

"I don't think I'll ever forget it. I'll be sure to keep you permanently stocked with flowers from here on out."

Ash laughed.

Sam kissed her neck, then nipped at her ear. Ash turned to face her. "You drive me crazy, you know that?"

"I hope so."

Ash crossed her arms behind Sam's neck and leaned into a deep kiss, balancing the coffee cup and spatula behind Sam's head. A few moments later, she broke the kiss and turned to glance at the pancakes. "I need to flip these. Would you grab the juice out of the fridge for me?"

Sam kissed her once more before letting go. "Sure." She walked over to the fridge and pulled out the orange juice and poured them each a glass. Pancakes done, they both sat at the table, with Goose at Sam's feet.

"Hey Ash?"

"Yeah?" she answered, smiling, but when she saw the look on Sam's face, her smile dimmed. "What is it?"

Sam wasn't sure how this was going to go, but she was exhausted from trying to balance Ash and Drea on Fridays and needed to find a better way to spend time with both of them. She took a deep breath.

"I was wondering if you'd like to go out with Drea and me next Friday." Ash blinked at her. "I know it might not be easy at first, but you both mean a lot to me. I want all three of us to be able to spend time together."

Ash looked uncertain, but forced a smile. "Okay . . ."

"Thank you."

"How does Drea feel about you and me?"

Sam wasn't sure how to answer that. "She . . . is probably going to need some time to get used to it."

Ash nodded and they were quiet for a few moments as they ate.

Sam thought about her struggle to balance all of the opposing forces in her life—Drea and Ash, Jake and work, Ash and Jake—it was exhausting. She needed to find a way to blend everything so she didn't always feel like she was failing everyone.

"Ash, there's some stuff you need to know about Drea."

A look of panic filled Ash's eyes. "No, nothing bad. I just need you to understand what she and I have been through together."

Ash set her fork down, paying full attention.

Sam, feeling her emotions stirring, clenched her jaw. "I told you that Drea and Anna worked together." Ash nodded. "Ash, Drea was there. When Anna had the aneurysm. She saw all of it. She was the one who called me. I rushed to the hospital," Sam bit the inside of her cheek. "But it was too late. She was already gone."

Ash took Sam's hand while tears spilled down Sam's cheeks. She tried to hold back the emotion. "I knew she was gone, but I just couldn't leave her. I sat next to her bed and held her hand." Sam wiped at the tears. "I kept wishing she'd just open her eyes. That it was all a big mistake. One of Drea's pranks."

She laughed and wiped away more tears. "I stayed with her for hours. Drea sat there with me the whole time. Long after the nurses stopped checking on us and the room had gone dark. If Drea hadn't put her hand on my back and told me it was time to go, I don't know if I ever would have left." Sam began sobbing.

Ash crouched next to Sam, wrapping her arms around her. "I'm so sorry, Sam."

Sam didn't know how long they stayed like that, but she finally sat up and tried wiping away her tears. Ash sat back down, but held onto her hand.

"Drea was the one who stayed with me the first few days. Making sure I ate something. Keeping me company the few times I did get out of bed." Sam bit the inside of her cheek and looked at her lap. "I will never know what Drea went through seeing her friend die right in front of her. Or how hard it must have been to be there for me and Jake when she was just as heartbroken."

Sam looked at Ash. "You remember when you said you felt jealous because you thought Drea and I were together?"

Ash nodded.

"Drea is my family. She and I have been through so much together and she's never given up on me. She will always be one of the most important people in my life."

Ash nodded.

"But that's why I want you two to get along. Because you're both important to me, and I don't want to lose either of you."

Sam stood and they wrapped their arms around each other.

Chapter 16

On Sunday, Ash joined Jake and Sam on their monthly visit to the aquarium. Ash hadn't been there since she moved back, so she was game to see what Jake was so excited about. They walked through the underwater tunnel as fish and stingrays swam over their heads. Sam smiled at the wonder on both Jake's and Ash's faces as they watched the animals glide past them.

"That's a stingray." Jake pointed at a ray swimming in front of them.

"Oh, cool," Ash responded.

As the ray started to glide up along the wall, Jake pointed at the slits on its belly. "Those are its gills. That's how it breathes."

"Wow, that's pretty interesting." She smiled at him.

They meandered through the different exhibits to the second level where Jake stood in a happy daze, watching the African penguins waddle along the rocks in their enclosure. As they dove into the water and used their flippers to swim gracefully along, Jake ran giggling alongside the glass wall to keep up with them.

Sam and Ash watched him for a few moments before Ash turned to Sam. "This place is really impressive."

Sam smiled at her. "Yeah, it's one of our faves."

Jake ran over to join them. "Mom, let's go to Parakeet Pointe," he said, jumping up and down.

As they approached the door to the open-air aviary, Ash turned to Sam. "They're in cages, right?" Sam grimaced and shook her head. Ash turned to Jake. "Jake, are you sure you don't want to go touch the stingrays instead?"

"Nope. Parakeets!" He ran ahead into the aviary.

Sam squeezed her hand. "They're really small. You'll be fine. I promise." Sam led Ash inside.

Sam bought three seed sticks so they could feed the parakeets. Ash watched, horrified, as a parakeet landed on Jake's head, flapping its wings in his hair, before flying down to his hand to eat the seeds. Two more parakeets joined the first and fought over the treat.

"Do you want one?" Sam asked, holding out a seed stick to Ash.

Without taking her widened eyes off Jake, she shook her head.

"It's really fun if you want to try. I'll be right next to you, I promise."

Ash looked at Sam for a moment and, heading for the door, announced, "I think I'll just wait for you by the stingrays."

Sam's smile disappeared, with a sinking feeling taking over. She turned to Jake. "Hey bud, I'm going to wait in the hall with Ash. You can see us through the door. Just come out when you're done, okay?"

Jake giggled at the parakeets perched on his arm. "Okay, Mom."

Sam jogged to catch up with Ash outside the aviary door. "Ash. Hey, I'm sorry. I just wanted us to do something fun together."

Ash gave her a small smile. "It's okay. I've just always had a thing with birds. When I was little, I saw a seagull pretty much attack a kid to steal his sandwich." She shrugged and laughed. "It's stupid, I know. But I've been terrified of birds ever since."

Sam squeezed her hand. "It's not stupid. Childhood memories like that can take a lot to get over." They held each other's gaze for a long moment.

"Mom!"

Sam's attention snapped back to Jake as he ran toward them, his hair sticking up at odd angles. Sam chuckled and helped smooth it back into place. "Did you have fun?"

"Yeah. Stingrays!" Before Sam could answer, he was running toward the touch tank in the next room.

Sam raised her eyebrows at Ash. "Stingrays it is."

"So it seems." Ash laughed.

After Jake managed to touch and name all of the stingrays in the tank, they headed for the exit. The bright sun and stifling heat accosted them as they walked across the brick plaza to look out at the

Mississippi River.

"Let's take a picture, Mom," Jake said excitedly.

Sam glanced at Ash, who shrugged with a smile.

"Okay, bud."

Sam handed her phone to Ash. "You have longer arms for the selfie."

Ash held out the phone and angled it down so she could get the river behind them. Jake stood in the middle, smiling. Ash and Sam wrapped an arm around each other's waists, and Sam draped her other arm across Jake's chest.

As they drove home, the sky darkened, a sure sign of a looming storm. When they were only a couple minutes from the house, the skies opened up with a torrential downpour. Sam parked at the highest point in the road in front of her house, as heavy downpours often resulted in flooding due to Uptown's slow drainage system. She handed the keys to Ash. "Can you go unlock the door while I help Jake out of his booster seat?"

"Sure." Ash opened her door and sprinted toward the house.

Sam leaned over the console to the back seat and unbuckled Jake's seat belt. "Okay, bud, I'm going to come around and help you out of your booster seat. When I put you on the ground, run as fast as you can inside. Don't stop to play in the rain. Okay?"

"Okay."

They were all soaked by the time they made it inside. Sam led Jake to the hall bathroom, then glanced back at Ash. "I'm going to get him into some dry clothes. You can grab something to wear out of my closet."

Sam stripped off Jake's soaked clothes and towel-dried his body, draping the towel over his head and rubbing vigorously as he giggled. She helped him change into a neon green T-shirt with a T-rex on it and khaki shorts, then went to her room and changed into a white T-shirt and dry jeans before meeting Jake and Ash in the kitchen.

Sam stopped abruptly in the kitchen doorway. She felt the blood drain from her face as she stared at Ash, who was pouring Jake some juice. She stopped immediately when she saw Sam's face. "What's wrong?"

Sam continued staring, still in shock.

"Sam, what is it?"

"You're, um, those were Anna's."

Ash glanced down at the forest green Tulane T-shirt and dark gray sweatpants she was wearing. She looked up at Sam with wide eyes. "I'm sorry. I didn't know. They were in a pile in the closet. I just assumed they were yours."

Sam shook her head, forcing a small smile. "It's okay. Let me get you something else to put on."

Ash followed her in silence, both of them knowing something huge had happened, but not knowing how to fix it. Sam grabbed some sweats and a T-shirt of hers. "Here you go."

"Sam . . ."

"It's okay." Sam smiled at her. "Really."

"Sam, I think . . ."

"Ash. Please. It's fine."

Sam couldn't have this conversation right now. Not like this. She knew Ash deserved more, but the shock of Ash in Anna's clothes was all she could handle at the moment.

Charlie's was lively. The bar was packed with people talking and laughing, the occasional clack of pool balls hitting each other. Music played in the background and voices hummed all around, but the silence at their table was the loudest thing in the room.

Ash had tried to prepare herself for tonight. She knew Drea would be standoffish at best, directly confrontational at worst. She knew she deserved that. Drea had only bad memories. She hadn't seen the side of her that Sam had. She just remembered the old Ashley. And she was right to hate her. Ash still hated herself. Even though she had worked through things over the years, she still hated how she had treated Sam back then.

But the tension was still a bit much. Drea sat across from her with Sam perched like a referee in the middle, looking back and forth between them.

"Well. Isn't this fun?" Sam tried to ease the awkwardness. Ash forced a smile at Sam's effort.

Sam went a few rounds trying to be the moderator. Getting Ash to talk about her business and Drea to talk about her latest graphic design endeavors. Pointing out how interesting it was that they were both designers of sorts. She tried Pickles and Goose. Surely, pets would break the ice. She was wrong. Drea's answers were all fairly short. She didn't look angry, just skeptical and maybe a little uncomfortable, which made Ash feel a little better. At least she wasn't the only one feeling awkward.

The whole night was going nowhere.

Sam finally gave up with an exasperated sigh and took a long sip of her margarita. "You know what? I'm going to the bathroom. Can I trust you both to play nice while I'm gone?"

Ash and Drea nodded, though Ash felt anxious.

Once Sam left, Drea leaned closer to the table. "Look, we don't have a lot of time, so I'm going to get to the point." Ash hadn't exactly imagined this curveball, but was ready to hear what Drea had to say. "You have no idea how much you hurt Sam back in high school. And you have no idea how much pain she's had to go through the past few years. I have no idea what she sees in you, but if you hurt her, I won't let you get away with it again."

They eyed each other for a moment as Drea sat back in her chair.

Ash took a breath. She had to admire Drea as a loyal and good friend to Sam. But Ash wasn't going to take any shit either.

"First of all, I know more than you think. I know you've been by Sam's side a long time and helped her pick up the pieces. And for the pain I caused her in high school, I am truly sorry. But I'm not that person anymore and Sam and I have dealt with this. I know you don't have much to go on besides what Sam tells you, but I think if you'd give me a chance, you'd see for yourself. I'm a different person."

Drea seemed unconvinced.

"And second, Sam doesn't need any more shit to deal with in her life. She hasn't said it directly, but I know this thing," she gestured between Drea and her, "is causing her more stress. So, if you really care about Sam, don't make this any harder than it needs to be. Maybe you should try trusting her judgment a bit. How is she ever going to believe in herself if her best friend doesn't even trust her?"

Drea was silent, but Ash could tell from the way her body slumped as she twirled her glass on the table, something she'd said had hit home.

When Sam returned and saw Drea's changed posture, she looked at Ash with wide open eyes. Ash just shrugged and sipped her drink.

Chapter 17

Over the next couple of weeks, Sam began feeling a sense of stability as she and Ash settled into more of a routine she could count on. She was happy to see Ash and Jake growing closer as well. Ash joined Jake and Sam on Sundays, some Saturdays too, and when Jake was with his grandparents on Friday nights, Sam stayed at Ash's house where they connected in more intimate ways. Even Drea was a little more flexible about Friday nights so Sam didn't always feel like a sex-crazed teenager knocking on her girlfriend's door late at night. As much as Sam enjoyed her nights out with Drea, she was growing very fond of the nights when she and Ash could relax over a lazy dinner, go to sleep together, and wake up in each other's arms. She hadn't realized how much she missed having someone there in the morning.

With a break from softball, Ash came over to Sam's place for dinner on Tuesday nights. Those were the toughest for Sam. As much as she cared for Ash, Sam still felt guilty thinking of Ash being in her bed. There was still a big part of her not ready to let that part of her life go. Things were usually fine until Sam put Jake to bed, but then she did mental acrobatics coming up with plausible excuses to make out on the sofa instead of in the bedroom. Thankfully, because they both worked the next day and Sam had to wake Jake up early for school, Ash never pushed to spend the night. She never said anything, but Sam was pretty sure she sensed there was something going on.

Sam knew she couldn't keep this up. She didn't want to, but she just wasn't ready to let all of her barriers down, and she tried hard not to think too much about why.

One night in late May, with only a few weeks left of school before summer break, Jake just didn't seem himself. Sam made fish sticks with tartar sauce for dinner, which he usually loved. She even let him have chocolate ice cream for dessert. When he still seemed down she pulled out the big guns: colored sprinkles. Though he didn't turn down the ice cream, his excitement was muted, and Sam felt helpless that she couldn't make him feel better.

Before bedtime, Jake cuddled with her on the sofa as they watched part of a documentary about penguins. Even the goofy, waddling little birds didn't brighten his mood.

As she tucked him into bed, Sam felt torn. He was clearly upset, but he'd evaded all her attempts to find out what the problem was. She decided to try one more time.

Moving a strand of hair out of his eyes, she asked, "Honey, you know I love you more than anything, right?"

He nodded.

"And you know you can tell me anything, right?"

He nodded, but avoided her eyes.

"I never want you to be sad. I will always be here to help, no matter what."

"I know, Mom," he said quietly.

"Good. So, is there anything you want to talk to me about?"

He shook his head. "No."

Damn. "All right, sweetheart. Just remember I'm here if you ever do want to talk . . . about anything." Sam leaned down and kissed his forehead. "Sweet dreams."

She hoped Jake would feel better in the morning, but a lingering sense of dread told her there was something pretty deep going on. She had no idea what it could be, and sincerely hoped she was wrong.

Ash waved hello to Jody, who was sliding a huge metal sheet pan full of bread dough into a massive oven in Daily Bread's kitchen. Jody smiled and waved back.

"Here you go, ma'am." Ash winced at the title as the college-aged barista handed her a large black coffee. *Ma'am. Damn. She was a ma'am now.* She wanted to tell the guy that "Miss" was fine. Or even "Ms." She was still young and cool, damn it. She looked at him, smiling at her, completely unaware of the effect his polite greeting caused. *Screw it.*

She smiled back. "Thanks."

Ash had made this place part of her morning routine ever since she stumbled across it with Goose. She was getting to know Jody, the owner and head baker. It felt nice to have a place she thought of as hers, where people knew her and lived in the same neighborhood. It made moving back a lot smoother. And it was nice to know other business owners. It was good for her professionally to be part of the business community.

As Ash walked to her car, a young lesbian couple hanging all over each other passed her on the sidewalk. She wished she could feel that way with Sam. To be head over heels in love. And some days, she felt like they were. But other times, it seemed they were in different places about the relationship.

That usually happened on Tuesday nights, like last night, when Sam did everything possible to find an excuse not to let Ash into her bedroom. Though they never talked about it directly, Ash understood it. She did. She tried to be patient, realizing it would probably take time. But as more and more time passed, Ash started to doubt whether Sam was ever going to let Anna go. She knew Sam could, but what worried Ash was that Sam didn't seem to want to.

Ash didn't want Sam to completely remove all traces of Anna from her life, she just wanted a commitment to move forward. Often, it felt like there were three adults in the relationship, with Sam treating her like the other woman. She didn't know what to do with that.

All the while, Ash and Jake had become really close. She loved the little guy. Her relationship with Sam included Jake too. And if Sam wasn't able or willing to move forward—if this relationship wasn't going anywhere—they needed to end it. Before anyone got hurt. Ash already feared the consequences of losing Sam and Jake. And she knew it would only get harder as time went on.

She hated feeling like this and wanted to believe in them as a couple. They were so amazing together in so many ways. But the more she tried to ignore the problems, the louder they became. On the day of the storm, when she had accidentally put on Anna's clothes, she really wanted to talk to Sam, but Sam shut that down right away. And as much as Ash tried to be patient, keeping quiet went against who she was. She had spent too much time addressing her own issues to return to a life of avoidance and lies. She needed to talk to Sam. Right away.

That afternoon, Ash leaned over her desk, one she had spent a lot of time searching for, the perfect desk, made from reclaimed wood from the surrounding area. She had also found a decent office space in an old mill overlooking the river. It was a short drive from her house, but worth it. The building seemed to house an assortment of young professionals, but Ash hadn't had time to get to know many of them yet. She had been working on Mrs. Devereaux's living room design all day. She felt good about what she had come up with so far and hoped Mrs. Devereaux would like it.

Ash's cell phone vibrated. She grabbed it, not recognizing the number. "Hello?"

"Hi, is this Ms. Ashley Valence?" It was a friendly older woman's voice.

"It is."

"Hi, Ms. Valence. This is Edna from St. Charles Elementary." She paused. "There's been an . . . incident between Jake Parker and another boy at school." Ash shuddered and envisioned the worst.

The woman paused a moment and softened her tone. "Jake is okay, but we can't reach his mother. You are the first person I've been able to reach from the pick-up list. Could you come speak to the principal and take Jake home?"

Ash took a moment with the information.

"Ms. Valence?"

"Yes. Sorry. I'll be right there."

She hurried through afternoon traffic, not knowing what had happened, but she felt pretty confident the other boy was that Max kid. *The little shit.* A sense of guilt washed over her. She shouldn't have kept Jake's secret. She should have told Sam. If something happened to Jake, it would be her fault.

When Ash reached the main office reception desk, she was led into the principal's office. Mr. Jackson, a balding man in his late forties, stood to shake her hand. "Ms. Valence, thank you for coming so quickly. I know you're not Jake's mom, but given the situation, I need to speak with an adult who's responsible for him."

Ash saw Jake, who sat in front of the desk with his head bowed. She sat down in the empty chair and put her arm around him. "Are you okay, Jake?" He didn't look up or respond. Ash looked at Mr. Jackson for details.

"I'm sorry, but Jake was involved in an incident with another boy in his class during recess. It seems the other boy, Max, called Jake names and hit him in the stomach."

Ash winced, squeezing Jake's shoulder.

"The nurse saw Jake and he's all right. Just had the wind knocked out of him and is in a bit of shock, I'm sure." He paused. "There was also some damage to a toy of Jake's. It was broken."

Ash rubbed Jake's shoulder again, trying to comfort him. She thought about Max, that nasty scowl, and anger spread through her body.

"Where is he?" she asked.

"Max?"

"Yes."

"I've already spoken with his parents and they took him home. Max might have involved some other kids on the playground, but he was the main one. He's been suspended for several days."

Ash shook her head. "Then what happens?"

"I'm sorry?"

"After Max's suspension is over. What happens? What are you going to do to protect Jake?"

He nodded. "I can assure you we will keep a close eye on the situation for the remainder of the year. We take bullying seriously here." So, *nothing*.

"Is there anything else?" Ash asked, sure nothing else was forthcoming.

"Um, no, that's all. Please let Ms. Parker know she can call me if she has any questions."

"Come on, Jake. Let's go," she said gently. Standing, she held out her hand to him. Jake took her hand but continued to stare at the ground as he walked. Only then did Ash notice the white plastic bag in his other hand. She could see blue and gray pieces through the plastic.

Her heart sank. *Tony.* She held back tears, knowing how much he meant to Jake.

"Where are we with the Thompson Dental campaign?"

It was Wednesday afternoon, and Sam sat with a few team members in the conference room. They would be pitching Thompson Dental, a local practice, in two weeks and this was their prep session.

While Sam had been with the company for several years and they were always pleased with her team's work, she worried. Given the recent changes, she wanted to make sure things didn't slip through the cracks as they all adjusted to the relative chaos with Pete at the helm.

Cassie, a bright and dedicated employee in her late twenties, answered for the others. "We've got two concepts sketched out, but need to put all hands on deck over the next week to make sure we're ready in time." Sam smiled. Cassie was her right-hand woman. In the two years Cassie had worked at the firm, Sam had learned to count on her. She was organized, reliable, and positive. A dream team member.

"Okay, let's run through what each of you needs to focus on to make sure we don't get behind."

By the time Sam returned to her desk a couple hours later, the team was well prepared for their deadline, and Sam felt good. She picked up her cell phone, not realizing she had left it on her desk.

Four missed calls. Damn. She saw who had called and felt alarms go off and fear grip her.

Oh no. Jake.

She listened to the first message. Edna from the principal's office. An incident between Jake and another boy. *Fuck.* But Jake was all right.

The second message was Edna again. No more details.

Every possible scenario Sam could imagine ran through her mind. Had there been a fight? But the woman said he was okay. What could it be?

Hands shaking, she played the third message. It was the school letting her know that Ash had come and got Jake.

Message four was from Ash, explaining what happened between

Jake and Max, and that they were at Ash's house.

Sam swallowed the lump in her throat, grabbed her bag, and told Cassie she had to get Jake. She wiped at the tears running down her face as she sped toward Ash's house. She wanted to kill Max, that little shit. She knew he was bad news. Why hadn't she listened to her gut? Now, Jake was hurt and could have been seriously injured, all because she worried he didn't have friends.

God, except Tony. The toy was Jake's best friend. Anna had given it to him for Easter. It was the last thing she gave him before she passed away. Though Jake liked the toy when he got it, after Anna died he kept it with him night and day, becoming obsessed with Transformers.

Sam went along with it though she worried whether it was impeding his grief process. But she decided it was his way of staying connected to Anna, and she knew he needed that.

Now, as much as Sam worried about what had happened to Jake—mentally, physically, and emotionally—she was even more worried about his reaction to the broken toy. Sam and Jake had both built a delicate wall around their memories of Anna, clinging to the things that kept her alive for them. Tony was a huge part of those memories.

When Sam arrived, Ash was waiting for her on the porch to give Sam details of what had happened. It was crushing to hear.

But when Ash handed her the plastic bag with the shattered pieces of Tony, the air left her body, and she had to hold onto the railing for a moment to steady herself.

Inside, she saw Jake sitting on the sofa, a dejected look on his face. Goose sat with him, but he hardly noticed. It broke her heart.

Sam thanked Ash for going to get Jake, but all she could think about was getting him home, where he was safe.

Jake was silent on the ride home, with Sam stealing glances at him in the rearview mirror as she drove. He mostly stared at his hands in his lap and occasionally looked out the window. It killed her to know he was hurting.

When they got home, Sam set him up on the sofa with popcorn and cuddled with him as they watched his favorite movie—*The Lion King.* Sam studied Jake throughout the movie. At times he seemed to be watching, during the exciting scenes at least, but then his expression would glaze over and she assumed he was replaying the day's terrible events. As the credits began to roll, she tried to get him to talk.

"That was fun." She tried to be enthusiastic, but the look in Jake's eyes told her he wasn't buying it.

"Listen, honey, I know today was rough. I'm so sorry you went through that."

He looked down at his hands.

"Do you want to talk about it?"

He shook his head.

Sam rubbed his back. "Sometimes it helps to talk about tough things. Should we try and see if it helps?"

He shook his head again.

Sam put her arm around his shoulders, leaning down to kiss the side of his forehead. "All right. So, which movie should we watch next?"

Jake finally glanced up. "Two movies?" he asked hopefully.

"Yeah. Why not?" Sam grinned at him and for the first time all afternoon, a small smile appeared on his face.

They spent the rest of the night on the sofa together in peaceful silence, though Sam knew both of them were torn up inside. They ate junk food and watched cartoons until Jake's bedtime.

As she tucked Jake into bed, Sam knew she had to talk to him about the events at school. "Jake, I want to talk to you about what happened today," she said gently. He avoided her eyes, focusing on the comforter.

"Can you tell me what happened?"

"I don't want to."

"I know, sweetie, but I need to know what happened." He didn't say anything. "Why was Max picking on you? I know you haven't been to any more sleepovers, and don't play after school anymore, but why was he picking on you?"

He shrugged.

His sadness and refusal to talk reminded Sam of her own trouble in high school, when she felt humiliated, heartbroken, and crushed by the things Jackie's posse had done to her. But no matter what her mom had tried, Sam wouldn't tell her what was going on.

Now Sam knew, *thank you Drea*, that at some point her mother *had* known what was going on. Why hadn't her mom given in and told Sam she knew? Instead, she let Sam dictate how she wanted to handle the situation. Looking at Jake now, Sam knew how hard that must have been. But maybe it was what Sam needed at the time. She had no idea if that was the right answer or not. So she tried again.

"This has been going on for a long time, hasn't it?"

This time Jake looked up at Sam and nodded.

She took his hand and they sat together in silence for a long time.

"Mom?" Jake finally said.

"Yes, sweetie?"

His face crumpled and he started bawling. She took him in her arms, holding him against her as he cried. She ached to her core to see him in such pain. Tears ran down her cheeks into his hair as she rocked him in her arms. When his sobs finally calmed a little, he spoke into her chest, his voice tiny. "He killed Tony."

"I know, baby. I'm so sorry." They cried together for a long time until Jake fell asleep in Sam's arms. She tucked him under the covers and laid down next to him, wrapping her arms around him. She lay awake wishing she could have done something to protect him, and feeling helpless knowing she couldn't.

Chapter 18

That night, Ash lay in bed for hours, thinking. When she got to the school, the look on Jake's face crushed her. He was so sad, so hurt, so . . . empty. So different from the sweet, happy little boy she was used to. She couldn't help but remember seeing Sam's face from so many years ago. She'd worn the same look Ash had seen today on Jake's face. Ash hated seeing Jake's humiliation today and she hated even more knowing she had made Sam suffer the same way long ago.

It had taken a lot of reflection to work through her past, accepting it and the reasons behind it, and trying to create a better future. She thought she had moved on, but seeing Jake today made her see events in a different light. She felt helpless. Helpless that she couldn't make Jake feel better and helpless that she couldn't take away the pain she had caused Sam. And she couldn't even imagine what Sam was going through.

Goose propped his head on her stomach and sighed. She almost forgot he was lying next to her. She stroked the soft fur on his head. "You were a good boy today, Goose. A very good boy. You were a good friend to Jake."

Ash bent down, kissing him on the head, as Goose's tail thudded against the bed.

Ash felt a little sad about how things had gone down when Sam showed up. She knew Sam was upset and her priority was taking care of Jake, but the events just seemed so cold and detached. Like she was just a babysitter watching Jake. Sam showed up, they had a brief conversation about what happened, then Sam got Jake and left. Ash felt selfish even being bothered by it in light of the situation, but it did bother her. She wasn't part of their family. She didn't know what she was.

That Friday night, Sam and Ash sat together on Ash's sofa, both still shaken by the events of the week. Sam had only slept an hour Wednesday night as she lay in bed with Jake, her mind constantly rewinding Ash's voicemail, the broken look on Jake's face, and the sound of his sobs as he cried in her arms. Thursday night was a little better. She at least got three hours of sleep, but still couldn't help beating herself up for not protecting him, for not knowing how to fix it.

By today, Friday, Jake seemed happier, looking forward to going to his grandparents' house for his weekly sleepover, but Sam was still shaken.

She knew Jake would be okay at school while Max was suspended, but Sam worried about what would happen when Max came back. At least there were only two more weeks of school left, but still, a lot could happen in a couple of weeks.

"I knew there was something wrong with Jake," she said quietly to Ash, "and I knew Max wasn't a good kid. I can't believe I missed this."

Ash looked at Sam for a moment. "I need to tell you something," she said hesitantly, the tone of her voice instantly putting Sam on edge. "The day I picked Jake up from school ... when you had to work late ... Jake told me about Max."

Sam sat up. "What?"

"I noticed a kid scowling at Jake. I asked him about it later and he told me Max had been making fun of him."

"Making fun of what?"

"That he had two moms." Ash looked down at her lap. "That his mom died."

"You knew what was happening and you didn't tell me?" Her voice went up an octave.

"Jake asked me not to tell you."

197

Sam stood, angry. "Are you kidding me? You of all people should know it was only going to get worse."

"What does that mean?"

"Well, you're pretty familiar with the art of bullying." Sam's tone was biting and she saw Ash wince.

Sam turned away, shaking her head. "And now you're back in my life telling me I should believe in myself." She turned to Ash. "Did you ever consider *why* that might be difficult for me?" Ash watched Sam but said nothing.

"Let me help you out then. You and your friends tore me down every chance you got. The way you treated me ripped away every ounce of self-esteem I had. You're seeing the effects of all your hard work now, right before your eyes." Sam held up her arms, as if introducing herself. "So, good job! You nailed it."

Ash was silent, looking down. They were on a speeding train now, with no brakes. Sam was going to take it all the way to the edge and derail them, leaving no survivors. Sam stared at Ash, who was still not looking at her. There was no coming back from this. Sam knew they were done. She just had to finish it.

"I can't believe I was stupid enough to let you into my life. Into Jake's life." All of Sam's anger—at Ash, at Max, at Anna for leaving her. All of it was exploding in one epic collapse.

Ash looked up at Sam, tears streaming down her face.

"I spent so much of my life trying to protect myself from you. And it never worked. How could I ever think it would be different now?" She shook her head. "Jake is my world. I've tried so hard to protect him from pain, but he's had so much more than any kid should have to face. We both have and you will never, ever understand!"

Ash shot to her feet, eyes dark with rage. "That's not fair. You know I love Jake, so don't pin this bullshit on me. And do you really believe you've let me into your life? Since we started seeing each other, you've kept one hand solidly on the door, ready to bail at any moment. You think I'm the one with walls up, the one who doesn't get it? Take a look in the mirror, Sam."

"What does that mean?"

"You can't even let me sleep in your bed. If that's not a metaphor for a wall to keep love out, I don't know what is. You won't even talk to me about it. You just shut me out. What are you so afraid of?"

They stared at each other, angry, tearful, silent. Sam looked down, searching for something to say, trying to recall the happiness and ease they had just days ago. But she was tired. She had spent her whole life fighting, first to survive high school and Jackie and Ashley, then to survive without Anna. She had nothing left. She was too broken from failing Jake—the one person who meant the world to her.

Sam felt the rage leave her body, replaced by defeat. Her whole body seemed to deflate as she looked at Ash.

Ash saw the change immediately. "Please, Sam," she pleaded.

Sam shook her head. "No. You're right. I'm sorry. I can't do this anymore."

Sam walked to the front door and opened it, glancing back over her shoulder at Ash. "Goodbye, Ash."

Chapter 19

Sam was exhausted and unhappy when Monday rolled around. She had hardly slept since ending it with Ash on Friday. For much of the weekend she lay in bed crying, missing her like crazy, thinking she made a huge mistake, before finding her anger again, for everything—how Ash treated her long ago, how she dared try to come back into Sam's life, and worst of all, how she made Sam fall for her.

At the office, Sam went to talk to Cassie about how things were progressing with the Thompson Dental campaign. When she reached Cassie's desk, Sam saw she was working on a different campaign.

"What happened to Thompson Dental?" Sam asked.

Cassie shifted in her seat, clearly uncomfortable, and bit her lip. *Uh-oh.* While Sam relied on and trusted all of her team members, Cassie was her go-to person, so if she couldn't tell Sam something, it was bad.

"Cassie, what is it?"

She let out a big sigh. "Pete met with us after you left and said we had to focus on the new Crescent City Tap Room campaign."

Sam raised a brow. "Did he?"

She nodded.

"So, who's on the Thompson Dental campaign?"

"Mike and Laila."

Sam shook her head. Mike and Laila were talented, but there was no way two people could put in enough hours on their own to complete the campaign in time for the pitch session. "All right, thanks."

She headed toward Pete's office, wanting to rip his sniveling little head off, but trying to stay calm.

"Pete, can you explain why you decided to take nearly every team member off the Thompson Dental campaign when we are staring at a deadline?"

Pete glanced up and a cocky grin spread across his face. "Sam, Crescent City Tap Room is a major client which could really boost our firm's reputation and revenue. We need to make sure we knock it out of the park and we need most of the team working to do that."

"Pete, you can't just abandon a client because you find another one with deeper pockets. This company is supposed to stand for more than that."

He just stared at her.

"When is the Crescent City pitch session?"

"Early July."

"That's a month away. We pitch Thompson Dental next Wednesday, and without the whole team, we might not be ready. Mike and Laila can't do it on their own. We need at least one more person full-time and one part-time to get it done. Give me Jess and Daniel."

He thought for a moment. "All right, but as soon as they're done, they're back on Crescent City."

"Fine." Sam started to walk away, then turned back to him. "I would appreciate it if you kept me in the loop with things affecting my team."

He shrugged. "You were gone—playing with your son or whatever."

At that, Sam clenched her jaw, ready to leap across the desk and strangle him with his stupid polka dot tie. She stared at him with balled fists, trying to remind herself that Pete wasn't worth prison.

"Sam, could you look over this design?"

The question grabbed Sam's attention and she turned to see Cassie standing a few feet away, clearly trying to defuse the situation. Sam was thankful for that. Sam unclenched her fists and started to walk away again.

"And Sam . . ."

She turned to see Pete leaning back in his chair with a smug grin. "Technically, it's my team, and I don't need to run any of my decisions by you."

Back home, Sam stewed, then got really angry again. Mostly at Pete, hating having to report to him and see the firm's reputation which they'd all worked so hard to build go by the wayside just to chase dollars.

Then, she thought about Max, fantasizing about ways to punish him, wanting to kill him for hurting Jake. Then she obsessed about her hatred for Pete again. Then Ash. But it was getting harder and harder to find reasons to hate her too. Every time she thought of something, she blamed herself instead.

Sam sighed. She had to let it go. She had broken up with Ash. She had said horrible, unforgivable things to her. There was no coming back from that. Sam vowed to focus on her son, who was still hurting. Focus on making his life better. Hers could go back to being an afterthought. She had tried finding love again—it just wasn't in the cards for her. She told herself that most people were lucky to even find it once. She needed to stop being greedy and just be happy for what she had shared with Anna and for the beautiful boy they had together. That would be enough. It had to be.

Drea suggested they play miniature golf in an effort to cheer Sam up, but Sam just didn't have it in her. So, they picked up daiquiris and went to the river, where they had worked through many of life's big issues. It was much warmer than the last time they had been here. Both Sam and Drea wore T-shirts and jeans, and they were still a bit hot. Summer hadn't technically started, since it was still only early June, but it sure felt like it. At least the light breeze off the river broke up the stickiness a little.

It wasn't dark yet, but dusk seemed like an appropriate time to be drinking. The beautiful interplay of pinks and purples in the sky seemed at odds with the sadness in Sam's heart. She sighed, seated next to Drea on their metal bench overlooking the Mississippi.

"Well, just say it," Sam said.

"Say what?" Drea asked.

"You told me so. I should have listened to you about Ash."

Drea turned to the river, sipping her drink. "Why is that?"

Sam wasn't sure if Drea was just dragging out Sam's misery from being wrong, but she played along. "I shouldn't have trusted her. She's not that different after all. She kept secrets from me about Jake that ended up hurting him. Um, take your pick."

Drea nodded and put her knee up on the bench so she was facing Sam. "She should have told you about Jake. That's true."

Sam mirrored Drea's position, facing her. "But?"

"But . . . I think I was wrong about Ash."

Sam held Drea's gaze for a moment, not understanding the change. "What?"

Drea huffed. She was never good at admitting when she was wrong. "I didn't give her a chance. You were right, Sam. She's *not* the same person."

"When exactly did you come to this realization?"

"After Charlie's."

Sam stared at her in disbelief. *Was Drea just screwing with her?* "What did Ash say to you that night?"

"It wasn't what she said exactly. It was more a feeling."

Sam arched a brow at her. "A feeling?"

Drea arched a brow back. "Yes."

Sam sighed, looking at the river, the boats in the distance, the current flowing steadily along. Everything seemed normal, but nothing was normal. She felt lost.

"Sam, you can do whatever you want about Ash. I will support whatever you decide. Just make sure you do it for the right reasons."

"Putting Jake in danger? Hurting me? Those aren't the right reasons?"

"Not everyone is naturally amazing with kids like us."

Sam choked on her drink, coughing. "Sorry, just went down the wrong tube."

"Anywaaay," Drea dragged out the word, "she messed up. I'm sure she regrets the hell out of it. If she had known what would happen with that little creep Max, do you really think she wouldn't have told you?"

Am I blaming Ash for something that wasn't her fault? She would never intentionally put Jake in danger.

Drea went on. "And as much as I hate to admit when I'm wrong…" Sam nodded in agreement. "I think she really cares about you."

Sam looked at her drink, biting the inside of her cheek to ward off tears as a wave of emotion washed over her.

"Do what you want. It was just nice to see you happy again, even for only a short time."

Ash parked along the grassy field. She had tried all week to focus on work, anything to keep her mind off Sam and Jake. During the week she stayed pretty busy, almost convincing herself she was okay. Then the weekend came. Saturday had been a mental tug of war, trying not to think about Sam. Now it was Sunday and she did everything she could to stay focused. She tried to work from home in the morning, but by one o'clock she gave up and went for a drive. No destination in mind. It didn't surprise her when her car seemed to drive itself to a familiar spot.

It was the big oak tree, her teenage place of escape, a place which sheltered her and reminded her not to give up. Things would get better. They had to. It was no surprise she had taken Sam to this spot on their first date.

Ash took off her flip flops, letting the warm blades of grass tickle her feet as she walked to the tree. She ran her hand along the rough bark, retracing the steps she had taken with Sam on their first date, closing her eyes and feeling the warmth from the sun-baked bark radiate against her palm.

She opened her eyes and walked over to where they had their picnic. She stared into the distance, waiting, until the giraffes appeared amongst the trees. She thought about Sam's smile. Heard her laugh. Felt her kiss. Sadness washed over her. She bent over and clutched her knees, trying to focus on her breathing. She had never felt so much loss after a breakup.

Ash sat on the grass, arms around her bent knees, watching the giraffes eating. She stayed for a long time, finally letting herself think through everything that had happened with Sam. Should she apologize and try to make things right again? She would if it could change anything. That's how much she wanted it to work out.

As much as Sam's words hurt her, Ash knew she could forgive her. She'd fallen in love with Sam and never got the chance to tell her. And even if Sam could forgive Ash for not telling her about Max, would it solve anything? Sam would still be afraid to move forward and let Anna go. As much as she wanted to, Ash knew it was something she couldn't fix. It was up to Sam now, to be the one to change if they had any hope of a future together. And after more than a week of no communication, Ash was pretty certain that would never happen.

She thought of never seeing Sam or Jake again and a lump formed in her throat. As the giraffes disappeared amongst the trees, she wiped away the tears running down her face, and stood to go home.

Sam had been really down all week, going through the daily motions as she reacquainted herself with life without Ash. Everything seemed mundane and joyless. Drea's comments swirled in her mind but she pushed them aside, avoiding her feelings for Ash. There was no point in focusing on them. Things hadn't worked out. It was over.

With only one week left of school before summer break, she signed Jake up for a week-long day camp starting the Monday after school let out. She hoped it would give him a chance to meet some new kids and have some fun—swimming, building robots, even a water balloon fight or two. He desperately needed to just be a kid again. And it would give them both a break from the massive hole left by Ash's absence.

"I get to ride a horse?" Jake asked excitedly as Sam tucked him into bed Sunday evening.

"Yep. I think there's even a petting zoo that day. You can hang out with pigs and goats and come home smelling absolutely amazing." She winked, tickling Jake as he giggled. "I think there's even a zombie apocalypse day. You can learn how to survive in case New Orleans is ever overrun by the undead." She glanced at him. "But don't worry, zombies aren't real. It's just for fun."

"I know that."

"You do?"

"Yeah . . . Drea always tells me they aren't real when we watch zombie movies. So I don't get scared."

Sam raised her brows. "Does she?"

Jake smiled shyly. "I wasn't supposed to tell you about that."

Sam shook her head, smiling. "Aunt D and I are going to have a talk about that."

Jake was quiet for a few moments. "Mom?"

"Yes, honey?"

"I miss Ash."

Damn it. They hadn't talked about Ash at all. As the week progressed, Sam thought maybe she had dodged a bullet and wouldn't have to acknowledge the breakup since Jake was so excited about summer camp.

She rubbed his arm. "I know, honey. I do too."

"Do you think she'll come over again when I finish camp?"

He was so hopeful, Sam didn't have the heart to tell him no. "I don't know, sweetie."

"Oh."

Sam hated him being sad, but knew there was nothing she could do to fix it. They just had to move on. It would hurt less at some point. She tousled his hair. "All right, get some sleep." She leaned down and kissed his forehead. "I love you."

"I love you, too."

She turned off the bedside lamp. "Sweet dreams."

Chapter 20

The following Wednesday morning, Pete called Sam into his office. The pitch with Thompson Dental was scheduled late morning so she was certain that would be the topic.

"Good morning Sam," Pete said, the start of a smirk on his lips. I just wanted you to know that I've cancelled the Thompson pitch today. In fact, the client is no longer with us."

"Pete, what the hell?" Sam asked.

"We don't have time to waste on small jobs with companies like that," he said curtly.

"Companies like *that?*"

"The little guys. We're not going to get anywhere if we focus on small campaigns for companies that can't afford to take it to the next level. We need the big companies, the movers and shakers in this town."

Sam's jaw gaped. She couldn't believe what he was saying. "Pete, *the little guys*, as you call them, are what make this city. Our company has always focused on quality campaigns for every client, regardless of their size or net worth."

"Correction, Sam. Our company used to focus on those things. Now that I'm in charge, we're taking a new direction. Focusing on the clients who will drive us to the top."

Sam narrowed her eyes and spoke through clenched teeth. "Last time I checked, Audrey was in charge."

His smug smile somehow turned up a notch. "Only in name. Bill wanted her to deal with all of the paperwork and ins and outs of keeping the business running, so I could focus on taking his company to the next level."

Sam's eyes widened. "Bill knows about this?"

"Of course, Sam. He knew I was the only one who had the balls to trim the fat and focus on catching the big fish."

Sam felt sick. Everything she believed in about the firm had just been turned on its head. It wasn't about keeping Pete from destroying the company anymore. He had Bill McGrady's full support to toss everything into the fire and become a soul-less company only concerned with prestige and money. She knew what she had to do.

"Excuse me."

Sam walked, determined, toward Audrey's office. Everyone busied themselves, trying to appear as if they hadn't been watching and listening. Sam knocked on the door as Audrey glanced up from her desk.

"Come in, Sam." She smiled warmly as Sam sat down in front of her.

"Audrey, I'm sorry to have to say this, but I've decided to resign. I'll stay to help finish up our current campaigns, then I need to move on." Sam felt horrible. She had devoted six years of her life to this place, but she was determined not to waver in her resolve.

Audrey sighed, clasping her hands on the desk. "Well, I hoped it wouldn't end like this, but I can't say I blame you."

"I'm sorry, Audrey. I've loved working here with you, but I don't share the same values with this company anymore. I used to believe in what we did, working with companies contributing to the heart of this city, seeing them grow and give back to the community."

Audrey nodded. "I wish there was something I could say to change your mind." She held Sam's gaze for a moment and then shook her head, a small smile spreading across her lips. "I wish you luck, Sam. You're one of the good ones. Frankly, I'm surprised you stayed with us this long."

That wasn't the response Sam had expected. "What do you mean?"

"Sam, you've kept your team running for years, almost single-handedly. *You* are why we have such great relationships with clients and why they are so happy with our work. Sure, there's a team behind you making quality campaigns, but you spend a lot of unlogged hours with clients trying to help them find their vision and making sure we create it for them."

Sam stared in surprise.

"You didn't think I knew about that, did you?" She flashed a mischievous smile. "This old bird's got some tricks up her sleeve, still. And I'm just biding my time until retirement. You can use your talents someplace else, someplace that appreciates you."

Sam smiled, taking a moment for Audrey's words to sink in. "Thank you, Audrey . . . for everything." Sam wasn't prepared for the rush of emotion overwhelming her. Looking down, she quickly blinked back tears.

"Sam," Audrey said gently, "I've been in this business long enough to know a success when I see one. Promise me you won't give up on yourself. This city needs people like you championing it."

Sam nodded and smiled. "I promise." She paused a moment. "Would it be all right if I headed out a little early today?"

"Of course. Go ahead and take the afternoon. I'll get your position posted and we can work out the details of finishing up the remaining campaigns tomorrow."

"Thanks, Audrey."

As Sam walked out into the bright June sun, pausing to feel the warmth against her face, the only emotion she felt was relief.

She headed across the parking lot to her car, turned on the engine, and rolled down the window. It was too beautiful not to enjoy the wind in her face as she drove. She flipped through the radio channels, landing on Bon Jovi's "It's My Life." She cranked up the volume and sang along as she pulled out of the parking lot, feeling, for the first time in ages, like she had the power to make all of her dreams come true. *I'm going to open my own marketing firm, damn it.*

Or not. By the time she pulled up in front of her house fifteen minutes later, her thoughts had flipped back and forth about twenty times from complete elation and unstoppable possibilities to absolute terror about making it work. Would she make a decent living? Would Audrey rehire her if she crawled back on her hands and knees? No, deep down, Sam knew she was done at McGrady Marketing. She was already a different person, simply by walking out that door, and she would never belittle herself by working with someone like that asshole Pete again.

"Asshole!" she yelled inside her empty car. An older woman walking her dog nearby gave Sam a concerned expression and quickened her pace. Sam smiled, put the car in park, and walked down the street to meet Jake.

Jake looked confused when he saw her waiting at the bus stop.

"Mom, why aren't you at work? Are you sick?" he asked, joining her on the sidewalk.

"Nope. I feel great. I just wanted to see my favorite guy. Is that okay?" She smiled as she slid his nearly empty backpack off and slung it over her shoulder.

"Yeah," he said shyly with a huge grin.

They walked hand-in-hand back to the house where Sam hung his backpack on the coat hook by the door. With only two days left of school, and the last day essentially a big party, summer was practically here.

"I was thinking . . ." She paused as Jake glanced up at her. "How'd you like to get some ice cream?"

She didn't think his grin could get any bigger as he jumped up and down. "Yay!"

They sat on a bench outside the Creole Creamery, with Jake's feet swinging merrily in the breeze as he filled Sam in on the events of his day. Sam smiled to herself. Mint chocolate chip never tasted so good.

Ash tossed the increasingly slobbery tennis ball to Goose as the pinks and purples of twilight cast shadows in her backyard. Time with Goose usually brightened her spirit, but she was struggling through each unenthusiastic toss.

The previous night had been hard. She'd started associating Tuesdays with Sam, first through softball, then through the dinners she had with Sam and Jake. With each passing Tuesday, Ash realized that maybe she and Sam really had been on different pages about their relationship. Ash started doubting whether Sam had feelings for her at all.

As much as she didn't want to, she knew she needed to let Sam and Jake go and try to move on. She was just wasting her time holding out for anything else. But it was a lot easier said than done. She'd have a few minutes where she felt fine, then something would remind her of Sam or Jake and she would be down again.

Goose dropped the soggy ball on her foot and watched it roll away. She stared blankly at him, no longer having the energy to laugh when he did silly things. "Come on, boy. Let's go inside." He tilted his head and followed her into the house.

When she went to bed that night, Ash felt tired, but she just lay there thinking, sleeplessly watching the hours pass. She finally fell asleep as the sun came up, having already decided to give herself a break and take the morning off.

When she awoke she took Goose for a short walk, then headed to Daily Bread, intent on sitting and enjoying a coffee outside. Jody was behind the counter when Ash walked into the café.

"Hey there." Jody greeted her with a big smile. She was probably the most upbeat person Ash had ever met.

"Hi." Ash tried to return at least a small smile. "Wow, you're tan." Jody was almost glowing—a deep bronze color having replaced her more typical pale white shade.

"Ha, yeah. I forced myself to take a vacation. Just got back."

"Nice. Did you have a good time?"

"Definitely. As much as I love it here, sometimes you just need some time away, ya know?"

Ash nodded.

"I even got to sleep in a bit."

"So, 7 a.m.?" Ash teased.

Jody tucked her head with a bashful smile. "Six."

Ash laughed. "Hey, that's really late for a baker," Jody responded. "I couldn't stand to be away for more than a week though. Had to get back to my baby." She rubbed her hand along the butcher block counter.

"Well, I'm glad you had a great time, but I'm definitely happy to have you back here."

"Thanks, Ash. Now. What can I get ya?"

Ash took her apple turnover and coffee, in a mug instead of a to-go cup for once, outside to one of the black metal tables along the front of the café. It was late morning, and since it was a weekday, there weren't many people around.

She sipped her coffee, tore off a piece of her turnover, and looked at the houses across the street. She tried hard to enjoy herself despite the emptiness she felt. She thought about what Jody had said. Maybe she should take a trip. A little time away to take her mind off Sam and Jake. Somewhere she wasn't constantly reminded of everything she had lost.

She popped another piece of turnover into her mouth, savoring the flaky sweetness. A trip might be nice.

Chapter 21

Very early Saturday morning, Sam's brother and their dad took Jake to Bayou Savage on a fishing trip. They had gone last year for the first time and had so much fun, it might become a tradition. It was only about forty minutes away, but gave Jake a chance to experience fishing beyond City Park.

They had scheduled the dawn outing to coincide with school getting out and the start of summer break. Given what Jake had been through over the past few weeks, Sam hoped this would be just what he needed.

Sam headed to her parents' house a little after nine o'clock so she would be there when the boys got back, and they could all have a late breakfast together. She found her mom making breakfast in the kitchen, the smell of warm biscuits and bacon filling the house.

"Hi, honey."

"Hey, Mom." Sam hugged her mom and glanced around at the different plates of food on the counter. "Is there anything I can do?"

"I just finished up in here. I'll put these in the oven to keep warm. Want to join me for coffee on the deck?" She took a sip from her already full black and gold Saints mug.

"Sounds good." Sam grabbed a Tulane mug out of the cupboard and filled it from the pot.

They sat down at the patio table, the sunbaked metal of Sam's chair burning the backs of her thighs for a few seconds.

"How was Jake last night?" Sam still worried about him, but at least school was out so he didn't have to see Max. As far as she knew, there hadn't been any other incidents with Max since he returned from suspension.

"He's just fine, honey. Don't worry." Sam gave her mom a look and she chuckled. "*Try* not to worry at least."

"I get the distinct feeling the only way we ever truly understand our parents is by becoming parents ourselves."

"Lord, isn't that the truth." Sam's mom shook her head and chuckled. "Grandchildren are the greatest justice in this world."

Sam laughed.

They sat in silence for a few minutes, taking in the already stifling humidity. It was going to be a long summer.

Sam's mom looked over and hesitated, settling on a smile. Sam smiled back and waited. Another minute went by as her mom perused the yard before she turned back to Sam, ready to say something.

Sam raised her brows, giving her the sign to proceed.

"Honey . . . I hope you know by now that you never have to hide anything from me and your father." She gave Sam a pointed look in case she had missed the not-so-subtle hint to fill her mom in on current events.

Sam tilted her head slightly. "I'm not so sure about that."

"Try me."

Sam looked down at her mug and shook her head.

"Is this about Ash?"

Sam looked up in surprise. "How did you know?"

She shrugged. "Well, Jake went on and on about someone named Ash teaching him to cook, and then you seemed happier than I'd seen you in years. After I saw Ashley Valence at the softball game, I put two and two together." She sipped her coffee.

"You remember Ash? And you were okay I was seeing her?" Sam was a bit shocked this conversation was even happening.

"I'll admit, I was ready to spit nails at first. But seeing how happy you and Jake were . . . I knew it meant something." She held Sam's gaze. "A parent never wants to watch their child suffer, knowing they can't do anything to change it. I've had to do that twice now—when you were being bullied, and then when Anna died. You've endured more than your fair share of pain, honey. You deserve to be happy again. And this time . . ." She looked out over the yard and when she faced Sam again, Sam could tell she was fighting back tears. "This time, I don't have to sit back helplessly. We all deserve a second chance." She took a deep breath. "So, if you can forgive Ash, for whatever it was that happened between the two of you, then I can swallow my pride and give her a chance as well."

Sam had no idea what to say, so she just stared into her coffee mug.

"Look, I don't know what went on, but if you can, you need to fix it. I saw how you were during the time y'all were together. I haven't seen you that happy since Anna. Maybe not even then. Don't let that slip away, honey. That's the whole point of all of this." She twirled her finger in a circle at the space around them.

Sam nodded, but didn't say anything.

"I know you loved Anna. I loved her too. She was an amazing woman . . . almost as amazing as you. But life is too short to live in the past."

Sam took a deep breath and let it out slowly. "I said something horrible. Something below the belt. I don't think Ash will ever forgive me."

Sam's mom nodded. "You know, we like to think we're good people, but when we get hurt, sometimes the not-so-pretty side shows itself." She took Sam's hand. "It doesn't mean you're a horrible person. It means you're human. And, if you're lucky enough to have a long relationship, you get more chances. To choose to do it better." She let go of Sam's hand and sipped her coffee.

Sam nodded, but doubted whether she'd get another chance with Ash.

"If you care about her, and I know that you do, make it right." Sam's mom started laughing, a good hearty laugh.

"What?"

"I just never thought I'd be telling you to apologize to Ashley Valence." She shook her head. "Life never ceases to surprise."

"Mom, she's not who she used to be."

"I know, honey. If she was, I'd drive you to the insane asylum myself."

Even though it had barely been a week since Sam gave her notice, a lot had transpired. Audrey and Sam worked out a plan for Sam to split her time evenly between working from home and being in the office. There were already quite a few applicants for her position, so she committed to working only until the end of the month to help the new person transition. Rumors about Sam leaving spread quickly, and John from Julie's Juice Company and Andrew Thompson from Thompson Dental had already called to tell her they'd follow her wherever she went next. Cassie also called. She was ready to leave McGrady and wanted to go with her as well. Sam wasn't prepared for the loyal following and couldn't help but feel proud. She also felt the need to plan her company's launch. Knowing she had clients let her rest easier about money, but she still wanted to open an actual office, making it official.

With Jake at camp, Sam used the time she wasn't working on campaigns to check out potential office sites and take care of logistical details. She spent her nights with Jake, hearing his excited retelling of his day as a camper.

But when she wasn't busy keeping busy, she kept hearing her mom's words. Sam had been happy with Ash. Sam wasn't sure if it was because she had known her since high school, or at least a version of her. Or if it was something else. Until the night they broke up, Sam was amazed at how easy things were when they were together. Sam never felt like Ash was out of her league or that she needed to impress her. Sam was just . . . Sam. Ash always made her feel like that was enough.

The more Sam thought about Ash, the more she missed her. She had been missing her since they broke up. A lot. But having her mom point out how truly rare it is to find someone you fit so perfectly with made her unable to think of anything but Ash.

Sam thought about how to get Ash back, how to apologize and make it up to her for how she had behaved. However, every scenario ended the same way: with Ash saying no.

Two weeks had already passed since their fight and Ash hadn't reached out to her once. Sam knew she had taken things too far and it was over. There were certain things you didn't say in a relationship. Sam knew Ash's weaknesses and she went for them without restraint. It was unforgivable. Ash was right not to want to be with her. Sam proved that all she would do is hurt her.

Sam went through all the reasons she and Ash shouldn't be together. But in the end, she kept returning to one fact. She missed Ash. When she let herself actually feel how much she missed her, it was crushing. There was an emptiness that reached depths she hadn't felt in a long time. After Anna died, she had spent three years trying to piece herself together and just be okay again. She was numb before Ash came back into her life, but at least she wasn't hurting anymore. Now she was mad at herself for letting someone else in enough to hurt her again.

Sam sat alone in the living room for a long time, finally letting herself feel the hurt. Fully. Her mind drifted to Ash's tears, the pleading in her eyes before Sam ended it. Her heart actually ached at the thought. It physically hurt to know she had hurt Ash. She closed her eyes, letting herself finally accept that she missed Ash because she was in love with her.

Now, there was only one thing she needed to figure out how to do.

It had been a few weeks since Sam saw Allison. As things grew more intense with Ash and busy at work, Sam had moved from weekly sessions to every two or three weeks. But after the events of the last couple weeks, Sam definitely needed an outside perspective.

"Hi, Sam. It's nice to see you." Allison smiled at Sam and adjusted her purple-rimmed glasses.

"New glasses?" Sam didn't remember ever seeing Allison wear glasses before.

Allison frowned. "Yes. Apparently I'm old enough to need reading glasses now." She pointed her pen to the legal pad resting on top of her crossed legs. "So I can take notes. You know, for when my memory fails, too." She rolled her eyes.

Sam laughed. She couldn't imagine Allison being any older than her. "Well, I like them. Makes you look distinguished."

Allison smiled. "Thanks. So. What can I help you with?"

Sam took a deep breath. "Well. There's a lot."

Sam filled Allison in on her relationship with Ash, giving notice at work, Jake being bullied, and how she had lashed out at Ash and broken up with her.

"Wow. That is a lot. I'm really sorry about Jake. I know that's tough to handle as a parent, and especially for someone who experienced that yourself."

"Thanks. I think I just couldn't justify my relationship with Ash once Jake was bullied. It felt like a betrayal in some weird way. And her not telling me about Max made me doubt whether I could trust her."

Allison nodded.

Sam looked away, suddenly feeling ashamed. "And a part of me was jealous that Jake told her about Max and not me."

"All of those feelings are perfectly natural, Sam. Did you ever consider that Jake may have had a reason he didn't tell you about Max? That it had nothing to do with you lacking in any way?"

"What do you mean?"

"Well, when you didn't tell your mom about being bullied, was it because she wasn't a good mom?"

"Of course not. I was ashamed and—" Sam's voice broke as her eyes filled with tears. She swallowed, trying to collect herself. "And I didn't want her to worry."

Allison handed her a box of tissues. "Could the same be true for Jake?"

Sam wiped her tears and nodded. After a moment, she took a steadying breath. "I blew up at Ash. It was pretty bad. I feel like all the progress I've made in therapy went out the window and I was back to lashing out. I said some horrible things. Things I didn't mean, but I said them anyway."

"Try not to be so hard on yourself, Sam. You've come a long way. You reacted in the moment, but you realized that pretty quickly."

Sam frowned. "I feel like I should be better than this by now, though. Better able to cope with everything."

Allison gave her a small smile. "You two have a lot of history, but you chose to give Ash a second chance and get to know her. Not many people could do that, Sam. It takes a lot of courage. Jake getting bullied probably shook you a lot and made you feel out of control. So when you found out Ash had kept something from you, especially something about Jake, it probably brought up that old version of Ash—the one who couldn't be trusted, who hurt you."

Sam nodded. It all made sense, though more than a little predictable in Allison's quick summary of her actions. *Am I that transparent?*

"I know what happened with Jake is different than what happened to me in high school. But that protective instinct just took over. I hated knowing that I missed it. I knew something was wrong. I should have made him tell me what was going on."

"Do you think that would have changed anything?"

Sam shook her head. "I don't know. But I could have tried harder." Sam's face crumpled as she sobbed into her tissue.

When her sobs quieted, Allison's voice was gentle. "What's upsetting you right now?"

Sam wiped her eyes, trying to collect herself. "I'm all Jake has now. I don't want to disappoint him . . . or Anna. But I just keep feeling like I'm failing." Sam shook her head. "She was a much better mom than me. She should be the one here with him. I can't even cook dinner without burning it."

"There are some excellent microwaveable meals out there." Allison's voice was light.

Sam snorted, then started crying again. "I burn those too."

"Sam, what matters is that you love Jake and you would do anything for him. You knew something was wrong, but you gave him the independence to talk about it, or not. No one's got it figured out. Every mother feels like she's failing. And if you didn't, then I'd worry."

Sam laughed lightly, wiping her tears, meeting Allison's warm gaze. "I care about Ash. I really do. But Jake is the most important person in the world to me. And as much as I would like to move forward, Anna is still tied into all of this. If we had broken up, that would be one thing. But I loved her and she died. A part of me will always love her. I haven't been able to figure out how to truly let Ash in without feeling guilty and hurting everyone."

"Have you told Ash that?"

Sam avoided eye contact. "No." She looked back up. "She tried to talk about it once, but I wasn't ready."

Allison nodded. "None of this is easy. You've been through a lot,

219

Sam. But it seems like there's something good between you and Ash. You have to decide if you want to pursue that and find a way to be true to Anna's memory without using it as a crutch to avoid getting hurt again."

Sam blew out a breath. "That was a bit direct."

Allison's hearty laugh filled the room. "Sorry, but I think you needed to hear it."

Sam sat with that for a long moment. "You're like a freakin' Jedi. You know that, right?"

Allison laughed. "That may be the nicest thing anyone's ever said to me."

That night, after Sam put Jake to bed, she sat down on the sofa. She thought about her session with Allison. About Ash. Jake. Her career. New Orleans. All the things she loved. And what she most wanted in her life and who she most wanted it with.

When Sam picked Jake up from camp on Friday, he was ecstatic about all the fun he'd had and the cool things he'd learned. Sam gave him an extra-long hug. It was good to see him so happy. Throughout the week, Jake had told Sam about all of the cool activities he did each day, but the space day was by far his favorite. He mentioned a few boys he hung out with, so Sam made sure to talk to their moms when she picked him up, hoping they could arrange some summer play dates. A couple of the boys went to his school, so Sam was hopeful that next year might be better for him with a few good friends around.

As much as Sam wanted to hang out with Jake after being home all day without him, she and Drea had something special planned for him. So, she dropped Jake off at her parents' house and headed home to meet Drea.

A few hours later, Drea put the finishing touches on an elaborate spaceship on Jake's wall. Sam stood on a chair sticking glow-in-the-dark stars to the ceiling in the formation of constellations.

"Jesus, they're all blending together." Sam stepped down from the chair, grabbing her beer off the dresser. She took a sip as she squinted at the ceiling, trying to tell them apart.

Drea glanced up. "It looks good. Don't forget Orion's Belt."

"Don't worry. That's the grand finale." Sam put her beer down and perused the constellation guide on her laptop. Memorizing it, she moved the chair a couple feet, and climbed back up. "I'm surprised these things don't come with a stick-by-number guide or anything."

Drea turned from her squatting position, her paint brush paused in the air. "Well, they do. These were a dollar less."

Sam stared at her. "I'm going to kill you."

When they both finished, Sam and Drea clinked their beers together, taking a celebratory sip. "That looks amazing, Drea. Jake's going to lose his mind."

Drea smiled at her painting. "Yeah, it turned out pretty good." She took another sip and turned to Sam. "So, any new thoughts on the Ash situation?"

Sam's smile disappeared. She'd avoided the subject since her therapy session Wednesday, not ready to face the next step. "I had a really good session with Allison this week that helped, but I really fucked up, Drea. I said some truly awful things. I don't know if she'll ever forgive me."

"You're human, Sam, and you were hurting. You forgave her for everything she put you through and gave her another chance. If you can do that, she can too."

Sam shook her head. "I'm scared she'll say no. And then I'll have no idea how to move on from that."

Drea put her hand on Sam's shoulder. "She might say no. Or she might say yes. It's a risk you have to take." Sam frowned as Drea continued. "You're one of the strongest people I know, Sam. I mean labor alone was god awful." She grimaced. "I saw things that day that will forever be etched in my brain. It made horror movies look G-rated."

Sam raised her brows. "Are you done?"

"No. It was atrocious."

Sam glared at her, and Drea laughed. "Okay, now I'm done. My point is, you made it through that, you survived losing Anna, and you've survived working with a complete idiot for years. You can handle this." She dipped her head, holding Sam's gaze. "But you have to try first."

Sam stared at the floor.

"What are you so afraid of?"

Sam shook her head, trying to hide the tears welling in her eyes.

"Sam, what is it?" Drea gripped her shoulder tighter.

"I can't go after Ash until I'm ready to really let her into my life. Fully into my life. I feel like I'm cheating on Anna. I can't even have Ash in my bed because it makes me feel so guilty."

"You know Anna would want you and Jake to be happy. She wouldn't expect you to be single for the rest of your life."

"My mind believes that, but my heart still has doubts."

"Sam, you have to let her go so you can live your life."

Sam felt the pain boiling up inside of her.

"Sam . . . why can't you let her go?" Drea's eyes were earnest, and Sam couldn't hold back her tears anymore. She burst into uncontrollable sobs as Drea took her in her arms.

Sam muttered through her sobs. "Because then she'll really be gone. I'll be on my own."

Drea held Sam for a long time. When her sobs eventually calmed, Drea took Sam by the shoulders, looking into her eyes.

"She *is* really gone, Sam, I'm so sorry. But you're not alone. In case you haven't noticed, there's been one person by your side all this time." She pointed to her chest. "Me. And I'm not going anywhere."

Sam wiped her nose with the back of her hand and wrapped her arms around Drea's neck, pulling her back into a hug.

When Sam let go, Drea met her eyes. "Anna will always be a part of you, Sam. Opening your heart to someone else doesn't mean you don't love her anymore. It just means you're willing to love again."

"I know, but even if Ash does forgive me, what if it doesn't work out? I don't know if I can survive that level of loss again."

"No one gets a guarantee on love, Sam. It's always a risk. But would you really rather never love anyone again to avoid the hurt? What kind of lesson is that for Jake?"

"You sound like my therapist."

"I read a lot. Women like smart chicks. And it doesn't hurt to have killer eyes and a body that won't quit." Drea struck a power pose and tossed her head back, pulling a laugh from Sam.

Sam sipped her beer, wondering if this intimate conversation could take another question.

"Hey, Drea?"

"Yes, ma'am?" She grinned at Sam.

"Why . . . don't you ever date anyone seriously?"

Drea shrugged. "Not everyone wants that, Sam."

"Yeah, but you are so amazing. It's sad that nobody will ever get close enough to really know you."

"Maybe one day, I'll feel differently . . ." She scrunched her nose. "But I doubt it. Besides, my life is pretty full with Pickles, my favorite furry feline. And you, and Jake. I've got all the family I need. Plus, I need time to myself to strategize. Those interns aren't gonna prank themselves."

Sam shook her head. "You really are special, Drea. In every sense of the word."

They both burst out laughing.

Ash felt lame, sitting at home, alone, on yet another Friday night. Here she was, in one of the most interesting and exciting places in the country, and she was a recluse.

She was still thinking about taking a trip, but hadn't actually done anything about it. She looked at Goose, who was resting his head against her thigh as they sat on the sofa together.

"You know what?"

Goose jumped to his feet, expecting to go outside.

"We'll do that in a minute, buddy. Momma's gonna plan a trip."

When Ash grabbed her laptop from the ottoman and failed to actually get up from the sofa, Goose laid back down and sighed.

"Sorry, bud."

Ash was thinking about somewhere with a beach, and started checking out destinations in California and Hawaii. But the more she searched, the more things she found that wouldn't be that wonderful by herself. She saw all kinds of things she knew Jake and Sam would love, which made her that much more depressed at the thought of going alone.

After a little while, Ash gave up and closed her laptop. Honestly, she hated trying so hard to move on and let Sam go. It had been three long weeks already and she told herself it was ridiculous to still hold out hope.

But deep down, she knew why she couldn't move on. She was in love with Sam and she wanted to be with her. She wanted a future with Sam and Jake. A family. She never knew how much she'd love family life until Sam and Jake came along.

She was always so afraid she'd pass on what her parents did to her that she had convinced herself she didn't want it. But, with the short time she'd spent with Sam and Jake, it turned out she did. And now, she couldn't move on because she hated the idea of a future without them. She was never so sure of anything in her life.

But it wasn't up to her. It was up to Sam. And holding out hope was only hurting her more every day.

Chapter 22

When they got home from her parents' house, Sam made elaborate excuses to keep Jake out of his bedroom. She wanted to wait until it was dark so he could get the full effect of the surprise she and Drea had made for him. But he was too smart for her. So, she had to tell him there was a surprise, but he could only get it after dark. He agreed, but time moved really slowly for them both.

When the sun finally went down, Jake and Sam turned to each other on the sofa. "Now?" Jake asked.

"Now." Sam smiled at him.

Outside his bedroom door, Sam covered his eyes with her hand. "No peeking."

She could feel Jake bouncing with excitement as she opened the door, flipped on the light, removed her hand and yelled, "Surprise!"

Jake blinked at the room for a minute, then squealed and ran to the spaceship, touching it with reverence. "Wow."

Sam smiled, so happy she and Drea could bring him some joy, especially after the past few weeks. The past few years, really. Drea had gone all out. The painting was almost to the top of the ceiling and she had even made a little window in the spaceship where the inside controls could be seen.

Sam laughed as Jake hugged the wall. "You like it?"

"It's so cool, Mom. I love it."

"Good. Remember to tell Aunt D that when you see her. This was her creation." Jake lifted his cheek off the wall to place a kiss on the painting.

"Aww. There is one more thing. You ready?"

Jake scanned the room eagerly, trying to find the rest of the surprise.

"Go lie down on the bed."

Sam turned off the lights and lay down next to him as they stared up at the stars glowing in the dark. Jake didn't make a sound. He just stared, his mouth hanging open, for a few moments.

"Do you like it?" He was usually so expressive. Sam was surprised by the silence and hoped it was a good reaction.

He turned to her with wide eyes, nodding, as a single tear trailed from the corner of his eye. "Oh Jake, come here." She hugged him tight. "I love you so much."

"I love you too, Mom."

They lay together, Jake snuggled against her, as he pointed out each constellation. Sam was amazed he knew so many.

"I don't know what that one is." Jake pointed to a cluster of stars in the corner where Sam had run out of ceiling space.

"That's Jake's Belt."

"Jake's Belt?"

"Yeah, it's like Orion's Belt. Just a little smaller." Sam winked, then tickled him until he couldn't take anymore, and they lay on the bed laughing.

"Thanks, Mom." His face turned serious. "I like it when you're happy. I don't want you to be sad."

Sam bit her lip to stop the tears from forming. "Then, let's both stay happy, okay?"

"Okay," Jake agreed enthusiastically.

After Jake fell asleep, Sam went into her bedroom and sat on the edge of her bed. She had taken the day to wrap her head around last night's conversation with Drea. She knew Drea was right—her only hope of moving forward in her life, with or without Ash, was to let Anna go. She never intentionally planned to enshrine Anna in her heart, leaving virtually no room for anyone else to enter, but that's where her grief took her. It was the only way she could survive, by holding Anna close, even if it was only in her heart and the carefully preserved vestiges of their life together.

Sam picked up the photograph of Anna and held it in her hands, tracing Anna's face and beautiful smile with her fingers. The all too familiar lump claimed her throat, her eyes welling with tears. Sam wondered if she would ever see a day when Anna's memory left her with more joy than pain. She was gone so suddenly, without any good-bye—to Sam or Jake. That was the hardest part. She went to work. And she never came home.

Sam had thought about that a lot over the years. In some ways, she knew it was a gift that Anna didn't suffer. But Sam was left to face everything—her life, her home, and her son—alone. Yet Anna was still everywhere around them. It was brutal.

She lay down on the bed for a while, clutching the frame, letting her emotions wash over her. When she finally felt ready, she carried Anna's photograph into the closet, placed it on top of the pile of her old clothes, and packed them in a box, which she put in the corner on the top shelf. She'd keep the clothes in case Jake ever wanted them, but out of sight so that she could move on without constant reminders of Anna.

On Sunday afternoon, Sam dropped Jake off at his new friend Danny's house for a sleepover. They had met at camp and Danny seemed like a good kid who was equally obsessed with astronauts and space. Sam indulged Jake with more than a few servings of astronaut ice cream over the past week, but drew the line at having dehydrated food packs for dinner—though they probably were an improvement on her cooking.

She went home and dawdled nervously for a couple of hours, going through different potential scenarios for a conversation with Ash—what to say, how Ash would react, how Sam would react to her reaction. Her brain started to hurt and it was all pointless. She needed to get up and go to Ash's house and hope she'd talk to her. She'd let her heart find the words.

Sam gripped the steering wheel and blew out a breath as her car inched lazily along the pothole-ridden streets. For once, she was grateful for the traffic slowing her down. As she passed several intersections, she considered bailing, but knew she would live in torment until she at least tried to tell Ash how she felt about her.

When she reached Ash's house, she sat in her car for a moment, still gripping the wheel, staring straight ahead. She took a deep breath, blew it out slowly, and opened the car door.

As she walked up to the house, she smelled the sweet, pungent aroma of hyacinths. Though it had only been a few weeks since she was last here, there was a strangeness and unfamiliarity to the house tonight. She stood at the door, hesitant to knock, then closed her eyes, steeling her resolve. Whatever happened from here on out, there was no going back. She had to tell Ash how she felt, and that would put Sam solidly in the most vulnerable position she had allowed herself to be in since Anna died.

She raised a trembling hand and knocked, the sound echoing around her. After a few moments, she began to worry Ash wasn't going to answer and she'd have to go through all of this again. She couldn't.

As she raised her hand to knock again, the door swung open, revealing Ash staring at Sam. She was as beautiful as ever in a deep purple shirt and faded jean shorts, her hair up in a ponytail, with a mix of hesitation, curiosity, and disappointment in her eyes. Despite her beauty, Sam noticed how tired she looked.

"Hi," Sam said hesitantly, ignoring the dread permeating her body. "I was hoping we could talk."

Ash stood still for a moment before stepping aside. "Come in," she said, her expression blank. Even Goose's energy seemed dampened as he stared at Sam, barely wriggling his little body.

Sam walked into the room and glanced back at Ash, who was still standing by the door. "Is it all right if I sit down?"

She nodded.

Sam sat on the light gray sofa, as uncomfortable as she remembered it, which seemed fitting right now. She met Ash's gaze again. "Would you sit with me?"

Ash walked slowly to the sofa and sat. Sam could see the raw pain in her eyes and Sam's heart ached knowing she had caused it.

Sam took a deep breath. "I know I'm probably the last person you want to see right now." Sam saw no indication in Ash's eyes that she was wrong. "But I need to tell you a few things. And then, if you want me to leave, well, I will honor that."

She glanced down at her hands, folded in her lap, knowing this was it—her one shot.

Sam raised her head, locking eyes with Ash. "Ash, I'm so incredibly sorry for how I acted and what I said to you." Sam shook her head. "It was horrible. Unforgivable. I know that. I was upset about Jake and I took it out on you. When really, I was mostly mad at myself. For not being able to protect Jake, for not being able to let you past the walls I built around myself, for not being able to let go of my past enough to enjoy the most wonderful person I'd met in years. Maybe ever. I couldn't move past my own guilt and shame to truly be with you." Her voice trembled. "You've been trying to show me all of this time how you've changed and I guess the sad part is that maybe I'm the one who's still the same."

Sam paused. "I built this wall around me when we were kids, trying to protect myself from the pain. But the truth is, I kept getting hurt. All I did was box myself in and make myself smaller. Thankfully, a few people were persistent enough to find their way in—Drea, and Anna ... and then *you*." Sam gave Ash a small smile. It wasn't returned.

She stared at her hands, fidgeting, willing herself not to give up, to finish what she had to say.

"When Anna died, I felt like I died right along with her. I couldn't imagine ever feeling love again or anyone ever wanting to love me like she did." A tear ran down Sam's cheek. She quickly brushed it away with the back of her hand. "But the truth is, I did find it again, with the least likely person, and in the least likely circumstance. And maybe that scared me more than anything. I didn't think I deserved to be lucky enough to be happy again. And to be honest, with you, I felt more like myself than I ever have before. You accepted me just as I was, broken as I was."

She forced herself to look up, tears running down her face now, to see Ash watching her with wet eyes.

Sam held her gaze, needing Ash to really hear her. "It wasn't fair to expect you to take the scraps of my heart while I held on to the memory of Anna. I know that now. And I'm truly sorry." Sam took Ash's hand in hers. "I wasn't ready then, but I am now. I put away Anna's picture, and those things that I kept. I let her go, Ash. Because

I want to move forward with my life. And more than anything, I want to move forward with you."

Sam squeezed her hand. "Ash, I'm in love with you. I have been for a while now. I'm just sorry I didn't say it sooner."

They stared at each other for what felt like an eternity. Sam couldn't read Ash's expression. She was still holding Sam's hand, so that was something. Though Sam wasn't positive she wouldn't momentarily snap one of her fingers off.

"I didn't want that."

Sam's heart sank, an entirely new lump forming in her throat. She dropped her head, and nodded. It had been her best shot, but it wasn't enough to make up for how much she had hurt Ash. It was time to crawl away and go home where she could cry in the comfort of her own bed. Sam stood to leave.

"No. *Sam.* You don't understand." Ash kept hold of her hand and looked at Sam with pleading eyes. Sam slowly sat back down.

"I didn't want you to put Anna's picture away . . . though moving it out of the bedroom would have been nice." A small smile spread across her lips for a brief moment before her expression turned serious again. "I never had a problem with you honoring her memory, because she mattered to you and Jake. I just needed there to be room for me in the relationship too."

"You know, I moved back here to create a home for myself. I spent so many years running from this place and my past . . . and I didn't want to run anymore." She rubbed her thumb gently along the back of Sam's hand. "You and Jake have been more of a home to me than anything I've ever known or even dreamed of." She shook her head. "I never imagined it was possible, but I fell in love with you too. A long time ago, actually."

Sam inhaled, feeling like she was taking her first breath after being held under water. "Does that mean you forgive me?"

Ash smiled warmly and nodded, her eyes holding back unshed tears. As Sam's face lit up with a huge grin, Ash slid her hand behind Sam's neck, pulling her into a gentle but sure kiss.

"Ash, I love you so much."

Ash stroked the backs of her fingers down Sam's cheek. "I love you too, Sam." And as she smiled at Sam, the unshed tears spilled from her eyes, streaming down her cheeks.

Goose barked at them from beside the sofa and stood up on his hind legs to be included, his little butt wriggling with excitement. "We love you too, Goose," Sam said, petting him as Ash laughed.

Chapter 23

"So what do you think?" Sam rested her arm across Jake's shoulders.

"This is all yours?" Jake asked in wonder, scanning the huge loft space Sam had leased for her business.

"Yep." Sam couldn't hide the pride in her voice. This was a big step. A scary, but awesome big step.

"I love it." Jake ran from one desk to the next, then stood on his tiptoes peering out the huge window onto the tree-lined street below.

Crescent City Marketing would officially launch on Monday, right after the July 4th holiday. In addition to Cassie, she'd hired Drea as her main graphic designer and quickly instigated a 'no pranking' rule to save any current or future interns. Word of mouth had spread over the past few weeks and Sam already had a handful of clients, mostly small and medium-sized companies as committed to New Orleans and its people as she was. It was going to be a great adventure, filled with like-minded people and rewarding work.

Also, Sam had made a point of finding office space within ten minutes of her house so she could be home each day to meet Jake at the bus stop.

"I think this is the last box from the car," Ash said, entering the office. She placed the box on Sam's new desk.

"Thanks, babe." Sam leaned in and kissed her.

"*Eww,*" Jake groaned from the window.

Sam and Ash pulled apart, grinning at Jake. "Just you wait. One day your views on kissing will change."

"I hope not!" Jake ran over to them. "Can we take Goose to the park?"

"Sure, bud. Let's go."

On Saturday afternoon, everyone crowded into Sam's backyard to celebrate Jake's sixth birthday. Sam's parents, Drea, Ash, and Goose were all there, as well as a bunch of kids from Jake's school, including Danny, his best friend.

Jake wanted a space-themed party, so Sam rented a bouncy castle—the closest thing to an anti-gravity chamber she could afford. The kids seemed satisfied, bouncing to their hearts' content.

Sam, Ash, and Drea went inside to get the cake ready. "Excellent choice to have an ice cream cake during one of the hottest months of the year," Drea said sarcastically as she watched the edges of the cake melt rapidly in front of them.

Sam scowled at Drea as she placed six candles into the frosting at the center of the cake, hoping it would hold up long enough for Jake to blow them out. "It's what Jake wanted."

Ash chuckled, sipping her wine, and wisely staying out of Sam and Drea's bickering. Sam smiled at her. "Hey, Ash, would you go gather everyone around the table? I think we're ready."

"Sure." She leaned over and kissed Sam before heading outside to the picnic table.

Sam caught Drea shaking her head. "What?"

"You two are just so adorable together. It's really . . . sickening."

Sam laughed and tossed an extra candle at her. "Shut up."

Sam lit the candles and carried the cake out to the group of smiling faces singing "Happy Birthday." Thankfully, the cake was still solid enough for Jake to make a wish and blow out the candles, Goose sitting loyally at his feet. Sam quickly cut enough slices for everyone before rushing the remaining cake back to the freezer. By the time she got back, her slice of yellow cake was floating on top of a puddle of chocolate ice cream. But, Jake seemed happy licking the melted ice cream off his plate, and that's all that mattered.

Later that night after Jake opened his presents and everyone had gone home, Ash and Sam tucked him into bed with Goose curled up next to him.

"There's actually a couple more presents," Ash said.

Jake's eyes went wide. "There are?"

"There are." Ash smiled at Sam, who reached under the bed and pulled out a package covered in spaceship wrapping paper.

"This is from Ash and me," Sam said, handing the gift to Jake.

Jake had the wrapping paper off in seconds. He stared, speechless, with his mouth hanging open for a moment before looking at Sam. She saw he was fighting back tears.

"I know how much he meant to you so Ash and I didn't want you to be without him." Sam smiled at Jake.

"Tony!" Jake hugged the toy to his chest and closed his eyes.

A tear ran down Sam's cheek and she quickly wiped it away. Ash took her hand, as they smiled at each other. They watched Jake run his fingers over Tony, bending his legs back and forth.

Then, Ash pulled a box from behind her back. It was wrapped in navy blue paper with moons and planets.

"Okay, last one," Ash said, handing the box to Jake, who squealed with excitement.

"What is it?" he asked.

"Open it and find out."

Jake gently placed Tony on the bed beside him before taking the gift from Ash. He ripped the paper in long swaths, gasping as he lifted the lid off the rectangular box underneath. He triumphantly held the gift so Sam could see it. "Look, Mom!"

Across a white apron that was actually his size, dark blue letters spelled out "Head Chef."

"Very cool! What do you say, bud?"

"Thanks Ash!" He leaned forward and wrapped his arms around her neck.

"You're welcome." Ash wrapped her arms around him. "Happy birthday, Jake."

After they said good night, Ash and Sam collapsed onto the sofa.

"Thank you for all of your help today. I couldn't have done it without you."

Ash kissed her forehead. "I loved it."

"You know, there is actually one more present . . ."

Ash looked at her, confused.

"And it's for you." Sam reached behind the pillow, pulling out a medium-sized rectangular box.

"For me?"

Sam nodded. "Open it."

Ash opened the box, tears coming to her eyes. "Sam," she whispered. "I love it."

She held up the wood-framed photograph of the three of them together by the river the day they went to the aquarium.

"I wanted you to have a picture of your family."

Tears escaped down Ash's cheeks. "Thank you. This is the best gift anyone has ever given me." She leaned toward Sam and kissed her gently. "I love you so much."

Sam placed her palm against Ash's cheek, holding her gaze with a warm smile. "I love you too, but . . ."

A look of concern crossed Ash's features. "But?"

Sam's smile widened. "But . . . there's more."

"What?"

"Turn it over."

Ash flashed Sam a cautious glance before flipping the frame over. On the back, a piece of clear tape secured a key. She looked up at Sam.

Sam took her hand. "You and Jake are my life, and I want you to be here with us, all the time, in our home. Will you move in with us?"

Ash nodded rapidly, a huge smile spanning her face. "I'll call my landlord tomorrow."

Sam took Ash's face in her hands, kissing her deeply. When they finally broke apart for air, a smirk crossed Ash's lips.

"What?"

"Would you be opposed to a minor kitchen renovation? Jake and I require certain accoutrements to keep our cooking skills up to par, you know." She grinned at Sam.

Sam rolled her eyes, but couldn't hide her smile. "I suppose that can be arranged."

"We can make this place the best of both worlds," Ash said as she carefully removed the tape and slid the key into her pocket. She took Sam's hand and led her over to the mantel where an assortment of framed photographs told the story of Sam's life and her heart.

Sam glanced at the faces staring back—her parents, Jake, Drea, Goose, and Ash. Even Anna—Ash had made Sam unpack Anna's picture and include it with the others.

Ash placed the new photograph up alongside the others. Sam and Ash stood together, arms wrapped around each other's waists, looking at the different pictures.

"Feels like a home." Ash smiled.

Sam kissed her cheek. "It is. Our home."

Acknowledgments

They say it takes a village. I think that's about raising kids or something, but it also applies to writing and publishing a book. Thank you to all of the fellow writers and readers I've met during this journey. Your support has meant more than you'll ever know.

Thank you to everyone at Bywater Books for helping this book become a reality. I'm honored to be part of the Bywater family. Thanks especially to Salem West, my publisher, and Fay Jacobs, my editor. Fay, I hope one day I write a joke that makes you laugh.

I must give a special thank you to Ann McMan, for believing in this book, and me, from the beginning. Every conversation we've had has made me laugh, think, and be awed, which is the same effect your books have on me. Thank you for helping me bring this story to life and designing a phenomenal cover to introduce it to the world. Your mentorship has meant so much to me.

An immense thank you also goes to Georgia Beers. Your writing found me during a particularly tough time in my life, and lit the flame that fueled everything to follow. I am so grateful for that, but even more grateful for your mentorship, support, and encouragement. Thank you.

To Lisa and Rose, whose friendship has been unwavering. If I've been even half the friend you've been to me, I'll count it a huge success.

Mary, though so much more could be said, I'll say only what matters to you, thank you for helping me.

Josh, thank you for understanding this whole crazy writing world and your solidarity in the struggle. I'm proud to call you my friend.

To my brother, you taught me early on the difference that one person can make when they fight for what they believe in. One voice. One life. Resist.

For my mom, who taught me to love books and has always supported me, even when she didn't understand or necessarily agree with my decisions. Thank you. Those have been the best gifts of all.

And though they will never read this, I would be remiss if I didn't mention Sevvie and Stripe, the two girls who have stayed by my side through every word of this book, reminding me (sometimes forcefully) to take breaks and laugh every day. I know that as long as I keep buying the good treats and not those grain-free ones, they will always have my back.

Lastly, it never ceases to amaze me the power and beauty that come when women lift each other up, rather than tear each other down. Thanks to all of the phenomenal women who have inspired and supported me. It has meant everything.

About the Author

Avery Brooks has a Ph.D. in evolutionary biology and has spent much of her life studying dominance, climate change, social justice issues, and human rights atrocities. She is a graduate of the Golden Crown Literary Society's Writing Academy. When she's not busy reading or writing, she enjoys hiking with her two dogs in Colorado. You can learn more about her at www.averybrooksauthor.com.

Bywater
BOOKS

At Bywater Books we love good books about lesbians just like you do, and we're committed to bringing the best of contemporary lesbian writing to our avid readers. Our editorial team is dedicated to finding and developing outstanding writers who create books you won't want to put down.

We sponsor the Bywater Prize for Fiction to help with this quest. Each prizewinner receives $1,000 and publication of their novel. We have already discovered amazing writers like Jill Malone, Sally Bellerose, and Hilary Sloin through the Bywater Prize. Which exciting new writer will we find next?

For more information about Bywater Books and the annual Bywater Prize for Fiction, please visit our website.

www.bywaterbooks.com